I0671288

Fields of Glass

PRESCOTT FAMILY ROMANCE

BOOK THREE

ALYSSA SCHWARZ

ALYSSA SCHWARZ

FIELDS OF GLASS

Copyright© 2023 by Alyssa Schwarz
All rights reserved

Editing by Caitlin Miller

ISBN-13: 978-1-7379788-6-2
ISBN-10: 1737978865

All rights reserved. No part of this publication may be reproduced in any form, stored in any retrieval system, posted on any website, or transmitted in any form or by any means, without written permission from the author, except for brief quotations in printed reviews and articles.

This is a work of fiction. Names, characters, places, incidents, and dialogues either are the products of the author's imagination or are used fictitiously. All characters are fictional, any resemblance to actual persons, living or dead, businesses, companies, events, or locales is entirely coincidental.

Scripture quotations and references are taken from THE HOLY BIBLE, NEW INTERNATIONAL VERSION®, NIV® Copyright © 1973, 1978, 1984, 2011 by Biblica, Inc.™ Used by permission. All rights reserved worldwide.

Library of Congress Control Number: **2023914602**

Cover image by Mike Pellinni on Unsplash
Cover design by Alyssa Schwarz

www.authoralyssaschwarz.com

PRAISE FOR FIELDS OF GLASS

"Alyssa pens an intriguing story full of interesting details and God moments that pull you in and won't let you go. From the first page until the very end, the plight of Grace kept me engaged in this superb story, especially while Grace experiences the kindness to a new friend and a growing relationship with Micah. This book is a roller coaster ride of emotions and mystery as both his and her pain keeps getting in the way until...redemption finds them choosing love." ~ Susan G Mathis, award-winning Thousand Islands Gilded Age author

"Fields of Glass is a beautiful journey alongside characters that feel like friends. Schwarz's vivid writing makes you feel as if you're right on that Colorado ranch, experiencing each moment for yourself. A heart-warming story of redemption, second chances, and love, Fields of Glass is a transportive read that deserves a special place on your shelf." ~ Caitlin Miller, author of *The Memories We Painted* and *Our Yellow Tape Letters*

"With heart, humor, and hope, Schwarz spins a tale of relatable flawed characters working to not only save their beautiful land but salvage their own hearts as well. Perfect for fans of inspirational romantic fiction, *Fields of Glass* reminds readers that redemption is always reaching for us and that the truest victory is often surrender." ~ Ashlyn McKayla Ohm, author of *When the Ice Melts* and *Where the Wings Rise*

PRAISE FOR ALYSSA SCHWARZ

"The letters penned in *Dear Beth* bring back a beautiful sense of nostalgia ... With well-developed characters and a handsome hero to fall in love with, readers will be rooting for Tye Prescott and Beth to get their happily-ever-after. I can't wait to read more of the Prescott Family romance series. *Dear Beth* is highly recommended for fans of inspirational contemporary romance, especially for readers who enjoy novels by authors such as **Denise Hunter, Becky Wade, Melissa Tagg, and Susan May Warren.**" ~ Goodreads reviewer

"If you enjoy an honest, thoughtful, character-driven story, *The Glass Cottage* will not disappoint. Debut author Alyssa Schwarz does an amazing job of balancing character development and plot while circling around romance, suspense, and small-town history. Simply spun, *The Glass Cottage* is a page turner with heart and a storyline like no other book I've read." ~ Becky Van Vleet, Award Winning Author

"Alyssa Schwarz has struck gold with a well-paced, intriguing tale that is sure to keep readers turning the pages. The Glass Cottage is a cozy, small town romance, with relatable characters and just the right combination of romance, mystery, and historical fiction." ~ Heidi Glick, Author of Dog Tags

"Alyssa Schwarz's debut novel, The Glass Cottage, reads like a Hallmark Channel movie. It's sure to make you laugh and possibly go out for a gourmet pizza. You may head straight to your favorite coffee shop for a latte and pastry too. Full of romance, suspense, and plot twists, it's definitely a must-read!" ~ Amanda Speights, Author

BOOKS BY ALYSSA SCHWARZ

A PRESCOTT FAMILY ROMANCE SERIES

To all the readers who find encouragement between the pages. Never stop believing in miracles.

"Then Jesus told them this parable: "Suppose one of you has a hundred sheep and loses one of them. Doesn't he leave the ninety-nine in the open country and go after the lost sheep until he finds it? And when he finds it, he joyfully puts it on his shoulders and goes home. Then he calls his friends and neighbors together and says, 'Rejoice with me; I have found my lost sheep."

—Luke 15:3-6

CHAPTER

One

GIVING UP WASN'T an option.

Despite what the parched earth might be telling him.

Kneeling, Micah Prescott scooped his hand into the dirt on the edge of the parking lot. The pale brown dust slipped through his fingers. Not a hint of moisture.

And, according to the wide blue, cloudless sky, nothing on the horizon either. Just perfect. Another drought was the last thing Micah needed on top of his growing mountain of problems.

He released the remaining handful to the wind and stood up. The bank papers in his jacket pocket crinkled with the movement.

It didn't matter what they all said. The ranch wasn't dead yet.

Micah shoved back his baseball cap and rubbed his forehead. The tension headache he'd been fighting all afternoon now pulsed at his temples.

"*I've never been late on a payment, not once in fifteen years—*"

He wanted to shake away the memory of his voice this morning at the bank. He hadn't been begging.

Just...reminding.

"*I'm sorry it's come to this...*" *Stupid Jackson, sitting behind his mahogany desk at Bank of the Rockies.*

"*Yeah, me too. How am I supposed to raise seventy-five thousand dollars in thirty days?*"

Jackson had left the question unanswered even as Micah stormed out of the office, not caring who might be watching.

Probably all of Lake City had figured it out, anyway.

He was about to lose the ranch that had been in his family for generations. Yeah, he was *that* son. Not the successful veterinarian like his younger brother Tye. He thought he'd finally been able to resurrect his father's legacy, if not his name. No wonder he felt their stares on his back, the cold shoulders from a town he'd grown up in.

Again, what did they expect from Micah Prescott?

He glanced at the digital display above the bank's sign, noting the late hour. Great. He'd already lost half a day in town, and all for a fool's errand.

Around him, the town buzzed with activity. Families and tourists popping in and out of shops. Noise spilled out from the open-air restaurants lining the streets on either side of him. On any other day, he could appreciate the perfectly clear fall day or the quaintly preserved mountain town.

He breathed in a steadying breath, and a faint tinge of smoke made his heart race. Turning, he spotted a handful of construction workers smoking beside their work trucks.

"Are you serious? One spark and you could light the entire county on fire!"

His warning barely lifted the head of one of the crew. He should march over there and put their cigarettes out himself. He took a step in their direction and halted, clenched fists relaxing a fraction. Confronting them would only amount to putting a Band-Aid over a gaping wound. Colorado faced droughts annually, and this year was no exception.

Only rain and a miracle could change that.

"Finn, come here boy." Micah blew a sharp whistle, and a mottled cattle dog with one blue eye and the other brown bounded toward him from behind a thicket of trees.

Micah opened the passenger door of his once-white '89 Dodge Ram, and with one solid leap, the animal hopped in. Finn barked excitedly at Micah, as if ready to get back to their sheep.

"Almost finished here, and then we can go home. I promise."

The dog calmed as if he understood—which, after a few years working the ranch with Micah, perhaps he did.

Micah stroked the dog's flat coat. *Just calm down. Think.*

The papers in his jacket pocket crinkled with the movement. Grabbing the bank's letter, he opened the glove box and shoved the stark white envelope in with the rest of his projections and ideas for the ranch he hadn't gotten to share with the managers at the meeting. The metal click of the latch echoed like a nail in a coffin.

Ready to leave everything from today behind him, Micah reversed his truck out of the bank's parking lot and drove as fast as the multiple stop lights and crosswalks allowed. A few miles south, he turned off the main highway and eased into his smaller hometown. Not much more than a few restaurants, a post office, a general store, and the all-important bait and tackle shop lined the street. A few new houses had sprouted up over the past decade, but besides that, it looked nearly the same as it had all his life.

Everywhere Micah looked, the place seemed... tired. A once-brilliant Main Street of Easter egg pastels now faded under the high-altitude sun. If it weren't for the summer tourists, the mining town of Lake City might have all but become a long-forgotten memory buried within the Colorado Rockies.

With Finn as his copilot, they slowed at the single stop sign and pulled into the parking lot of the Gold Bar Café. Its log exterior and rustic mountain character made it a popular place with locals and tourists alike, and the barbecue burger with homemade fries could nearly make a man forget his problems.

Nearly. But he'd give it a try.

Finn lifted his nose and wined as the smell of bacon and fried potatoes wafted into the car.

Micah only planned to be gone for a few minutes. Twenty, tops. But between the dry heat outside and the pathetic look Finn was sending him, how could he say no? Besides, he knew from experience that Pauline wouldn't bat an eyelash. Micah patted his thigh, and the dog immediately jumped down from the seat as if having expected the invitation all along.

A little bell above the door announced their arrival.

Even in September, hardly a table or booth sat empty. He caught a few familiar faces as he looked around the room. Jenny from the post office glanced at him, then turned away from where she sat at the counter. Wayne and Joe sat at the corner table, drinking coffee. A few groups of unfamiliar faces gathered around the larger tables, backpacks slung over their chairs, conversation and laughter erupting in busts like a tractor backfiring. Tourists.

Pauline pointed to his regular stool, as if he'd ever sit anywhere else. "I'll get you a coke."

He just might survive the day, given the smell escaping the kitchen. Barbecue and buttery biscuits.

He walked to the end of the bar, and like the socially outcasted leper he was, no one stopped to say hi. Fine. It wasn't like he needed or expected friends—he knew what the Prescott name meant in this town. And his scars certainly didn't help ease up on that general opinion.

Micah sank onto the vinyl seat, and within minutes, a waitress he hadn't seen there before greeted him.

"Howdy. What can I get for you?" The girl slid a pen from behind her ear.

He checked to make sure Finn was settled on the floor beside him before placing his order. "I'll have the rancher's special, but without the mushrooms."

"Great choice. Anything to drink?" She couldn't have been older than eighteen, but the way she smiled at him—young and innocent and a little flirtatious—made him feel guilty for even stepping foot inside.

"Just a bowl of water for Finn."

She smiled at Finn, who was already fast asleep, and returned her gaze to Micah. "I meant for you, silly." A slight flush colored her youthful face. She had to have been at least a decade younger than him, but that didn't seem to stop those fluttering eyelashes. He envied her carefree attitude; he just didn't want it directed at him so intently.

"Just a coffee, thank you." Anything with enough caffeine to tame his mounting headache.

Her airy chuckle followed her toward the kitchen, leaving him alone to stew over his thoughts.

Once she was gone, he pulled his phone from his pocket and stared at his reflection in the blank screen. He had to make the call eventually. But the thought of admitting to his younger brother that he'd failed rankled. He was the oldest, the one who was supposed to have all the answers. He'd taken over the ranch when Dad died, made sure Tye went to veterinary school.

He raised the phone to place the call, which felt like a brick in his hand, when the screen lit up with a text from Caden.

Oh, no. What had that cousin of his gotten himself into this time?

God knew he shouldn't trust Caden to operate the hay baler on his own, let alone manage the ranch for an entire day. With Micah's recent luck, he'd come back home to a half-plowed field or the hayloft in flames.

Sure, Callie would be nearby in case things went sideways, but he could only infringe on his neighbor's goodwill for so long.

"Storm's coming. I can feel it." Pauline herself stepped up to the bar, red-and-white-checkered apron tied around her waist. The skin around her eyes wrinkled as she smiled—something sweet, almost forgiving in it—and she tipped the coffee carafe to fill his cup.

If only that were true. While sitting in the bank's lobby, the local radio station had predicted nothing but hot weather and laughable humidity levels. But if Pauline from the diner thought she knew better...

"Don't give me that look," she said, handing him a plate of steaming hash brown and her famous brisket. "The last time my knee acted up like this, it rained for two days straight. The river nearly flooded its banks, unless you've forgotten." She rubbed her knee as if to support her statement. "And based on how it's hurtin', I'd say we're in for a real doozy."

Micah picked at the pile of hash browns before moving to the brisket. He understood a lot of things, but how an arthritic knee could predict the weather with more accuracy than a team of meteorologists and all their fancy equipment was not one of them.

"Mark my words. That drought everyone's been talking about, the one that's got all of you frowning into your coffee cups as if they hold the answers, it's about to end." She bobbed her salt-and-pepper head, making her aquamarine earrings sway like raindrops, before disappearing through the swinging kitchen door. A few seconds later, she returned and propped a plate of blackberry pie topped with whipped cream in front of him.

"What's this for?" He eyed the glossy berries and tried to remember the last time he'd splurged on something so sweet. Not that he'd turn up his nose to a slice of Pauline's pie.

"It's on the house. A thank you for working on those cabinets in the kitchen. I don't know how you managed it, but they're almost as good as new."

Micah's face grew warm. "There's really no need. All I did was tighten a few screws and sand some edges. Anyone could have done it."

"Nonsense. Now, eat up. I know you've got more than enough room in that stomach of yours." The bell above the door chimed, and she waved toward whoever had entered. "I'll leave you to it. But when I come back, I'd better see both those plates licked clean." Whisking the coffee carafe from the counter, she sauntered toward one of the booths by the window to greet the newcomers.

Micah chuckled at the woman's determination to see the good in everybody. He'd like to believe that as well, but despite his best attempts, he'd learned the hard way that people, no matter their intentions, would let you down one way or another. Best to be as self-sufficient as possible and leave the rest to God.

Micah nursed the remainder of his coffee and, having finished his meal, turned to the pie before him. Despite the meal he'd just eaten, Micah's stomach gurgled at the tempting scent of warm pastry and jammy blackberry. Unable to resist, he dug in, savoring each bite before he had to make the hour-long drive back to the ranch.

Micah paid for the rest of his meal, slipping a generous tip to compensate for the slice of pie, and ducked out the front door with Finn on his heels.

"Come on, buddy. Let's go home." In one leap, the dog jumped through the open car door and crawled to his spot in the middle of the bench seat. When he turned around, his tongue lolled to the side, a wide grin spreading across his face if ever Micah saw one.

For what was hopefully the last time that day, Micah climbed into his truck and started the ignition.

The paved road soon gave way to dirt, and they continued up the narrow, winding valley. With few cars and fewer people, he could finally breathe again. These days, the town held precious little attraction to him, and even less so when the only reason for him going was to sort out his financial troubles.

He'd pray for a miracle every day if he thought it would help. No matter how hard he tried, how many seasons he worked the earth and tended the sheep, he only ever managed to scrape by.

A few years ago, he and his mom had finally surfaced for air long enough to make a few much-needed repairs to the barn and outbuildings. He couldn't begin to describe the waves of relief he'd felt then. For once, everything was right in the world. His mother was happier than ever, managing almost an entire year without slumping into one of her moods, and he finally had the time and resources to start planning for the future.

All seemed fine until the bank sent him notice that they were recalling the loan.

Apparently, the threat of another drought was enough to make the managers quake in their polished leather loafers. He bet none of them even owned a decent pair of boots or knew a thing about a hard day's work.

Micah frowned and slowed his vehicle as it rumbled across a series of deep washboards in the road. Finn sat up at the noise and pressed his wet nose against the glass.

Micah released a pent-up breath. At least his mom didn't have to suffer through this again. Aunt Nora and Uncle Greg had been kind enough to invite her down to their place in Florida. As much as he missed having her around, he knew the distance was good for her. Staying in a guest house on the beach, all she had to worry about would be when to go golfing and which drink to order at the country club.

He almost smiled at the thought. His mom would sooner fight a bear than lug around a bag of irons. But if she was happy there, so was he.

The road smoothed out once again, and they picked up speed on the straightaway. His headache dulled to a faint pulse, likely due to the three cups of coffee he'd downed at the café, and he tried to focus his thoughts on a solution.

He and Caden had a healthy flock of sheep this year, and if things went as planned, they'd also have the alfalfa harvest come October. He could sell off part of the flock and make a decent profit if need be. He'd hate to lose so many good sheep, but they were far easier to replace than land. It might take some calling around, but surely he could find a buyer this late in the year.

His mind flicked back to the series of emails he'd received recently from a company interested in buying a portion of his land. After reading the first one a few months back, he'd forwarded the rest to his spam folder. He'd rather sell his property to the bank than palm off a piece to some unknown corporate entity. Mr. Francis G. Riley could email him all he liked, but that was one thing Micah would not budge on.

He drove past the gated entrance to the Landry's old ranch, the *For Sale* sign staked into the earth, and a twinge of uncertainty tightened in his gut. If all else failed, he might not have the luxury of that decision.

"Well, Finn." Micah turned to face his companion. "It looks like we have the next month cut out for us. Do you think we can do it?"

Finn wagged his short tail, and Micah took that as a *yes*. He smiled. "Look at me, taking advice from a dog. I really must be going crazy."

Finn barked again, and Micah laughed.

Praying for a miracle, he returned his sights to the upcoming month. Thirty days was more than enough to bring in the harvest, get the sheep ready, and find a buyer. He'd been through rough patches before, and he'd always found a way through. This time wouldn't be any different. And with Caden's help, it was as sure as done.

At least, so he hoped.

They crossed the next bridge and veered up the rise when the first raindrop splashed against his windshield.

CHAPTER

Two

"DON'T QUIT ON me now," Grace pleaded with her glitchy phone while doing fifty down a country road in the middle of nowhere. She smashed her thumb against the dark screen, and her maps program lit up long enough for her to catch the words *Lost Canyon* before it blacked out.

Pellets of liquid sleet pattered against the windshield of her orange VW bug, her wipers doing double-time to keep up with the torrential downpour. Grace squinted ahead at the road, gripping the steering wheel white-knuckles. Where did this storm come from? She'd made certain it wasn't going to rain when she set out for this trip, double-checking both weather apps on her phone before leaving home.

A bolt of lightning lit up the sky, followed by a deafening explosion of thunder. Suddenly, she was eight again. Similar car, similar storm. The last time she'd driven through something like this had been with her parents. The memory was foggy at best, but she'd never forget the rain. Or the headlights that had come out of nowhere.

Hands slick with sweat, she cranked the defrost to its highest setting, not caring that her fan had threatened to give out ever since the last snowstorm back in May. A wave of damp air filled the car, coating the windows with a thin film of moisture. Worry mounting, she wiped her hand across the cool glass to restore her vision of the road.

Soggy nothingness greeted her. Not even an illuminated sign to indicate she was heading in the right direction. She'd turned off the main highway a few miles back, crossing the dry riverbed on one of those rickety bridges often seen in the movies. The last car she'd spotted had been heading in the opposite direction toward town. And that was over half an hour ago.

Radio static blared in the background, an unwelcome reminder that she's volunteered for this assignment.

"Nice job, Francis Grace Riley. You sure know how to pick 'em." She squeezed the steering wheel, causing the black leather to dimple under her palms. Her life had been a series of poor decisions, and she prayed this spontaneous trip wasn't one to add to the list.

The least she could have done was notify her boss about her impromptu site drop-in. One week of unpaid leave to track down a stubborn rancher and persuade him to sell—that's what she'd convinced herself she had to do. So far, she hadn't gotten a single reply from Mr. Prescott about her company's proposal.

Either the man didn't have decent Wi-Fi or was as stubborn as the cowboys in the movies. But one way or another, he'd have no choice but to listen to her once she showed up on his doorstep.

Betsy, a friend and coworker, had warned her, "Leave the big decisions to the executives. Why worry over something you can't control?" Unlike Grace, Betsy had everything going for her—a wonderful husband and a stable family. Not to mention her uncle owned half of the business. God had handed life to her on a silver platter, not the flimsy paper plate that had been Grace's life so far.

On the other hand, her boss Katrina, would have understood and supported the assertive business move. This was Grace's chance to show the partners at Prospect & Gould she had exactly what it took to secure this deal. She'd prove to everyone just how much she had to offer, and if that meant driving three hours over treacherous mountain passes and back roads to get there, so be it.

That is, if she ever managed to find her way out of this winding canyon.

The headlights flickered against the uneven road like a bad horror film.

"Come on, Cordelia. Just a little farther." Grace gave the dashboard a good smack, and the flickering stopped. This car had been a lemon when she'd purchased it from her aunt ten years ago, and it wasn't about to start making lemonade anytime soon.

The engine rattled as she drove over the rutted road, and another pang of doubt crept in. Maybe she shouldn't have gone about this alone. If she'd been willing to wait, she could have notified her boss about her plans and borrowed one of the company trucks instead. But with Katrina out on another project, now seemed like the perfect opportunity to take some initiative.

She'd made it this far. No reason to turn back now.

The road curved ahead, and Grace pumped her foot against the brakes. The lights on her dashboard dimmed a few seconds before a new noise began—something that could only be described as an angry monster growling from beneath the hood.

An indicator light flashed red above the steering wheel. Panicked, Grace navigated the car toward the gravel shoulder and pulled the emergency brake. The headlights flickered and went out, the engine's horrible clatter dying with them.

Grace fumbled with the keys in the ignition and turned.

Nothing.

She tried again.

Silence—not even the clicking sounds of the engine trying to turn over.

"No, no, no!" Grace squeezed her eyes shut and rubbed a shaky hand across her forehead and into her straw-colored hair. *This can't be happening. Not now. Not here.* She tried to look down the stretch of road. The darkness seemed to engulf her like a blackout curtain. Had she not looked at the clock minutes before, she would have thought it well past midnight, not early afternoon.

She reached for her purse and spilled its contents across the passenger seat. Without a light to go by, it took her a minute to sort through the mess of crumpled receipts, business cards, and a bottle of allergy medicine before she found the one map she'd printed out before leaving her apartment. Squinting at the small print, she went to click on the overhead light, only to remember it wouldn't turn on with a dead battery.

Can this day get any worse? Releasing a heavy breath, she grabbed her phone and tapped the screen until a picture of a mountain meadow illuminated the darkness. She quickly swiped through her contacts list, bypassing her coworkers' numbers before dialing her aunt. Not that she needed to check in with her. It had been years since she'd moved out, but she could really use a friendly voice right now.

After the second ring, it went silent, and Grace stared at the dark screen.

Call disconnected.

"It's okay, Grace. Just calm down. I'm sure once the storm clears, someone will show up. You'll see." But the idea of accepting help from a total stranger churned her stomach.

Grace bit her bottom lip and pulled her arms in tight to her side. She was not about to have an emotional breakdown. Not while stranded alone on a mountain backroad. There had to be something she could do to fix this, anything to get her back on the road and to her destination.

If it was even possible, the sky grew darker. The wind bore down on her small car and pelted the windows with water from all sides. Was this her punishment for trying to do something on her own? God's way of telling her she was better off pushing papers as nothing better than a glorified assistant?

God, if you're there, I could really use some help right about now.

Another bolt of lightning flashed over the trees. Grace held back a yelp. She tried to regain the composure she'd fought so hard to perfect, but her shaky hands would not cooperate. So much for that prayer. What had she been expecting, her car to magically start up again? She might as well wish for a corner office and premium parking while she was at it.

Thunder rolled down the valley and vibrated through her bones. A warning to turn back.

She glanced up, half expecting to see a monster lurking in the shadows with her luck, and gasped as the glow of a car appeared beyond the trees.

Twin headlights glared in the rearview mirror. She watched with mixed emotions as a truck crept to a stop behind her. Grace held her breath and waited, heart pounding rapidly against her chest. She'd seen this movie—the girl stranded on the side of the road only for an ax-murderer to find her. Grace didn't want to end up on the front-page news. At least, not for something like that.

An excruciating minute went by without any movement from the mystery driver. Perhaps he had chosen to wait out the storm like her.

Grace scanned the inside of her car for anything that could be used for self-defense if necessary. Too bad she'd packed her curling iron away in the trunk. With few options, she settled on the compact umbrella tucked behind her seat, locked the doors, and waited.

A door opened behind her, and a giant shadow of a man stepped out. With the headlights behind him, Grace couldn't make out his features beyond a set of wide shoulders that would have dwarfed her five-foot-six stature. In his left hand, he carried something with a long handle that may or may not have been a dangerous weapon. A crowbar? Maybe a bat?

She looked down at her hands, and suddenly her collapsible umbrella seemed like a not-so-perfect form of defense.

Holding her breath, she imagined every crunch of his boots against the gravel until his large shadow fell across her window. He rapped on the glass twice, but the pounding rain distorted whatever he said.

The man jiggled the locked door handle and then pounded his fist harder against the drenched window.

Please, God.

Grace's heart was in her throat. She knew she shouldn't have come out here on her own. It had been a foolhardy idea to make a name for herself. And she most definitely shouldn't have skipped that last oil change. But she couldn't change the past. God help her, if she survived this, she'd do whatever He asked—go back to church, volunteer more, donate half her shoe collection...

In an act of uncharacteristic courage, she pushed the door open and jumped out, swinging the umbrella in a wild arc at the stranger.

The man raised his hands to block the unexpected blow, grunting at the dull impact, and dropped what was in his hand. The object clattered onto the pavement. Grace shifted and took aim before the man could charge. Brandishing the umbrella like a baseball bat, she stepped forward and her shoe collided with something heavy. She gasped at the sharp pain in her toes and watched as the object skidded across the ground and stopped beneath the sole of a leather cowboy boot. The stranger lowered his hands with caution and bent to pick up what appeared to be a heavy-duty flashlight.

Time seemed to slow as he stepped back into the light, the truck's headlamps illuminating his features with long shadows. Despite the water clumping on her eyelashes, her gaze traveled the length of the man's flannel-cased arms to his broad shoulders and up his shadowed face. His gaze locked with hers for a moment before a dog's excited yip broke the tension.

Grace's mind fought to catch up with reality. The animal leaped from the man's truck and trotted in her direction as the rain soaked into her shirt and shoes. The man made no move to intervene as his dog shoved a wet nose against her knee.

Grace shivered. She relaxed her grip a fraction on the umbrella and, with caution, reached down to stroke the animal's damp fur. The man remained at a respectable distance, for which she was grateful. When the dog seemed satisfied with her greeting, he turned and trotted back toward his owner.

The stranger didn't speak, but the dog seemed to calm down the moment his free hand lowered toward its upturned head. He made no attempt to approach her again, but a series of silent questions seemed to radiate from him.

She looked down at the umbrella still clenched in her fist. Grace's face and ears grew impossibly warm despite the cold rain soaking her to the skin. Dozens of reprimands flooded through her mind for her hasty overreaction, but none of them assuaged the embarrassment that threatened to overwhelm her.

She dropped the umbrella like it was a snake and looked once more into the face of a man who was decidedly not an ax-wielding murderer.

CHAPTER

Three

MICAH RUBBED THE sore spot above his temple and peered down at the woman in front of him. Not much taller than the faded orange Volkswagen she'd jumped out from, but she sure knew how to handle herself with an umbrella. She had a fighting spirit. He'd give her that much, although why she'd attacked him in the first place was beyond him.

Finn's tail thumped against his drenched boot as if prompting him to speak.

Micah cleared his throat. "Sorry for startling you, miss. Not many people take this road, so when I spotted your car on the shoulder, I figured maybe you'd gotten lost or something. But by the looks of things, I'd say your car gave out instead."

The woman's smooth forehead dipped into a frown. Her weary gaze flitted between him and Finn once more, as if they were the ones who didn't belong. Like her wedged heels and silk blouse were any better suited to the rain and rugged mountainside.

Micah reined in his thoughts and tried again. "Would you like me to call you a tow truck? Or do you have family around here?" An unlikely theory since he knew most of the people who called the valley home.

When she didn't so much as respond, he decided he'd take his chances against her and her dangerous umbrella and stepped toward her car.

"Hey, what are you doing?" She raced ahead and cut him off in front of her door.

He crossed his arms over his chest and stared her down. Enough was enough. He wasn't about to spend all afternoon in the rain waiting for her to answer his questions. "I thought I'd take a look at your car, if you don't mind. If it's something simple, I might be able to fix it and send you on your way."

She could give him the silent treatment all she liked, but he was not leaving without at least seeing if he could help.

She seemed to realize as much and finally stepped aside.

Regretting his good intentions of earlier, he reached through the open driver's side door and popped the hood. A dark cloud rose from the engine compartment as soon as he lifted the rounded cover. Micah choked on the pungent odor and stepped back. After the worst of the smoke had dissipated, he drew in a lungful of humid yet clean air, ducked his head, and stepped forward once again.

Micah squinted against the darkness and turned to the woman huddled behind him.

"Do you have a flashlight?" he asked.

He sensed more than saw her shift closer. "What about yours?"

"You mean the one that cracked on the asphalt when you came at me with your umbrella?"

"Oh, right. Sorry about that." There was an uncomfortable pause. "I have one in the glove compartment." She hovered beside him under the meager shelter the open hood provided.

Surely, she didn't expect him to rifle through her things to find it. He turned his face toward the engine so not to frighten her with his deepening frown. "Would you mind bringing it to me? It'll be easier to inspect if I can see what I'm looking at."

Another pause, followed by the crunch of her heels against the gravel, signaled her compliance. The passenger door clicked open and slammed shut seconds later. "Will this work?" She held out a compact penlight which, when clicked on, provided a pitiful excuse of a light source.

Micah sighed. It was better than nothing. He grabbed the pocket-sized flashlight and angled its LED beam beneath the hood.

He didn't need the light to identify the scent of burnt plastic lingering in the air. First, he examined the electrical system and found a blown fuse connected to the radiator fan. *Well, that would explain the smoke.* He moved the beam slowly over the engine block and paused at the sight of a hairline fracture across the aged surface. Not that a single crack was a deal breaker, per se, but if her car had completely given out...

He continued his rough inspection, buying time before he had to break the news. After he'd checked the oil and transmission fluid levels, along with all the exposed belts and hoses, he finally addressed the woman hovering beside him. "I'm afraid it's more than an overheated engine."

She sidled up closer to him and squinted through the rising steam. Her flowery-scented perfume wafted toward him. "How bad is it?" she asked.

He massaged a hand over the back of his neck and frowned. "I'd say you probably have a busted engine block, likely the electrical system, too."

"Is that bad?" She asked the question with such innocence he couldn't tell if she was joking or serious.

"It's not good. Definitely beyond my abilities. Exactly what happened before you pulled over?" He wiped his hands against his jeans while she rattled off the symptoms, each further driving home his initial diagnosis.

"Based on what you just told me, I'd say there's a good chance your engine might be shot. I'll give my buddy a call and see if he can tow it to his place. But I expect it could take at least a week to fix. If not more."

"A week?" she squeaked out.

He winced at the way her eyebrows shot up at the news. He didn't have the heart to tell her how much a repair like that would cost her as well. "Maybe two. And that's *if* Tony happens to have the correct parts available. If not—" he looked once more

ALYSSA SCHWARZ

over the classic '97 VW Beetle, from the canvas convertible top to the bright orange paint—"he'll most likely have to order a used engine, and a decent one can be hard to find."

She groaned and buried her face in her hands, into which she mumbled, "I can't believe this is happening to me. Today of all days." A line of mascara smudged beneath her fingers as she pulled them away. He doubted she even realized it.

Micah shifted beside her, uncomfortable with her sudden distress. Give him a herd of unruly sheep any day, but a woman in tears? He'd had his hands full learning to live with his mother's seasonal mood swings. Never one to parade her emotions, she'd mostly keep to her room until she felt more like herself again, leaving him to do what he knew best—keep the ranch running.

She hiccupped back a sniffle and smoothed a hand down her soaked navy blouse. "I'm sorry. I'm not usually this emotional." Her eyes seemed to rove the gravel at her feet, no doubt embarrassed by her outburst.

"It's fine. Happens to the best of us." In a way, he could relate to her misery.

Her fingers traced beneath her lashes and swiped the watery lines from her face. This woman sure was a mystery. One minute, armed with an umbrella, set on taking off his head, and the next, she all but fell apart at his feet. Now, aside from the rain wreaking havoc with her hair and makeup, she appeared almost normal.

"By the way, my name's Micah—Micah Prescott." He swiped the grease from his hand and offered it to her. He could have sworn she flinched when he said his name, but she gripped his hand in a surprisingly firm shake.

"Grace."

The name suited her willowy yet petite frame. Without the umbrella, she seemed quite the elegant and charming woman. Which piqued his curiosity all the more as to why she was all the way out here.

"Grace. I assume there's a last name that goes with it?"

"There might be." She smiled then, making him nearly forget about his earlier troubles at the bank.

"Fair enough. Well, Grace. What'll it be? Dry off at my place and wait there, or stay here in the rain until the tow truck arrives?" Micah backed up toward his truck to give her space to think. He didn't want to force her to do anything she didn't want, but he'd be lying if he said he'd be okay leaving her on her own.

A spark of something flashed across her expressive eyes—a striking bluish green he couldn't quite place—as if his offer was the lifeline she'd been hoping for. "I don't want to inconvenience you any further than I already have."

Micah studied the woman before him. The last thing he needed was to get saddled with a lost tourist, but between her broken-down convertible and the limp blonde hair plastered to her cheeks, he couldn't abandon her.

"Absolutely. My place isn't much farther down the road. We can get there in no time. I would offer to give you a lift to a hotel in town, but it's too dangerous to drive that far in this rain." He waited for her answer while she fidgeted with the stacked rings on her slender fingers. "If it helps," he interrupted, "I promise I've never, nor do I ever, intend to kidnap anyone."

Grace laughed, and the last of the shadows seemed to fall from her face. "In that case, how can I say no?"

With that settled, he closed and latched the hood, then moved to assist her with her suitcase. Purse clutched to her chest, Grace climbed into the passenger seat with Finn, where the dog welcomed her with a few well-placed licks to the face. Micah couldn't hold back his smile. He might not have been able to solve his own problems of the day, but at least he could help someone else for a change. The sooner they got on the road, the quicker he'd place that call and see her settled.

He was looking forward to a hot shower and a change of clothes himself. Not to mention another cup of coffee.

He met her gaze. "Ready to head out?"

She nodded. "Anything to get out of this rain."

With her assent, Micah directed the truck back onto the road toward home. In a matter of minutes, he'd make the necessary phone calls and leave Grace to tidy up on her own. Now all he had to do was figure out what to tell his cousin Caden when he showed up at the ranch with an unannounced, sopping, and beautiful woman at his side.

"You look like you could use some dry clothes and a hot cup of coffee, or whatever you prefer to drink."

Grace propped her suitcase against the wall by the door where Finn lay curled up on a simple quilted dog bed. After the day she'd had so far, she envied the dog. Her tense muscles had begun to relax on their short drive over, and all she wanted was to curl up with something warm to drink and throw on the cozy cashmere sweater she'd bought for her twenty-ninth birthday last March. "Coffee sounds great, actually. Thanks."

Micah busied himself in the kitchen, scooping out a heap of coffee grounds into the machine. "Bathroom is down the hall and to the left. Clean towels are in the adjacent closet if you want to take a shower. And if you need any dry clothes, just let me know. I'm sure I could find something that might fit."

"Thanks. I've got other clothes, so no need." Grace placed her wet shoes beside Micah's discarded cowboy boots. She inwardly groaned at the dirt and water stains on her pumps' delicate finish, chastising herself for not thinking to bring more appropriate footwear. *You're not in the city anymore, Grace.* No doubt she'd guessed wrong when she'd thought business-formal attire would impress someone like Micah Prescott.

Of all the people to show up to her rescue, it had to be him. Of course, she hadn't known right away that her not-so-dangerous rescuer was the same rancher she'd sent over a dozen emails to in the past month. When he'd finally introduced himself, she'd panicked. The man currently pouring tap water into the ancient percolator knew her better as Francis G. Riley, an associate at Prospect & Gould, not *just Grace.*

She unzipped her bag and pulled out a pair of slacks and her beloved sweater. When Micah had finished with the coffeemaker and disappeared somewhere else in the house, she gathered her things and slipped into the hall bathroom.

"What are you doing, Grace?" Her reflection stared back at her through the small mirror over the sink, as lost for an explanation as she was. She clutched the dark green towel to her chest. The raw wood cabinets bespoke the same rustic mountain feel as the rest of the house. A far cry from her modern apartment in Denver's Washington Park.

Her gaze dipped to the pine-slat walls and the timber floorboards at her feet. She shifted her weight and listened to the melodic squeaks and groans that seemed to speak to her. Voices of all the generations that had lived here before, perhaps?

"Don't be silly, Grace. It's only a house, same as any other."

Finishing her conversation with the hundred-year-old floor, she walked the two steps to the shower and cranked the temperature as hot as it could go. Steam rose from the ceramic tub basin, and she let the hot waters wash away her reservations.

Ten minutes later, she toweled off and changed into clean and dry clothes. She slipped the sweater over her head and tucked her loose strands of wet hair behind her ears. This time, Grace smiled at her reflection. She felt more like herself against the soft lilac material. Feminine, confident, in control.

So, maybe things hadn't gone according to plan, but this unexpected turn didn't mean her efforts would result in a dead-end. She was, after all, standing in the man's house. The

Grace of this morning would have been proud of that accomplishment. Besides, Micah seemed like a reasonable enough person. He'd understand the situation. Maybe even laugh about it.

Revived by the shower and subsequent pep-talk, Grace swiped on a thin layer of mascara, ready to face whatever life threw at her.

Micah was already seated and waiting for her at the counter when she emerged from the steaming bathroom. A brown, knit sweater stretched across his broad shoulders, a few shades darker than the ends of his wet hair, and he nursed a mug of coffee in front of him. Without his baseball cap on from earlier, the ends had begun to curl at the edges, making the faint scar she'd noticed before a touch more visible.

Along with the red mark from where she'd struck him with her umbrella.

His eyes connected with hers as she stepped into the kitchen. He offered her a cup as she sank into the seat beside him. "Better?" he asked.

"Mm, much. Thanks for the coffee, by the way."

He shrugged. "Don't mention it. I would have brewed a pot, anyway." He took another sip, and she followed his lead.

Grace had wondered the entire drive up here what kind of person Micah Prescott was. Now that she sat mere feet from him, the mental image she'd put together—old, crotchety, unwelcoming—was nothing like the man beside her.

"I'm sorry about earlier. You know, for attacking you and all. Once I knew you were there to help and not kidnap me—not that you look like the kind of person who would, but you never can be too safe, you know?" Her face grew warm, and she continued her rambling string of thought before her better sense could tell her to stop. "Anyway, I feel like an idiot for jumping to such quick conclusions. Not everyone's first impressions of a person are correct."

She clamped her mouth shut and stared at the mug clasped between her hands. What was wrong with her? She didn't usually prattle away like this, especially not with a prospective client.

Micah's soft laughter peeled her attention away from her coffee, and she relaxed under the warmth of his gaze. "Don't worry. It wasn't the first time I've taken a beating." He chuckled. "And I'm sure it won't be the last."

She only hoped his good opinion of her wouldn't pop the moment she told him who she really was. The longer she waited, the worse it would be. *Better to rip the Band-Aid off, I suppose.*

Grace inhaled a fortifying breath, but Micah cut her off before she could get a word out.

"I left a message with my friend Tony about your car. I'd expect him to call back fairly soon, but in the meantime, I've got to go check on a few things. You think you'll be okay here on your own?"

Grace was more than relieved. The quick change in subject might have derailed her attempt to set the record straight, but another hour or two wouldn't hurt. "I promise not to burn the place down in the next hour," she said with a laugh.

Micah frowned. Okay, so maybe that had been the wrong choice of words.

"I mean, don't worry about me. I have a book, so I'm all set." She tapped her purse where a copy of *Count Your Gifts: 90 Days to a More Positive You* sat buried beneath the folder of paperwork. She'd planned to finish chapter four, "How to Count Your Blessings," in her hotel room later that evening. An extra chapter now wouldn't hurt. "Besides, Finn will keep me company."

At the mention of his name, the dog's ears perked up. He looked between the two of them, tilting his head as if waiting for some cue.

From his seat, Micah studied her the same way the kids on the playground did when she'd switched schools in second grade. She wanted to squirm beneath his intent gaze, but she instead ran through her rehearsed checklist as her doubts tried to surface. She had her dream job, an apartment she adored, her aunt's old VW Bug... Well, after today, she might have to remove that last item from her list. But she could add *surprise rescuer* in its place.

Seemingly satisfied with her response and subsequent silence, Micah dipped his head. "Okay, then. Feel free to make yourself at home. Extra blankets are behind the sofa in the basket, and there's some food in the fridge in case you get hungry. I'll be back in an hour or so, and hopefully by then, I'll have heard back from Tony." He slipped his arms into the sleeves of his rain jacket and prepared to leave, Finn close on his heels.

With his back turned, she withdrew the book from her bag. The manila folder with the contract slipped out, and she quickly shoved it back in, careful not to bend the edges.

"Oh, and Grace?"

Her head shot up to see him halfway through the open back door. Had he seen the company logo on the folder?

He angled his body toward her and paused. "I expect to see the place still standing when I return."

A faint smile played at the corners of his mouth, and Grace couldn't help but like him a little more—a feeling which was soon eclipsed by her guilt the moment he and Finn walked out the door.

So much for Finn keeping her company.

Grace dropped the unopened book on her lap and stared out the sliding glass door at their retreating forms.

The man didn't deserve this duplicity. For all her earlier misgivings, Micah Prescott seemed to be a decent person. After all, he'd been kind enough to pull over in the rain to help her. He'd stayed, even after she'd gone after him like a crazy person. After voluntarily inspecting her car, he'd offered her a ride out of the rain and called in a favor to have her car checked out. Now she was sitting in his kitchen drinking his coffee while he trusted her enough to see to his other responsibilities.

Katrina might have praised her results, but all Grace could focus on was the sickening sensation in her stomach that grew with every sip. And it wasn't because the coffee was bad. In fact, it was surprisingly good for drip. She hadn't set out to manipulate the situation, but that was exactly what she was doing. She'd let the charade go on long enough.

Next time she saw Micah, she'd confess and explain everything.

CHAPTER

Four

GRACE DID NOT, in fact, tell Micah about her secret the next time she saw him.

The moment he returned from wherever he'd disappeared to, he promptly filled her in on the latest update. "Good news: my friend was able to tow your car to his place. Bad news: he just got word from the sheriff that the bridge between here and Lake City washed out from the rain. It could be days before anyone comes to fix it. Until then, it looks like you're stuck here."

"What do you mean by stuck?" She'd prepared for anything besides that. The car would no doubt be a major financial setback, but she was willing to foot the bill for it if it got her one step closer to closing this deal and one step closer to that promotion. She was already giving up a week of her vacation time to be here. And now her rancher-in-shining-armor was saying a flood had taken out her only way home?

He gave her the same look as when she'd asked him if a cracked engine block was bad, then continued. "The only way out of this valley is currently resting under a few feet of running water."

"What about the Department of Transportation or the National Guard? Don't they usually handle these sorts of things?" Maybe if she got Katrina on the phone and explained the situation, she'd find a way to help. With all her connections, they were sure to come up with a solution.

Micah huffed and peeled off his rain-soaked jacket. "Not here. Our county has the lowest population in the state, so we don't rank very high on the political-aid totem pole."

The wind wailed against the windows, a second wave rolling off the nearby mountains as dusk settled over the valley and Grace's fledgling hope. Finn paced in circles in the living room, whining as the storm intensified. After a few more turns, he plopped onto his pillow in the corner and seemed to settle for the time being.

Down the hall, a door opened and closed. Finn's head shot up as a pair of voices carried from the outside and into the living room, one deep and masculine, the other light and airy. A few seconds later, a woman with flaming curls sailed into the kitchen, followed by a man who shared a slight familial resemblance to Micah. A brother, perhaps?

They both had their hands full with wooden crates that jangled when they walked.

"I see you found them," Micah spoke, nodding toward the wooden boxes.

"Yeah, right next to Aunt Ruth's rhubarb wine. The least you could have done was warn us about the spiders in the cellar." Despite the man's cringe, he laughed and set his rain-drenched box down beside the back door with ease.

"Oh, it was nothing but a few daddy longlegs," the girl teased and readjusted her grip on the box in her arms. The contents clinked together as they shifted. Sensing her struggle, Grace pushed her purse toward the edge of the concrete countertop just in time for her to set her armload of goods.

"Who thought a few dozen empty mason jars could weigh so much?" Her arms moved while she talked, settling just long enough to shove a wayward red curl behind her ear.

Micah clicked open a can of soda and offered one to the guy leaning against the countertop. "I tried to warn you two. Imagine how much they'll weigh once you've filled them all with honey."

"Ugh, don't remind me. I'd prefer to exist in a perpetual state of bliss until the time comes when I need to think about such things." The girl sidestepped Micah and opened the fridge to retrieve a pitcher of lemon water from the top shelf.

Grace leaned against the far wall of the kitchen-diner and watched. This woman was something else. A few inches taller than Grace, and of similar age, she wore a pair of army green overalls over a sunny yellow T-shirt. Bits of dirt clung to the tops of her leather boots, and her curly hair—which Grace would have described as a cross between auburn and copper—threatened to spring free of the braid hanging down her back.

She didn't miss the fact that every inch of her exposed skin seemed covered in freckles, as if she'd stood behind a truck while its rear wheels spun in the mud. Nor did she miss the way Micah's posture seemed to relax while in her presence.

The girl continued talking and sipping her water between breaths when she spotted Grace tucked in the corner. "Oh, I'm sorry. We haven't been introduced. I'm Callie." She stuck out her hand and took Grace's in hers. Her smile was warm and inviting, and Grace couldn't help but return the gesture.

"Grace."

"Ooh, I love your name. My parents decided to raid the time capsule and call me Calliope. Like anyone's had that name in over a hundred years. But around here, everyone just calls me Callie." She made a face that made Grace's smile deepen. Oddly enough, she could imagine this woman standing beside her namesake at a carnival, lively music spilling from its organ-like whistles in a loud yet cheery tune.

"And I'm Caden," the other man interrupted. "Micah's younger, but far better looking, cousin." He flashed her a grin that was no doubt meant to make her swoon.

"Don't forget humble, too," Callie added. "I seem to recall a certain someone who refuses to let us forget about the time he single-handedly saved the sheep herd."

"Look who's bringing it up now?" He waggled his eyebrows in her direction as her face turned a light shade of pink.

Micah slid Grace an apologetic look and turned toward Callie, interrupting the banter. "Are you planning to stay for dinner?" he asked. "I was thinking about making enchiladas."

"Hmm, sounds great. And I don't particularly like the thought of sloshing through the mud to get back home at the moment." She filled a second glass with lemon water and plopped it in front of Grace. "What about you, Grace? Are you staying?"

Grace opened and closed her mouth when it dawned on her she hadn't thought that far ahead.

Micah shifted beside her and spoke first. "She's sort of stuck here for the time being."

"Oh?" Callie turned her curious gaze his way. "What happened?"

Micah returned the half-empty pitcher to the fridge and shrugged. "Bridge is out."

"Again?" Callie's shoulders slumped. "That's the second time in three years. Any idea how long it'll take to fix this time?"

"Like I was telling Grace, it's anyone's guess."

Callie shook her head, sending a few curls flying. "You know what would really fix our issues? Someone on the Planning Commission who actually knows what it's like to live off the land."

"Not this again." He glanced at Caden, but he'd conveniently snuck away to the kitchen dine-in table. No help there.

Callie raced ahead, hands flying as she spoke. "But you'd be perfect. Who else is more in touch with what's really happening up here? Jack Flanagan has hardly set foot in this valley since the day he was voted in. All he cares about is lining his own pockets, not the people who call this valley home. You could even put in a good word for me about my business proposal. It'd be a win-win!"

A tug of familiarity pulled at the corners of Grace's memory at the mention of a Mr. Flanagan, but it was gone just as quickly.

"I've already made up my mind, Cal. And the answer is still no. Besides, I'm the last person people would vote for." Micah's lips formed a firm line, telling her he'd said all he intended about the subject.

Callie harrumphed, but she slid Grace a look that indicated the subject was far from finished and turned back to Micah.

He ignored her pointed expression and popped open the freezer. Cool air seeped into the compact farmhouse kitchen as he pulled out something wrapped in brown paper, and he closed the door with a little more force than necessary. "How about instead of badgering me, you make yourself useful and help with dinner?"

Either the girl didn't notice his foul mood, or she didn't care. Whatever the case, she didn't appear to be giving up so easily. Callie turned to Grace. "What do you think? Should we put him out of his misery?" Her stage whisper was loud enough to be heard down the hall, and her conspiratorial grin said she knew it.

Grace held her laughter in check at Callie's spunk. She glanced between them and pretended to think through her answer. Callie was all rosy smiles while Micah waited in silence for her response. She could add patience to her quickly growing list of attributes about the man. "I think he's earned himself at least a few hours' respite. After all, he did save me from being stuck on the side of the road in the rain."

Micah's gaze held hers for a moment. Was that a ghost of a smile?

Callie sipped on her water and plunked the glass down onto the counter. "I suppose you're right. Although it is fun to see him all worked up sometimes."

Micah cleared his throat. "I'm standing right here."

She waved a hand dismissively in his direction, not one bit intimidated by his impressive height or stern expression, then returned to Grace. "Don't mind him. He's just moody because he knows I'm right."

"Again, right here."

"Give it up, man," Caden commented, jumping into the conversation. "You'll never win that argument." He crossed his arms across his chest, the long sleeves pulling back enough to reveal part of a tattoo above his wrist.

Shaking his head, Micah gave up his defense and went back to working on dinner. When he started to pull more ingredients out of the cupboard, Callie spun on Grace.

"Come on. Help me pick out some veggies from the cellar, and you can tell me all about what brought you here and your subsequent heroic rescue. You don't mind spiders, do you?" With a wink, she looped her arm through Grace's and pulled her toward the hallway she'd emerged from moments earlier.

Micah's and Caden's voices soon faded behind them as they made their way to the other side of the house. In fact, Grace *did* mind spiders. Very much. But she kept her mouth shut and followed Callie outside and toward the weathered cellar door.

A low roof slanted over a set of double doors that protruded from the ground at the base of the house, shielding them from the worst of the rain. Callie fiddled with the ancient latch as fat droplets of water soaked into their clothes.

"So, what's this I hear of a rescue?" Callie asked over the echo of raindrops on the corrugated aluminum above them. "Must be quite the story if you managed to drag Micah into it. I want all the details."

The latch clicked, and she pried open the two doors. Musty air greeted them as they descended the half-flight of steps into the darkness. Callie reached for a cord that hung to their right, and yellow light illuminated the earthen root cellar. Wooden shelves lined the far wall, stacked two rows deep with glass jars and bottles of various sizes and colors. To the left of the steps were more crates like the ones Callie and Caden had carried into the kitchen, only these were filled with assorted fruits and vegetables instead of empty mason jars.

Brushing past Grace, Callie made a beeline for the bottom shelf and selected two jars whose contents looked vaguely like tomatoes and salsa in the dim light. "I could about live off his mom's salsa. Just wait 'til you try this with some homemade tortilla chips. I firmly believe this is how God intended for us to use tomatoes and jalapeños." Sitting back on her haunches, she handed Grace one of the jars and brushed the dirt from her overalls with her free hand. "Now, about that story."

There was something innocent in Callie's relaxed smile that made Grace feel she was talking with a close friend instead of a total stranger. Sheltered from the storm in the dry confines of the cellar, Grace repeated the story of her car breaking down in the middle of the forest and how Micah had shown up moments later. Despite her embarrassment, she even told her about the incident with the umbrella and how she'd stood there like an idiot when he'd offered to inspect her car.

"Just when you think chivalry is dead, then comes someone like Micah to prove you wrong." Callie plopped onto the bottom step and propped her elbows on the wood slat behind her.

"You said it." Grace joined her, careful not to snag the fabric of her slacks on the long splinters, and lowered herself onto the narrow ledge. "Back home in Denver, you'd be lucky if a serial killer pulled over to check on you."

"Sounds, um... nice?" Callie snorted a laugh, then forced her face into a look of contrition. "I'm sorry. I shouldn't laugh, but that sounds terrible. I couldn't live in the city if you paid me to."

"It's not all bad. There are the parks, the museums ... Not to mention, there's always something going on."

Callie scrunched her face, unconvinced. "I think I'll stick to my honeybees and garden."

"Don't forget your tourist-rescuing neighbor," Grace teased. "In all honesty, though, you're lucky to have someone like Micah in your life. He seems like a nice and understanding kind of person."

"You forgot stubborn, pig-headed at times, and often unreasonable," she added with a smile.

Based on all the ignored emails she'd sent him in the past month, Grace couldn't help but agree with that least one. She mirrored Callie's posture and leaned back against the next step. "I suppose they can't all be perfect."

"Exactly. What are men compared to bees and honey?" Callie smiled, and her mind seemed to drift beyond the cellar walls. Her fingers toyed with the raised lettering of the glass jar, slowly tracing the cursive design. "One of these days, he'll make some woman happy. He just has to settle down long enough to look up from his ranch for more than a second. And Caden?" She shook her head. "Don't even get me started on him."

Grace frowned. "But I thought... you and Micah seem so close..."

The girl laughed, a light and airy sound that filled the cavernous space. "Me and Micah? Now that would be something, wouldn't it?" The very idea seemed to brighten her spirits. After a few more suppressed giggles, she went back to tracing the lettering with an amused smile. "We've known each other a long time, but he's been more like a brother to me these past years than anyone else. And I have two, so I speak from experience."

"Oh, I didn't mean to assume." She'd already been too quick to judge Micah earlier, and now this. She might as well keep her foot in her mouth for the rest of the day at this rate.

Callie waved aside the apology. "Nothing to apologize for. To tell you the truth, I don't know what I'd do without him. He's helped me out more times than I can count, and I hope can to repay the favor someday."

After everything Micah had done for her this afternoon, Grace could only imagine what he'd be willing to do for a friend. It had been a long time since she'd known that kind of loyalty. She was much more accustomed to empty promises and toughing it out on her own.

Callie swiveled to face her on the step. "So, what are your plans now that the bridge is out?"

For as much as she'd been enjoying their conversation, the reality of her situation came crashing back down on her. Grace fought the urge to hug her knees to her chest and shrugged instead. "I haven't quite worked that out. I have a reservation at the Granite Lodge in town, but I suppose that's not really an option now, with the bridge out and all."

"Perfect. You can stay with me, then."

Grace shook her head. "I can't ask that of you."

Callie set the jar at her feet. "Nonsense. We girls have to stick together out here in the country. Besides, as much as I talk about them, bees don't keep that great of company."

She couldn't help but stare in disbelief. "Just like that? You don't even know me."

"Of course. I have good instincts when it comes to people, and I have a feeling we could be great friends. What do you say?"

Grace remained seated, as if a splinter had snagged on her slacks and was holding her hostage on the steps. Maybe her prayers had been heard, after all. How else could she explain Micah's rescue and now this? It would be so easy to take Callie up on her offer. And it wasn't like she had many other options at the moment.

She swallowed the lump in her throat and nodded. "I'd love to. That is, if you're certain about it."

"Completely." Callie jumped from the bottom step, the jars of tomatoes and salsa tucked beneath her left arm and her right extended toward Grace. "Let's go tell the boys the good news."

CHAPTER

Five

"WHAT DO YOU think they're talking about?" Caden sidled up to Micah at the counter and took another sip of his soda. He leaned a hip against the solid edge and peered down the hall, a pensive look on his otherwise relaxed face.

Micah busied himself chopping onions while the meat seared in a pan on the stove. Despite lunch and Pauline's pie at The Gold Bar, his stomach rumbled with the fragrances spicing the air. "Definitely you and your sheep rescue story." That incident from Caden's first week on the ranch would be seared into his memory as long as he drew breath. "I seem to recall finding you knee-deep in manure when all was said and done."

"Hey, I managed to get all the sheep back in their pens in time for the shearing, didn't I? And, if I might add, all while wearing sandals. How's that for impressive?" Caden snatched a bag of tortilla chips from the counter and washed one down with a swig of soda. Despite the fact he was nearly twenty-eight, the guy still ate like a college student.

"Right. Was that before or after you lost a shoe in the sheep dung?"

Caden frowned, a single line indented between his eyebrows on his otherwise smooth face. "I never did find that sandal, by the way. Shame. I bought those out in California while I was working for the winery. They had this cool logo of an octopus fighting a shark and everything." He munched on another chip and buried his hand back in the plastic bag.

It was a wonder Caden stayed so thin. The Prescott gene, perhaps. "Make sure to leave some for the girls."

Caden propped his hip against the countertop and made a show of eating another chip. "You know Callie only likes those organic tortilla chips, and Grace doesn't strike me as a junk food kind of person. The way I see it, I'm doing everyone a service by finishing off these sub-par snacks."

Micah rolled his eyes and went back to chopping onions. That cousin of his had an answer for everything.

"Besides, I think I missed lunch, so I've got some catching up to do before dinner."

"You *think* you missed lunch?" Micah laughed under his breath. "What about the leftover pasta salad I saw in the fridge this morning?"

Caden shrugged. "I got hungry halfway through baling hay, but that was hardly a meal's worth." He paused and reached for another chip. "Say, how did the meeting with the bank manager go?"

Micah clenched his jaw and ran a spatula over the pan to break up the bits of ground beef. Leave it to Caden to bring up the one topic he'd hoped to avoid for a single evening.

"That bad, huh?"

The crunch of overly processed corn chips echoed beside him. Caden's cavalier attitude grated on his nerves as much as the crinkle of the plastic bag, but that wasn't the real source of his discomfort. Micah forced his jaw to relax while he methodically grated a block of pepper jack cheese into a bowl.

"The man wouldn't budge on the deadline. He didn't so much as look at my projections for the year. There's still the upper hay field to harvest, and that always brings in some extra money. If I could somehow prove to him we're not a risky investment, I'd bet that'd be enough to make him see reason."

Caden crumpled the empty bag and tossed it in the trash bin.

"That's tough, man. But what I don't understand is how they could increase the mortgage payment in the first place. You and Aunt Ruth have been breaking your backs to keep the ranch going for years, not to mention you've never been late for anything in your life. Let alone a payment."

A question Micah had been asking himself ever since he received the notice in the mail.

"You know, I was thinking," Caden continued. "I could take a look at the contract. Wouldn't hurt to get a second pair of eyes on it. After all, I did spend a year in college working for an accounting firm in Temecula. It's worth a shot."

All of Caden's ideas were *worth a shot*. Like when he'd skipped a semester of college to work the ski lifts in Taos. Or when he wasted his graduation money on a trip to Hawaii and ended up staying for three months giving surfing lessons to tourists. In his memory, the ranch was the longest-lasting job Caden had held down since high school, and if he was going to help his cousin keep that streak, there had to still *be* a ranch to work at when this was all over.

"Thanks, but I think it's best if I handle this myself. The ranch is my responsibility, not yours. Besides, you're already helping me enough as it is."

Caden leaned back and shoved his hands in his pockets. "Your call. But my offer still stands. If you'd ever like some additional help..."

"I'll know where to find you." Micah smiled his thanks and dumped the sliced onions into the hot pan.

After heating everything through and preheating the oven, he and Caden laid out the rest of the ingredients in assembly-line formation. All they were waiting on now was the tomatoes and salsa. Micah checked the clock on the stove, surprised to see more than twenty minutes had passed since Callie and Grace had gone down to the cellar.

"Keep an eye on the food. I'm going to go see what's taking them so long." He sidestepped around Caden, and his elbow snagged on Grace's oversized purse sitting on the counter. It toppled over the edge and onto the tile, sending its contents in every direction. Micah bit back a groan. Just what he needed, another mess to clean up.

Kneeling, he rooted around the floor to collect the spilled papers, phone, keys, and the spare change that had rolled beneath the bar stools. When he'd found the last penny, he scooped everything into his hands and was about to dump them back into the leather bag when his eye caught on a manila folder. A name and address were printed across the top, and recognition flooded his senses.

Without pause, he snatched the folder from her bag and stared in disbelief at Prospect & Gould's logo. The very same company who'd been hounding him all summer about buying his property. The same company he'd flat out denied and told in the nicest way possible to shove off.

Why would Grace, of all people, have something from them?

"What's that you have there?" Caden asked. He stepped around the counter and joined Micah by the barstools, pausing to examine what had captured his attention.

"I'm not sure." The word *Confidential* was stamped in red beneath the company name. He flipped the packet over and paused at the handwriting scrawled across the front.

"What's your address doing there?" Caden leaned closer and pointed toward the two lines scribbled at the bottom of the envelope. Sure enough, it was a series of directions to the ranch.

But why?

Something about this didn't sit right. Micah's fingers itched to open the envelope and understand what was going on, but his conscience held him in check. Whatever this was, he had no right going through Grace's personal things. No matter how much his gut told him to.

The front door opened, and a burst of cool air carried the girls' voices into the kitchen. Their light footsteps clicked down the hallway until they reached the wool rug. Callie sailed into the room on a wave of laughter with Grace right behind her.

"We come bearing gifts." She plopped her jar of salsa on the table, followed by the tomatoes. "And just in time, too. It smells amazing in here." Callie pulled two bowls from the nearest cupboard and went in search of the organic tortilla chips.

Smiling, Grace popped the two lids and poured out the jars' contents before peering up at Micah. Her eyes dropped to the envelope in his hand and grew wide. Just as quickly, her forehead dipped into a frown. "Why are you going through my purse?"

Micah bristled at the accusation. She was the one who needed to explain herself, not him.

"I accidentally knocked over your bag and was trying to put things to rights when I saw this." He held up the envelope, and the look in Grace's eyes reminded him of a caged animal: unpredictable and dangerous. Whatever was in this envelope was serious enough to set her on edge, which meant he'd be wise to take it seriously as well. "If there's a simple explanation, now would be the time to share it."

He didn't want to think the worst of people, but circumstances had taught him otherwise. If Grace had anything to do with Prospect & Gould's attempts to take his ranch, he deserved to know. Now.

Grace peeled her stunned expression from him to Callie, who stood unusually quiet at her side. Even Finn seemed to sense the tension in the room. Grace's eyes seemed to scan the small kitchen before flitting back to Micah. After a minute of uncomfortable silence, her shoulders dropped in defeat.

"I work for Prospect & Gould."

The truth hit him with full force, nearly knocking the air from him as she raced ahead.

"I've tried emailing you the past few months, but after the first email, you stopped responding, so I thought if I came up here and spoke to you in person—"

"Wait," Micah interrupted, his thoughts trying to make sense of everything she was saying. "You're the one who's been sending me all those emails? You're Francis G. Riley?"

Her gaze dipped to the tile floor and settled on Finn. "Francis Grace, actually."

All this time, he'd thought his tormentor as a pencil-pushing bureaucrat with a formal suit and tie and non-distinct facial features. Over the months, that image had somehow morphed into that of the bank manager and his father all rolled into one. Disapproving, judgmental, and distant.

Her pleading eyes found his once more. Now he remembered what the pale bluish green color reminded him of—silvery lupine. From a distance, the plant with purple flowers seemed harmless enough, but it was deadly to livestock. Especially sheep.

"I really do go by Grace. So technically, I never lied to you."

"A lie of omission is still a lie." Micah dropped the envelope onto the counter and crossed his arms over his chest, mouth set in a firm line. He'd been a fool to trust her. No doubt she'd planned the whole thing—the car on the side of the road, coming back to the ranch with him... He couldn't go so far as to blame her for the washed-out bridge, but if he could, he would.

"Micah, I can explain." She stepped toward him and stopped, wrapping her arms around her body instead. "When you drove up, I didn't know who you were. As soon as you introduced yourself, I planned to tell you everything, but—"

"Was that before or after you took me for a fool? I was the one who stopped for you. I helped get your car towed. I even invited you into my home, for goodness' sake." His fists clenched at his sides, begging for something to take out his frustration on. He couldn't stand here any longer. He needed to clear his head away from the house, rain or no rain.

He pushed past Caden toward the back door.

"Micah, I'm sorry." Grace raced after him. "I made a mistake, but I'm sure there's a way we can work this out." Her hand landed on his shoulder as he reached for the door handle.

He shrugged her off and turned around, trying to restrain his mounting frustration. "When will you people get it into your heads? I would rather lose the entire ranch to the bank than sell it to some soulless company set on subdividing it into a hundred lots, or whatever it is you're already planning for it. I never should have trusted you."

"Micah."

Callie's soft tone cut like a reprimand, and he stopped. A muscle ticked in his jaw, a whole slew of choice words to be said, but he held his tongue. This was exactly why he needed to get away. As much as he hated to admit it, he didn't trust himself enough not to say something he'd later regret.

Callie's hand settled on Grace's arm. She gave a gentle squeeze and directed her next comments toward Micah. "How about, instead of blaming everyone, we figure out a way to get along? However it may have happened, Grace is here now. I've already offered for her to stay with me while the bridge is out and her car's getting worked on."

"Are you sure?" Grace asked timidly, her defenses of earlier quickly receding under Callie's warm smile.

"Of course. A promise is a promise." Callie looped her arm through Grace's once more and turned a challenging look toward Micah. One would have thought he was the big bad wolf in this scenario. "I think we'll leave you two to your dinner, and maybe in the morning, we can all see reason."

"Sounds reasonable enough to me," Caden cut in for the first time, taking Callie's and Grace's side.

Micah stared at the three of them. Were they all nuts? He was not the one who was in the wrong here, but for some reason, they all seemed to think so. Had they completely missed the fact that Grace, or whatever her name was, was here under false pretense?

Without a parting concession, he forced open the door and strode out into the rain in search of a project, any project, to distract himself from his growing mountain of problems.

CHAPTER

Six

GRACE SLUNG HER purse across her body and stepped out of the truck. Although smaller than Micah's white pickup, Callie's was a bright robin's-egg blue with a white stripe down each side. The bobblehead sunflower attached to the dashboard was another difference, along with the sachet of lavender stuffed into the cup holder and the two crates of glass mason jars rattling in the backseat. Grace was about to reach for the nearest container when Callie climbed out of the driver's side.

"Don't worry about those," Callie said. The bobblehead danced as the door shut behind her. "We can come back for them and your suitcase later once it's stopped raining."

Happy to leave the heavy items for later, Grace took off after Callie into the drizzly mist. Mud squished around her shoes along the country driveway until they reached the bottom of the hill. A small clapboard house came into view. The white paint peeked through the foliage like a daisy in spring, full of hope and promise.

The groan of an old hinge tore her attention away from the building before Callie stepped through a wooden gate. Grace followed her lead, latched the gate behind her, and almost ran straight into Callie, who had stopped only feet ahead.

"Watch your step." Callie tiptoed around the trickle of water cutting across the path. With ease, she skipped ahead, missing the puddles and pockets of mud as if she performed this dance on a regular basis. She sidestepped a large puddle in the middle of the trail and walked across the wooden beams of the raised flower beds. "I know I should be thankful for the rain, and I am, truly. It's our lifeblood up here," she said over her shoulder. "God knows we've been hanging on by a thread the past few years. But it would be nice if it didn't have to all come down at once, you know?"

Grace followed, albeit a little slower, as she tried her best to mirror the woman's delicate balance on the narrow slats of wood. The scent of lavender tickled her nose as she brushed past a row of green-and-purple mounds, the surrounding air loud with the buzzing of honeybees. Something tickled the back of her arm, and she swatted her hand at it to shoo the insect away.

"Don't worry about the bees," Callie said over her shoulder. "They won't sting unless provoked."

They wove through the maze of a garden, passing beneath sunflowers the size of dinner plates. Despite the ongoing drought, it looked like a chef's paradise. The colorful patches of multi-colored lettuces, kale, and tomato vines reminded Grace of the salad bar at her favorite vegan restaurant in Denver.

Aside from the sound of their footsteps and the low drone of insects, a peaceful hush seemed to drape its arms around the place. Grace couldn't remember the last time she'd experienced such quiet. She'd lived in cities most of her life since she'd first moved in with her aunt as a kid. At first, the noise had been unbearable, but over the years, she'd learned to tune out the car horns and late-night pub-crawlers from the comfort of her downtown apartment.

"Do you live out here all by yourself?" she asked, slowly piecing together this woman who'd invite a near-stranger into her house.

"Yep, just me and the bees. I grew up here, but after the fire, my parents decided to move us closer to the city. It wasn't until after college that I decided to come back."

"Doesn't it get lonely?" Life in the city could get a little claustrophobic at times, but she'd always found comfort in knowing she was surrounded by others, even if she didn't interact with them much.

"It's not too bad. It can get a little quiet sometimes, but I don't mind. And besides, I've got Caden and Micah to keep me company. There's never a boring day with them around." She leaped onto a patch of relatively dry earth, copper curls frizzing around her face in the late evening humidity.

"Hard to picture Micah as a friendly neighbor. Caden, though, I would believe. He seems nice enough." Without the same ease, Grace hopped down from the raised bed and landed with a splash. She cringed at the dirty water spilling into her now-ruined shoes, but Callie only laughed and wiped a few brown droplets from her overalls.

"Caden is great, and so is Micah. Don't worry about him. He'll cool down once he's had time to think about it, so don't write him off just yet. His bark is far worse than his bite. Believe me."

For the sake of her job, she hoped so. At this point, Grace would be lucky if he let her step foot on his property again. She'd need a healthy dose of good luck, or a miracle for that matter, for him to ever agree to hear her out now.

A glimmer of gold seeped through the clouds, causing the moisture on the plants to almost to glisten. Everything about this little garden made Grace want to believe in second chances, but the dark clouds overhead warned her not to get her hopes up.

"Hey, Callie? Why did you stick up for me back there with Micah? I mean, you could have easily turned me out, same as him." As much as she appreciated the woman's support, she knew enough not to trust handouts.

Callie turned away from the flowering beds and offered her a small smile. "I never asked what brought you here, so as far as I'm concerned, we're all good."

Grace averted her gaze to study the rows of squash, suddenly uncomfortable. Everything about Callie was innocent and trusting, and at the moment, Grace felt anything but worthy of such kindness.

"For what it's worth, I'm still sorry. Nothing about this trip has gone how I'd planned, least of all starting off with a lie." She kicked a pebble and watched as it bounced down the path. Coming here had been a long shot of an idea, anyway. "Maybe this is a sign I should give up."

"Don't say that. You've only just gotten here." Callie reached inside one of the covered bins flanking the yard and pulled out two pairs of leather gloves. "And besides, what do you plan to do with the bridge flooded and your car out of commission? Hike out on foot?" She smiled and plucked a yellow-and-pink-striped tomato from the vine at her feet. "You hungry? It's not Micah's famous enchiladas, but I do make a mean goat cheese and tomato pizza."

A woman after her own heart. "How can I say no to that?"

"If you did, I'd say we couldn't be friends," Callie teased. "Come on, help me pick out a few more of these, and I'll show you inside so we can get started." Tomatoes in hand, along with a sprig of fresh basil and a freshly unearthed onion bulb, the two of them took in the last rays of sunlight before they ducked inside.

It couldn't have been more than a two-bedroom house, but between the blue front door, the bundles of hydrangeas and lilies lay strewn across the farmhouse table, and the soft butter-colored wall paint, it felt to Grace like a cottage straight out of a storybook.

Just inside, they shed their muddy shoes, the cool of the tile floor a welcome relief to her aching feet.

Once in the kitchen, Callie cleared a space on the countertop and deposited their meager harvest in a heap. Grace unloaded her handful of tomatoes and took her time inspecting the cozy kitchen-diner. Bushels of dried flowers and herbs hung from the ceiling rafters. Jars filled with amber liquid glowed along the windowsills, casting streaks of golden light onto the timber floor. Everywhere Grace turned, glass dropper bottles sat in rows across the counter, along with stacks of compact aluminum tins of various sizes.

She might not be an expert in country living, but even this seemed a tad excessive for one person. "Back at Micah's place, you mentioned something about a business plan. What's that all about?" Grace asked.

Callie smiled and spread her arms wide as she did a slow twirl in the middle of the room. "This is it."

There must have been an order to the madness. But the cluttered kitchen reminded Grace of a hoarder's paradise. "So, your plan is to.... What, exactly?"

Callie stopped mid-spin, a silly grin glued to her face. "I know it doesn't look like much yet, but I have big plans. Despite my parents' best attempts to dissuade me, I intend to make a life for myself up here with my plants and bees. After only a year, the hives are producing more honey than I know what to do with, and I've already got a dozen or so teas, tinctures, and salves ready and waiting. There's a reason civilizations have utilized the medicinal properties of herbs and plants for centuries, and I intend to share that knowledge with the community."

After pausing her speech to straighten a stack of boxes on the table, she turned back to Grace, a look of apology tugging at her brow. "I'm sorry. I tend to ramble when I get excited. But I truly believe the natural approach to health isn't something we should leave to the history books. Here, smell this." She plucked a bundle of lavender from a string of dried herbs above the counter and handed it to Grace, who breathed in the flowers' perfume.

It wasn't the lavender that made her feel relaxed and welcomed, but she couldn't deny the pleasant memories brought on by the sweet aroma. Long summer days by the lake. The smell of her mom's perfume as she laid out the picnic blanket. Her father grinning as he strode up the beach empty-handed but paused to lay a kiss on each of their heads. It was a faint memory. A lifetime ago, really. Yet she'd go back there in a heartbeat if she could.

While she tried to capture the peaceful memory before the moment passed, Callie chatted away about the plant's health benefits. "... It's great for stress, minor skin irritations, and it's even been shown to help alleviate headaches."

Grace inhaled another lungful of the soothing fragrance, then frowned. "I could serve Micah all the lavender tea in the world, and I don't think that would make a dent in the headache I've caused him."

Callie released an audible breath, her face softening. "He's really not as bad as you think. He might seem gruff at times, but he's as loyal a friend as they come." In a heartbeat, she reached for a covered bowl on the counter, scooped out a lump of dough, and began to shape it to fit a large circular pan already waiting on the stovetop.

Unsure what to do, Grace watched the process of pulling and kneading, the repetitive motion lulling her into a false sense of peace.

"I'm sure you're right. It's just..." What was it exactly? She'd faced difficult clients before, but this felt different. As it so happened, she'd never found herself in the situation of being rescued by a client, hiding her true motives for being there, and then having it all blow up in her face in a matter of hours. And to top it all off, she hadn't expected to be holed up in the house next door with the man's close friend.

She blinked and peered down at her bare feet. "If I were in his shoes, I wouldn't trust me either."

Callie stopped her task and laid a flour-dusted hand on Grace's arm. "How about I go back over and smooth over the ruffled feathers? Who knows—maybe he'll come around."

"I appreciate the offer, but I don't want to cause any trouble between the two of you. You've already stuck up for me enough by letting me stay here."

"Nonsense. I have some things I'd planned to take over, anyway. And perhaps I'll slip in a bag of *Tension Tamer* tea for good measure." Callie winked and reached for a jar in one of the upper cabinets. Uncapping the lid, she poured what smelled like lavender, peppermint, and chamomile into a small bag and tossed it into a box beside a large tub of honey. "I'll head on over once we've had dinner and try talking some sense into him."

"You're sure?" Grace asked, skeptical of the offer. The idea of being left alone in Callie's house didn't sit well with her, either. Despite the unwarranted invitation, they were hardly more than strangers. Callie had no reason to trust her. No reason to be helping her the way she was. However much her heart craved the friendship, she knew better than to believe it was real.

Callie tilted her head and smiled. "Of course. What are friends for?"

As soon as they'd cleaned up their plates and the rain had stopped, Callie stepped outside into the humid evening air and made a beeline for her truck. Sure, she had planned to take over some honey later in the week, but her main reason for going back to Micah's place had been purely for Grace's sake.

And maybe she didn't mind the idea of seeing Caden again as well.

A gust of wind blew through the trees and danced with the ends of her hair as she climbed into the cab. The daisy bobblehead bounced in welcome, ready for another adventure.

"You agree with me, right?" The crocheted figurine nodded, and she took that to mean *yes*. "Good, that's what I thought."

Despite her assurances to Grace, she was not immune to Micah's moods. It had been a long time since she'd been on the receiving end of his anger, and while she stood by her decisions, she also wanted to mend the rift between them sooner rather than later.

Callie stole one last look at the house before reversing out of the gravel driveway.

Grace would be fine on her own for an hour or so. No doubt she was tired and could use the time to unwind. Before Callie left, she'd made sure to show her around the house and the guest bedroom upstairs. At her own prompting, she'd even pulled down a mug and brewed a cup of her favorite tea—raspberry rose—in the hopes that it would help alleviate the day's worries.

Even if what Micah said was true, and Grace was trying to convince him to sell the ranch to her company, she was still human. The least Callie could do was show her some kindness. And based on Grace's reaction to her initial invitation, she'd make a guess the woman could use a friend.

Callie rolled down the windows, letting the cool breeze wash over her skin. The surrounding forest blurred into a mosaic of greens and shadows as she traveled down the short stretch of dirt road. In the distance, she could make out a few dozen curly-haired sheep calmly munching on the wild grass. A few lambs frolicked around the meadow, their stubby tails flicking back and forth as they played. With no one else on the road, she took a few minutes on the short drive to smile at their innocent joy.

She'd been called many things in the past—a dreamer, idealist, naïve—but never once had she been accused of not caring for those around her. If Micah had an issue with her taking Grace in, that was his problem, but she knew a hurting soul when she saw one. And Micah and Grace were *both* hurting in different ways. She could sense it as clearly as Pauline's arthritis could predict a storm.

Brushing a curl from her face, she slowed at the entrance to the ranch and turned up the long drive. The lights were off in the house, so she drove around back. She pulled up next to Micah's truck, and with honey and tea in hand, went in search of the two cousins.

Grace stood in the corner of Callie's living room, the only place in the house with a decent cell signal.

She clutched the phone to her ear and paused, studying Callie's bookshelf on herbal remedies and farm life while trying to think of a way to explain her current predicament to her boss. All her well-thought-out explanations seemed dwarfed by the voice echoing inside her head, throwing out accusations. Bold. Assertive. Rash. Words that made her feel as small as the grape tomatoes clinging to the vines beyond the window.

Reaching for a book on beekeeping, she thumbed through the first few pages before returning it to the shelf.

At least Katrina wasn't here to see her failed attempt. Grace had put off the call long enough, and she sighed a breath of relief when the call had clicked over to voicemail. She wasn't so sure how an open return date would be received, especially since she hadn't told anyone about her impromptu weekend trip in the first place.

Get in. Get the job done. And get out. That had been the plan.

But apparently, God had other ideas.

"Hey, Katrina. I'm sorry for the late notice, but I won't be in the office next week." Coward. "I'm busy following up a lead, and it's taking a bit longer than anticipated. But don't worry, I'm on it." It wasn't exactly a lie, per se. Who knew? Maybe in the morning, Micah would come around and decide to hear her out.

Grace could just see it—him standing on Callie's porch in his cowboy boots, ready to put the past behind them. They'd laugh about it for a minute or two, exchange pleasantries, and she'd be on her way, signed contract in hand.

Or so she hoped.

She tried to envision how that conversation would play out, but his smile quickly turned sour even in her fantasy.

Who was she kidding? The man hated her and with good reason.

"This deal is as good as settled." She wasn't sure why she'd said that. It most assuredly was *not* a done deal. But she needed to reassure herself more than her boss that she hadn't taken such a gamble on nothing.

CHAPTER

Seven

"DID YOU HAVE to be so harsh back there?" Caden asked as he and Micah sloshed through the mud behind the barn. He'd been as surprised as the rest of them to hear about Grace's reasons for being there, but in his opinion, his cousin could have handled things a lot better.

Micah grunted as he hefted a square bale of hay to his shoulder and onto the growing stack near the barn door. After nearly two hours of back-breaking work, Caden's muscles were close to maxing out, but Micah seemed to have caught a second wind. Normally, they would have let the hay dry another day or two before stacking it with the rest of their winter stores, but he knew better than to get in Micah's way when he was in a funk.

The way he'd snapped at Callie, however, was not cool.

"She was only trying to help, you know." Caden sidestepped Finn, who'd planted himself in front of the trailer, and grabbed the next bale, using his knees to lift it on top of the others. The seventy-pound bundle landed with a thud, sending bits of hay dust flying in all directions. He tried not to choke on the chaff and held his breath until it settled to the barn floor.

The remaining bales sat in the trailer beneath a large tarp, protected from the rain. He almost hadn't finished in time, what with how fast that storm rolled in earlier and Micah having gone into town, but he'd managed. Maybe with a few more sore muscles than he'd care to admit, but a job was a job.

A bead of sweat crawled down his temple. Dropping onto the nearest hay bale, he swiped a gritty forearm across his forehead and reached for his water bottle.

"Don't tell me you're giving up already," Micah groused. Like Superman, he marched past, one bale thrown over each shoulder. He unloaded them one by one, and they fell with a loud *whomp* beside Caden.

"Well, if you're gonna choke me to death with hay dust, I just might." Coughing, he buried his face in his shirt until the dust settled once more.

"Sorry about that." Micah plucked at a frayed string tied around the bale and frowned. "Pass me the baling twine."

Caden raised an eyebrow before reaching for the large spool at his feet. His back protested the simple movement. He'd put on some muscle in the past year working around the ranch, enough to carry out his share of the chores and then some. But even he had his limits. With a dramatic groan, he cut a length of roughly ten feet of twine and handed it over.

Micah shot him a look as he straddled the square bale. He threaded the blue cord around the length of the bundle, wrapping one end around his right hand. He cinched it tight with a twist and wrapping motion and tied off the two loose ends of the knot.

Finn's excited yips echoed through the open barn door. The speckled dog came bounding inside, followed by light footsteps. Rising to his feet, Caden looked up to see Callie striding toward them. Her hair practically glowed under the barn's exposed lights. Even in her overalls and mud-caked work boots, she somehow exuded sunshine itself.

"Twice in one day. To what do we owe the pleasure?" Her very presence seemed to lift his spirits, and he found himself crossing the barn floor. Grateful for the reprieve, he met her on the threshold and smiled down at the box's contents in her arms—honey, some teas, and what looked like two jars of jam. Having missed dinner because Micah, in his sour mood, refused to eat dinner and went to work instead, Caden's stomach grumbled at the very sight.

"Oh, you know me. Can't stay away from the smell of hay and manure."

"Right. Maybe you should find a way to bottle that and sell it to tourists. You could market it as *Fresh Country Living* or something like that. I bet you would make a fortune."

Her musical laugh filled the entryway. "Well, it's not quite *eau de ranch*, but I did finish another batch of jam. I thought I'd bring over more samples. This one," she said, pointing to the jar on the right, "is rhubarb, honey, and thyme. I'm still experimenting with the recipe, so let me know what you think."

He, for one, didn't mind being used as a guinea pig. If the food she kept bringing them were her *experiments*, then he had no doubt she'd succeed once she got her business up and running. Honey, teas, jams... The Colorado Front Range wouldn't know what hit them.

Micah trudged up behind him, and Callie put on her sunniest smile. "I also brought you a few more teas to try. With any luck, one of them will work for those headaches of yours."

Caden read the label *Tension Tamer* and grinned. Micah, on the other hand, didn't seem amused. "If it's all the same, Callie, I'd like to finish up here before midnight."

"So you don't want to hear me out?" She set down the box of goodies. Finn sniffed the bags of tea before meandering out the open barn door.

Micah sighed and pinched the bridge of his nose. "You're just going to say something to try to get me to change my mind about Grace. I barely have enough time to keep this place running, let alone play nice with someone out to take the land from right under me. Unless you've forgotten why she's really here."

"I never said you'd have to make daisy chains together." She crossed her arms over her chest.

Caden bit back a laugh. His cousin wouldn't be caught dead wearing such a frilly thing, but the mental image would give him a chuckle through the rest of the evening hauling hay on an empty stomach.

Micah shook his head, brushing off the remark as if it were nothing but a fly. "Look, there's no way I'd even consider her company's offer to buy the place, so why should I pretend to like her? We're already late in shearing the sheep, and there's still the upper meadow to be harvested before the frost sets in. The proceeds would go a long way to getting us through to another year."

"I'm trying to come up with a solution that works for everyone here."

"Meaning..."

Callie chewed on her bottom lip as if debating whether to voice her idea. Caden had seen that expression countless times to know Micah was not about to enjoy what she had to say. He, however, couldn't wait to hear it.

"What if I told you I already knew someone who could help? And I happen to know for a fact they are available to start immediately."

"Who?" Micah made a show of peering around the cavernous barn as if people were lining up for manual labor. When he looked back at Callie, she seemed anything but amused.

"Grace."

Micah made a grunt of disapproval. "Be serious. I doubt she's ever seen a hard day's work in her life. The last thing I need is to have to baby-sit someone who doesn't know a shovel from a pickax."

"You won't have to. I'll make sure she knows what to do. Besides, you said it yourself. You need more help here on the ranch. And who knows? She could be the answer to our prayers." She placed her hands on her hips, as stubborn as ever, and continued. "The way I see it, you have two options: ignore each other until the bridge is up and running again—which, let's face it, might be a while—or learn to get along."

Micah didn't appear impressed by her suggestion, so Caden jumped on board. "Yeah, unless someone hires a helicopter to get Grace out of here, which is highly unlikely, she's stuck here. And unless she can work her job remotely, she's probably going to need a way to earn some money to cover expenses."

"Exactly!" Callie readily agreed. "It can be a sort of trade—her help on the ranch in exchange for free rent and meals at my place. Show her what the ranch is like. Make her fall in love with the land and maybe she'll forget all about selling you her pitch. And if you don't have the money for the loan repayment at the end of the month, you hear her out."

If anyone could teach someone how to work a ranch, it was Callie. If it hadn't been for her, Caden probably would have floundered during his first week there. Micah's philosophy had been sink or swim, but she'd been the one to show him how to do more than survive. That was one of the things he admired most about her—her willingness to see the good in people and cultivate it to its fullest potential. No matter if anyone else did or not. He might still be on the fence about her new housemate, but if Callie was willing to give her a chance, so was he.

Caden watched as she stood toe-to-toe with Micah. Before Micah could pop a blood vessel, he stepped in once more. "I can help as well."

Micah stared at him as if he'd grown a pair of horns and shook his head. "You two really think you can convince her of this crazy idea?"

Callie looked to Caden with appreciation and back to Micah. "Absolutely."

Caden could almost hear the gears turning inside that head of hers while Micah, no doubt, was regretting his decision before he'd even made it. It might be a recipe for disaster, but the idea of spending a little extra time with Callie, no matter how that came about, was good enough for him.

He couldn't wait to get started.

"You told him I'd do what?" Grace stared open-mouthed at Callie. What had she been thinking? Her working on a ranch? That's what she got for falling asleep before Callie got home last night and talking about it now, not hours before she was supposed to show up at the ranch. "I'd rather take my chances and hike out of here than embarrass myself further."

Callie gave her a skeptical look and ladled another spoonful of pancake batter onto the griddle. A bowl of warm blueberry syrup glistened on the table, and the batter's cinnamon vanilla aroma filled the cozy kitchen. One by one, she slid the steaming pancakes on top of the others, then whisked them toward the back patio.

Still waiting for a reply, Grace reached for the syrup and coffee and followed her outside into the cool morning sunshine. Callie was already dividing the stack between their two plates, a peace offering if ever there was one. "Don't worry," she said, pouring Grace a mug. "It wouldn't be any of the hard stuff. Just feeding the sheep and things like that. I already told Micah you'd be up to the challenge. And he's willing to be civil, which is a feat in and of itself."

Grace knew a guilty stack of pancakes when she saw one, but it all smelled too good to turn down. She sighed. If her new friend had gone through the trouble of working out an arrangement, in addition to welcoming her into her home, the least she could do was hear her out. Even if she already knew her answer.

"And what makes you think I'd be any good on a ranch? If you haven't noticed, I'm not exactly the ranching type." She glanced down at her two-hundred-dollar cashmere sweater and back to Callie's overalls and work boots. This morning, Grace had swapped out the green pair from yesterday for one with flowers embroidered over the pockets. Pair that with her leather boots, and she looked ready for a day spent wrist-deep in the garden.

"That's exactly what Caden said when he first got here, and now he's practically running the place with Micah. Besides"—Callie waved a pancake-speared fork while she talked—"didn't you say you wanted a way to earn back his trust? Well, I can't think of a better alternative. And who knows? Maybe you'll actually have fun." She wiggled her eyebrows with a hint of mischief and dug into her breakfast.

Even though the very idea made Grace's skin crawl, Callie wasn't wrong. Based on what Micah said yesterday, it could be days, if not longer, before she could leave. The least she could do was find a way to put a positive spin on what had quickly turned into a disaster. Even if it did mean losing out on that promotion she'd been counting on.

A lone honeybee buzzed over the blueberry syrup and toward the first row of flowers in the raised beds. Grace watched the fuzzy insect disappear into the hollyhocks, then turned her attention to the rest of the garden. Moisture from yesterday's rain sparkled against the tall grass like a carpet of small glass beads. A wall of aspens and wild brambles seemed to blend the edges of the yard with the surrounding forest. With all its fairy tale charm, she wouldn't have been surprised to see a family of gnomes emerge from the thicket.

Grace washed down her pancakes with the rest of her sweetened coffee. "Hmm. This is delicious. Did you buy it in town? This isn't like any coffee I've ever had before." She took another sip, noticing the floral notes and surprising lack of bitterness.

Callie topped off her cup and plunked the carafe beside the syrup. "I'm glad you like it. However, it's not coffee."

"What do you mean?" Grace frowned, peeling her gaze away from the garden. Grace took another sip of the dark brew, testing the sweet yet bitter notes on her tongue. "If it's not coffee, what *exactly* am I drinking?"

Callie chuckled. "Dandelion and chicory root tea. But don't worry," she added before Grace could object. "It's completely safe and has loads of health benefits without the added caffeine."

Grace spied a cluster of yellow buds in the corner of the yard and turned back to her mug. "By dandelion, you mean the *weed*?"

"The *flower*," Callie corrected, "which, might I point out, you already claimed to be delicious."

Grace had to give it to her. Despite Callie's innocent, homegrown appearance, she had more than a few tricks up her sleeves. Grace leaned back against the wrought-iron chair and took another tentative sip. Now that Callie mentioned it, there was something different about the flavor. She tested it on her tongue once more and relented as one sip turned into another. "I suppose you're right. Whatever this is, it *is* pretty good."

"Right! Most people wouldn't give it the time of day, but if they can put aside their pre-determined assumptions and give it a chance, they might find they actually enjoy it."

Grace scrunched her nose and tried not to grimace. "I have a feeling we're not talking about dandelion coffee anymore."

"Maybe I am. Maybe I'm not." Her innocent expression wouldn't fool a fly. "But what would you think if I weren't talking about coffee? If, oh, I don't know..." She waved a hand in the air as if searching for her own thoughts. "Let's say a certain landowner got off on the wrong foot with a certain visitor from out of town. In a small community, it only makes sense for the two of them to give each other a second chance. Either that, or they could always start their own feud and divide the valley like the Montagues and Capulets. Now that would make for an exciting change." She smirked behind her mug as if meddling in other people's business was a common pastime.

"Are you really comparing Micah and me to Romeo and Juliet?" Grace couldn't help but laugh. She had no idea why the rest of the world was set on romanticizing the Shakespearean tragedy. Self-reliance and reason had been her guideposts through life, and she wasn't about to throw them aside any time soon. "I always thought they'd have been better off if they'd kept to their own families. That way, everyone would have at least lived to the end of the book."

Callie played with the end of a creeping vine that had wandered across the patio. "You may have a point there, but there's nothing wrong with following your heart." For a moment, her mind seemed lost on other things. Carefully, she wound the vine of honeysuckle around her fingers and threaded it back through its wooden trellis.

As much as Grace hated the idea of facing Micah again, she loathed the thought of going home empty-handed. Grace turned from the garden to look at her curious new friend and frowned. "Why are you helping me? Aren't I supposed to be the enemy or something? I could be planning to buy up the entire valley and subdivide it with condos, for all you know.

"First of all," Callie started, a faint smile on her lips, "never in a million years would I believe that many people would want to move out here in the middle of nowhere." She chuckled. "And second..." She studied Grace for a long moment before proceeding. "It might sound strange, since we hardly know each other, but I have a feeling God brought you here for a reason."

More like a misguided sense of ambition and a broken-down VW Bug, but who was counting?

"Look. It's no secret that ranching is a difficult life. It's unreliable, a lot of hard work, and often lonely, but it's rewarding in its own way as well. To see the seeds you plant grow into fields of gold or when you bite into that first juicy tomato from your own garden ... It reminds us that we are part of something bigger. We're blessed to call this place home. And if there's a way to save that for anyone, even if only a part of it, I'm all in." Callie looked out over her garden and the surrounding forest, and a peace seemed to settle over Grace.

If Micah cared for his land as much as Callie did, then maybe there was still a chance he'd listen to her proposal. Every person had their price, and if things were as difficult for the Prescott Ranch as Callie let on, this could very well be the answer to both of their problems. After all, Prospect & Gould wasn't interested in developing the land, nor did they need all of it. "I'm not making any promises, but if he's willing to give it a try, then so am I."

"Does that mean you're staying?" Callie asked.

In all honesty, if it hadn't been for Callie, she didn't know what she would have done. She still didn't understand this unearned kindness but owed it to Callie and herself to see where this opportunity led her. "At least until my car and the road are repaired. After that, I guess we'll both find out."

Callie squealed and threw her arms around Grace in a hug. The action caught her off guard, but her arms instinctively returned the gesture. A surge of memories threatened to force its way to the surface—her mother's comforting arms, her father's rich laugh. Those seemed as much a fairytale as the garden she found herself in.

Moisture tickled her lashes, and she quickly blinked it away before pulling back.

Callie looked between them and, for the first time, seemed to notice the difference in their attire. "First things first. We need to find you some appropriate clothing. But don't worry, I think we're about the same size. Pants might be a little long, but you can always cuff them."

Grace only hoped Callie owned more than overalls. The boots, however, she could live with. "I think my shoes would thank you."

Callie laughed. "I'll bet. I've got just the thing."

With the energy of a forest sprite, Callie cleared the table of their dishes and skipped back inside, leaving Grace once more to follow behind.

CHAPTER

Eight

"FINN. LOOK BACK." Micah raised his voice over the sound of the herd and watched as Finn raced toward the edge of the field. Micah let out a loud whistle, and Finn responded by moving in a counterclockwise circle, driving the stragglers back up the hill toward the rest of the sheep. Once they were safely with the others, he called the dog off.

Finn pivoted as if a switch had flipped and raced to catch up with Micah and his horse. He trotted beside them, grinning in self-satisfaction at a job well done. The seven-year-old cattle dog was a huge part of the ranch's success, but more so, he was a part of the family. No fancy pedigree or professional training, but he was loyal and true, and that was far more than any man could hope to ask for—four legs or two.

"Do you think we got them all?" Caden asked from astride his horse. The buckskin quarter horse stood a hand shorter than Micah's bay, Roper, but its quick gait could give Micah a run for his money any day. As usual, Caden kept a firm hold on the reins in case Dune got spooked and decided to bolt. Again.

"Looks like it." From beneath his baseball cap, Micah looked out over the rocky field and the sea of white. Together, the herd of five hundred moved like a flock of starlings. As a kid, he'd been mesmerized by how so many animals could move together as one. Sheep, birds, fish... He'd noted similar behaviors across species, but he'd yet to find the same camaraderie between people—Caden and Callie not included.

After discovering a portion of downed fence by the river, he'd gone in search of Caden. It had taken the better part of the morning to round up the flock, but after a rough head count, everything appeared as it should. He hadn't intended to rotate them into the upper pasture until next month, however. He'd been banking on that last harvest and its proceeds to go toward the loan, but he'd figure out their next move once they got there. He could always grow more crops. The sheep, on the other hand, were far more important.

One fire at a time.

"Once we get them settled, I'd like to inspect the rest of the southern fence line. If any other sections are down, we need to know." Even a single hole was enough for a pack of coyotes to find their way in. Or a mountain lion. Micah's chest tightened. If one of those got to the herd, he may as well kiss the ranch goodbye.

"How much do you think that's gonna set us back?" Caden asked.

"If we do most of the work ourselves, I'm hoping not much." There was plenty of leftover fencing back at the barn. Enough for a temporary fix, at least. "I figure we can make do with what we've got and go from there."

Micah ducked beneath a protruding branch, letting Caden go ahead through the narrow path in the trees. Only another mile of forested hills and they'd reach the eastern gate.

Without instruction, Finn pushed the herd from behind while Micah and Caden skirted them around the base of the granite outcrop. The San Juan Mountains towered above them like sentinels standing watch over the narrow valley.

The sun was directly overhead when they reached the upper pasture an hour later, A bead of sweat slid between Micah's shoulder blades, reminding him that September was well underway. Once he accounted for every sheep, Micah secured the gate and opted for the long way home. As much as he needed to repair the fence, the last thing he wanted was another run-in with Grace. A futile hope to delay the inevitable, he supposed, but a man could dream. Somehow, Callie had roped him into this plan of hers, and if he hadn't already given her his word, he'd have tossed Grace off his property the next time he saw her.

Micah didn't need someone telling him he'd overreacted. In fact, he seemed to be the only one concerned about the fate of their futures. If the ranch went down, there went his home, Caden's reason to stay, and even the land Callie had been leasing from him for the past few years. They were the ones not taking this seriously enough.

"Want to talk about it?" Caden seemed to read between the lines of Micah's silence. "You're extra quiet this morning, which means you're either worrying about the ranch or Grace."

Could this week get any worse? Micah ground his teeth, keeping the sarcastic comment to himself. He'd mulled it over all night, and the way he saw it, Grace would spend one day getting her hands dirty and be done with this whole thing.

"Not worried. Just being realistic."

"Then why do you look like someone put salt in your coffee?"

Unfortunately for Micah, he knew exactly what that was like. "Like the time you switched it for sugar when the whole family went camping?"

Caden laughed. "I'll never forget Tess's face when she took that first sip of her *sweet* tea."

"If I remember correctly, your sister chased you into the lake a few seconds after that. The rest of us would have, too, if we weren't gagging on our drinks."

"It was totally worth it." Caden flashed him a boyish grin, a reminder of the five-year age gap between them. Closer to thirty now than twenty-five, there were times Caden still seemed like the same little punk who couldn't go a day without getting into mischief.

"Anyway," Caden roped the conversation back in. "Whatever happens, I know you'll find a way to fix it. You always do."

Dune snorted beside him, chomping at the bit to go faster. Happy to oblige, Caden kicked his heels and trotted ahead.

Despite his desire to race across the field and away from his problems, Micah held the reins with a relaxed grip and kept his pace steady.

After another half mile on horseback, they neared the house where Callie's blue truck was already waiting for them. Squinting against the sun, Micah could see both her and Grace sitting inside. From the looks of the fresh mud on the tires, they hadn't been there long. When the passenger door swung open, Finn took off running to greet them.

"Traitor," Micah mumbled under his breath. He scratched the line of puckered skin along his temple and tugged his baseball cap lower over his forehead.

Caden had already dismounted by the back gate and was busy chatting up Callie by the barn when Micah joined them.

"So. You convinced her to agree to this crazy plan of yours?" he interrupted. Something clanged against the metal truck bed, and he looked over to see Grace rummaging around in the back for who knew what.

Callie shifted her weight to face him and stuck a hand to her hip. "Who says it's crazy?" Her smile held nothing but warmth, but her tone said not to argue with her.

"Fine. Just so long as I don't have to deal with her." Grace could muck out stalls or paint fences for all he cared. Maybe after a day of menial labor, she'd change her mind and leave him alone for good. Then again, she'd already shown an unnatural determination by sticking around. No doubt a skill she'd honed over the years—tricking ranchers into signing over their land had to require a backbone of steel. But it didn't change the fact that she'd lied to him.

Beside him, Caden cleared his throat and bumped him on the shoulder. "You'd have better luck getting him to warm up to her if she had four legs and a wool coat."

Callie laughed. "I'll keep that in mind." Her face relaxed into a soft smile, easing the thick tension around their conversation. "Well, I guess I'll let you two get back to work. I've got a whole day planned for Grace and me, so we might as well get started."

She turned to head back to her truck a few moments before Caden led the horses to their stalls.

Grabbing Roper's reins, Micah pivoted in the dirt and took off toward the open barn door. From the corner of his eye, he caught Grace's gaze, but she quickly averted it, pretending she hadn't been watching him from behind the truck. A tight grin tugged at the corners of his mouth. It was just as well. It was going to be a long day.

She had no idea what she'd signed up for.

Grace wrapped her fingers around a prickly weed, cursing the plant's stubbornness. Already, she was second-guessing this plan, and it wasn't even noon.

As far as she'd been concerned, she had already done the hard part. She'd stayed. The rest was just details. After changing into some clothes Callie lent her back at the house, they'd driven north along the backcountry road to Micah's. Despite her misgivings, there was no sense in hiding out at Callie's little cottage any longer.

She peered down at her jean overalls, flecks of fresh mud already decorating the cuffs, and sighed. Micah might have agreed to this plan, but she would bet he was just as unhappy about it as she was. He'd made it very clear she wasn't welcome, and she hadn't helped matters by hiding her identity in the first place.

Her stomach tightened. She'd been so certain of her path most of her adult life. *Driven*, her aunt called it. Never once had she doubted her decisions, but this time felt different. Grace bit her lip, forcing back the negative thoughts. That wasn't an option, not anymore. Not only was she here, but she was staying. Even if the whole thing fell apart, she'd go down fighting.

Her palms slick with sweat, she gripped the trowel tighter and went after the bushy undergrowth. The plant's small yellow flowers seemed to mock her progress, the hard clay earth reluctant to release its hold. "Why are we doing this, again?" she asked, sweltering under the sun's intense heat and her layers of cotton clothing. "We're in a field in the middle of the mountains. Don't weeds sort of come with the territory?"

With one final yank, the soil released its hold on the roots, and Grace fell back onto her butt with an *oomph*.

Callie stopped her humming and looked behind her. "Believe it or not, that little plant has the ability to wipe out an entire herd of cattle. Imagine what it can do to a flock of sheep."

Grace peered at the seemingly harmless plant clenched in her fist and let it fall to the ground.

"Don't worry. It's only poisonous if you eat it. So I don't suggest trying to make a salad out of it or anything." Callie shoved her spade into the crusty earth and yanked the weed out with a single heave. She tossed a handful of leaves and stems behind her and swiped the back of her hand over the floral headband that was fighting—and failing—to keep her curls in check.

"How do you know so much about plants?" Grace asked, curious to know more about her new friend. They may have only known each other for less than twenty-four hours, but her warm enthusiasm and unusually welcoming demeanor were hard to resist.

Callie shrugged. "I guess a lot of it comes from growing up out here. Spend enough time outside, and you eventually learn a thing or two."

"Maybe, but I don't see Micah making coffee out of dandelions."

Callie released a laugh that startled a few nearby sheep. "Micah *refuses* to drink the stuff even though I've told him a hundred times it's better for him than the caffeinated coffee he downs by the cupful." She made a face that said how much she disapproved of the stuff before she tackled another cluster of weeds.

Growing up in the city, Grace had never been much of a gardener. In fact, she could hardly keep a succulent alive, let alone identify the flowers in her neighbor's window box. She looked out over the field, noticing the hundreds of yellow-flower-specked weeds, and fought the urge to groan.

A bead of sweat traced between her shoulder blades, and she peeled off the warm leather gloves. "By the way, how did you convince him to let me come back here? I thought he made his feelings perfectly clear yesterday." She stretched her arms over her head, the muscles in her back protesting the movement. Every cloud seemed to have evaporated overnight, and an endless blue sky towered above them and the mountain-flanked valley.

"He *is* okay with me being here, right?" Grace asked, suddenly worried at Callie's silence.

"Of course he's okay with it." Callie added another weed to her growing pile, her back turned to Grace as she worked. "He just needed a little persuading, that's all."

Grace frowned. She had a hard time accepting that Micah had suddenly come to appreciate her presence overnight. Especially after his cold treatment that morning. "Seems to me he could hire anyone for the job. So why me?"

When they'd cleared every weed in a three-foot radius, Callie finally dug her trowel into the dirt and turned to face Grace. "Look, instead of questioning everything, you should count your blessings. I thought this was what you wanted. A chance to earn back his respect."

Grace flexed her hands, positive she could feel a few blisters already forming beneath the skin despite the thick gloves Callie had lent her. Another few hours of this, and she'd be lucky to make it out with a part of her that didn't hurt. "I don't know if that's even possible at this point. He blames me for trying to steal his land."

"And are you?" Callie asked, the question firm but without accusation.

"Of course not." Despite her honest attempts to contact the man, she'd never stoop that low to secure the deal. Promotion or not. "I'm sure you've heard about the water shortages across the state?" It was no secret. Colorado had been courting this drought for decades like a hesitant debutante at a ball. Even with the seasonal monsoons, there was no denying the future of their state seemed at risk. "Colorado and seven other western states have been told to cut their water usage by at least fifteen percent in the next few years. *Fifteen percent*. That's almost one million acre-feet worth of water."

"I don't see how that's possible," cut in Callie. "Do they have any ideas about how they plan to do that?"

"That's the thing." Grace charged ahead, the same sense of excitement stirring within her that she always felt when starting a new project. And compared to her company's usual interests, this was one she could really get behind. "Everyone is arguing about policy and change, but if Prospect & Gould can secure the water rights, then they might be able to win a government contract to relocate water from lesser-stressed regions to the cities."

"Won't that take water away from the communities that rely on those sources?" Callie asked.

It was a question Grace had heard a thousand times, and she dove into the pitch she'd rehearsed months ago ago.

"Not at all. They'd only pump a sustainable amount from the rivers and aquifers. Just think, millions of gallons of water are lost every year to leaky pipes and water mains. This would cut out that number entirely and provide real drinking water to places that actually need it."

Callie was quiet for a moment, no doubt absorbing the information Grace had thrown at her. Her left hand twirled the end of a wild curl that had fallen from her braid. "Sounds reasonable to me," she finally said. "Does Micah know all that? I'm sure if you explain it all to him, he'd understand."

"Highly unlikely."

"You never know. Last time I checked, he did rescue you on the side of the road. He might not have ridden in on a white steed, but around here, a truck's as good as gold. Or water, for that matter."

That may be true, but that was before yesterday's incident.

As much as she hoped otherwise, she was too well acquainted with disappointment to get her hopes up. In her experience, people didn't change. The world would try to say differently, with all its self-help books and promises to transform lives, but she'd yet to meet someone to prove her wrong. People made decisions every day, usually with their own desires in mind. The consequences of those decisions determined their future, and those around them, for better or for worse.

Across the field, a family of prairie dogs scurried between the grass's weak shadows, occasionally poking their heads above the grass and scampering back into their holes. Even all the way out here, the reminder of what she didn't have found a way to haunt her.

She blinked back the sting in her eyes. "Allergies. Must be from all the grasses and weeds." She rubbed the knuckles of her right hand across her nose and put on a convincing smile—for her or Callie, she wasn't entirely sure.

A truck rumbled to a stop in the distance. Grace lifted her head to see Micah and Caden getting out of the white pickup. Callie turned and waved, drawing Caden's attention. He smiled back and covered the space between them and the truck as Micah led Finn toward the barn.

"How's it going here, you two?" He surveyed the yard before his gaze finally rested on them. "With the way Micah's going after those fences, I think I'd rather stay here and pull weeds. Anyone want to trade?" He flashed them a toothy smile.

"I don't think either of us are falling for that trick." Callie was all smiles, which wasn't saying much as Grace had yet to see her without one. But if it were possible, she'd have sworn her eyes had an extra sparkle in them at the moment.

Caden raised his hands with feigned innocence. "No tricks. Only a fair and equal trade."

Grace looked toward the barn and back. "It can't be that bad."

"Oh, believe me, it can." Caden raised an eyebrow that said otherwise and returned his attention to Callie. "I already told him we don't have enough material, but he's ready to break his back—and mine, for that matter—to prove me wrong."

"Somehow, I don't feel sorry for you," Callie teased.

Micah exited the barn, laden with an armload of posts and wire. Grace couldn't make out his expression from beneath the hat, but she could imagine him scowling at her even from here.

"Fine," Caden said in mock defeat. "You two have fun with your little shovels. But if I don't make it back, think of me with fond memories."

Callie laughed as he skipped back toward the truck. Grace studied her friend's sappy expression and couldn't help but smile. "So, what was that all about?" she finally asked.

"The fence repairs?" She sent Caden and Micah a final wave before they packed up the truck and drove off again. "There's always something that needs fixing on a ranch."

She wasn't fooling anyone, least of all her. "No, I mean between you and Caden."

Callie's green eyes rounded. "Oh, it's nothing. We're just friends."

"But you like him, I can tell."

Callie blushed, making her freckles stand out more than usual. "Can you blame a girl?"

Grace laughed. "I suppose not. And for what it's worth, I think the feeling's mutual."

"What? No. That's just Caden. Friendly to everyone." Her earlier enthusiasm seemed to dim, and she plucked a pink clover bud from the ground, twirling it between her thumb and forefinger as she grew suspiciously quiet.

"Anyway..." Callie said, changing the subject. "I'd say we've earned ourselves a little break. How about we raid Micah's kitchen and rustle up whatever we can find?" Callie scooped together an armload of weeds and began to shove them into trash bags. The plastic stretched, threatening to burst, but it held its own against the onslaught of spiky branches.

"You don't think he'll mind?" Grace asked. The idea of stepping foot in his house uninvited sent shivers down her spine. She much preferred her earlier line of questioning.

Callie shook the bag at her feet to consolidate its contents. When satisfied, she wiped her hands on her thighs and looked up. "Not at all. I happen to know he has a whole box of tea and local honey just waiting to be dug into."

"Well, when you put it that way..." Grace mirrored Callie's grin. It may have only been a day, but she had a growing sense that Callie had a gift when it came to persuasion. It was a talent she'd love to possess if it helped win over Micah.

CHAPTER

Nine

CALLIE COULDN'T HELP but notice the moment Caden walked into a room. His larger-than-life personality usually announced his presence, but there had always been more with him, some invisible connection between them since the moment he'd stepped foot on the ranch.

It had been this way for over a year... and yet nothing had changed.

When Grace asked her point-blank about it yesterday morning, she'd panicked. Of course, she liked Caden. She'd be an idiot not to. He was kind, sweet, and he always knew how to make her laugh. She would *not* dwell on the fact that he was drop-dead gorgeous or that his smile could make her toes tingle—blame it on the high altitude or her lack of human interaction. Physical attraction a relationship did not make. Even if nothing ever happened between them, she was content having him as her friend.

Perfectly content.

Callie raised onto her toes and reached across the top shelf. She fished around in the dark for the last jar of canned peaches and grinned triumphantly when her fingers grazed the cool glass. She mentally promised to make Micah an extra-large batch this next fall, easing her conscience as she pulled the jar down from its dusty perch.

"It's for a worthy cause," she whispered. Somehow, she'd talked Grace into inviting Micah and Caden over to her place for dessert, and she knew exactly which dish to make for such an occasion.

"I'd say your peach crisp is a worthy cause, any day."

She screeched, a sound any Jane Austen heroine would never have made, and turned on the intruder. Caden stood in the doorway to the cellar. Well, stooped, really. He had more than a couple of inches on the six-foot ceiling, his large frame filling the small space.

"Would you stop sneaking up on me like that?" Her heart pulsed in her throat, and she swallowed her surprise.

"What would be the fun in that?" Caden smiled, and Callie felt something tug against her ribcage like a fishhook.

Yep. She was a goner.

"I told Micah I'd find you down here, and there you are."

"Here I am." She lifted her arms like a child discovered in a game of hide-and-seek. Ever since Grace's question about her and Caden, she couldn't push the idea from her mind. But the way his eyes held hers in the darkness had her rethinking her earlier assumptions about their friendship.

"Did you need something?" she asked, suddenly aware of her frizzy hair and ratty overalls. She wished she'd worn something nicer—knowing she'd most likely run into him at the ranch—but she'd already loaned her new overalls to Grace. There was no use worrying about it now. Her fingers plucked at a frayed seam, the floral patch the only truly unique thing about her outfit.

"What makes you think I need something? Maybe I came looking for you." His eyes searched hers, and for a moment, something seemed to pass between them.

The little voice inside her head told her not to fall for his charm. She'd do anything not to risk their friendship. But if that voice could see how he looked at her, it might say differently.

The moment was gone in a breath, and Callie wondered if she'd imagined the whole thing.

"Actually, you're right." Caden shifted and touched the tattoo below his right elbow. She'd often wondered about the story behind the compass but had never asked. Another of the many lines she'd yet to cross. He rubbed the skin, twisting the usually straight lines of ink before letting go. "I asked Grace to help change one of the tires on the tractor, but it turns out we need another set of hands. Better to be safe than sorry." He readjusted his stance until he could almost stand up straight. "Shouldn't take but a few minutes. I promise you'll have more than enough time to make dessert afterward."

His lopsided grin was her undoing. Even if she had a dozen peach crisps to make before nightfall, she'd still say yes to Caden. Besides, the peaches could wait another hour.

"Sure. Not a problem." She set her jar on the bottom step and followed him out of the dingy cellar and into the bright afternoon sunshine.

The only reason Micah had agreed to this was because Callie had promised to clean out the water troughs for a week. Based on the knot in his gut, he should have pushed for two. It sure wasn't out of the goodness of his heart that he and Caden were standing on Callie's doorstep about to have dessert with her and Grace.

Beside him, Caden scuffed his boots together and knocked off the last of the mud from working in the fields. One day in and they'd managed to re-string a whopping fifty feet of fence line. That hardly made a dent in the two-hundred-fifty-foot stretch along the river. By his estimates, they'd be at it for at least a week, a chunk of precious time he didn't have to spare. Just before heading out, he'd received yet another email from the bank. In no kind terms, they'd reminded him of the fast-approaching deadline. Between the fence that needed replacing and the road that was still out, he couldn't help but worry. He could do all the work in the world, but if he didn't find a buyer for part of her flock come the end of the month, the ranch was as good as gone.

Footsteps sounded inside. Micah readjusted his grip on the bottle of rhubarb wine he'd pulled up from the cellar moments before Grace opened the door. She'd changed out of her dirty overalls and now wore a pair of high-waisted capris and some sort of wrapped shirt covered in pink flowers. The ends of her blonde hair hung in damp waves as if she'd recently taken a shower, and he could make out the faintest scent of jasmine.

"Making yourself at home, I see." The comment was out before he could stop himself.

Grace's smile slipped, and the prickly exterior settled back in place. Not too dissimilar to the barbed wire fence they'd spent the day taking down. "Callie's busy in the kitchen."

Caden swiped the bottle of wine from his hands and strolled into the house, making a beeline for the kitchen. Grace didn't so much as look at Micah before she retreated back inside.

Way to start things off. He knew this was a bad idea. He hadn't meant to come across as harsh, but he couldn't help it. Her presence brought out an inner hostility he didn't particularly like. He offered up a quick prayer for strength and closed the door behind him.

Inside, the smell of butter and peaches was a welcome relief to that of the ranch. He closed his eyes and, for a moment, forgot about the ranch and the loan. How easy it would be to step away and forget his responsibilities for an hour or so.

"Well, are you coming or not?" Caden shouted from the kitchen, crashing through his moment of peace.

Micah opened his eyes to see Grace disappear through the open patio doors, then sighed. *So much for that.* The sight of her retreating ponytail reminded him once again of everything he stood to lose.

Callie walked toward him, a playful smile on her lips, and shoved a stack of plates into his hands. "If you're just going to stand there, you might as well make yourself useful."

He relaxed and looked over her shoulder to see Caden, hands already full with utensils, napkins, and a pitcher of iced tea. If his cousin had a hand free, he might have tried to carry out the dessert as well, but Grace had already beaten him to it.

No matter his own feelings, Micah knew Callie was trying her best to help everyone get along. The least he could do was try to be civil.

"Lead the way."

Micah followed Callie through the dining room, avoiding the stacks of boxes and dried herbs resting on the edge of the old farm table, and stepped out onto the back patio. Without warning, Callie skipped ahead of him and took her seat between Caden and Grace. He dropped his gaze to the remaining chair on the other side of Grace and knew he'd walked right into a trap.

One hour and a half-eaten peach crisp later, the four of them sat around Callie's patio table in the shade of her climbing trumpet vine. The pink and orange bell-shaped flowers bobbed in the light breeze, taunting him with their peaceful wave.

"Grace and I came up with a name for my business this afternoon." Callie interrupted the group's quiet eating.

Micah raised an eyebrow in question, but it was Caden who jumped ahead.

"That's great. What did you decide on?" He'd finished off his helping in record time and was currently nursing a glass of sweetened sun tea. The amber liquid glistened in the late afternoon sunshine, and a bead of condensation slowly dripped onto the table.

Micah glanced at Grace, who looked about ready to shove a forkful of peaches in her mouth to avoid the attention. He could almost feel the warmth radiating off her skin as she squirmed under his gaze. When all eyes were on her, though, she rested her fork on the edge of her plate and slid Micah a challenging stare.

Grace fidgeted in the chair beside him, apparently as equally uncomfortable with this conversation as he was. "Among the Bees," she said, fingers clasped together in her lap. "Honey & Herbal Remedies by Callie."

"Brilliant." Caden beamed at the women across the table. "That's exactly the kind of thing you were looking for, Cal."

"I know, right?" Callie practically jumped in her seat. "It ties together the hives *and* the garden. I could have done without my name in the title, but Grace said it's the personal touches that connect a business to its customers."

Her innocent smile took him back to when they were kids—untouched by the harsh realities of this world. Even though it warmed him to see her so happy, concern still nagged him. If she knew the statistics of how many small businesses failed in their first year, she might not be as enthusiastic. The fact that Grace was fueling this whole thing made it worse. She was only there until her car and the bridge were repaired. After that, she'd be gone, as would her interest in helping Callie, and he'd be left to pick up the pieces as always.

Micah's skin grew warm. He downed a large gulp of water, letting it cool his suddenly parched throat.

Callie continued to speak, her forkful of peaches and crumb topping threatening to fly off at any minute as she moved her arms about. "We've even started talking about a possible business plan, although that's been mostly Grace. I'm like a tomato vine without a lattice when it comes to numbers and spreadsheets. I'm in it for the people, and if I can make any sort of difference through all this, then I'll be happy." She smiled and took another bite.

Micah held his tongue for Callie's sake. A business plan? More like a takeover from where he sat. Grace wasn't here to be their friend. He knew her type. She'd do anything to get what she wanted and then be gone the first chance she got. He muttered under his breath about empty promises and tipped his hat lower to block out the encroaching sunlight.

"What was that?" All eyes turned to him, and the gnawing in his gut intensified. From Grace's hard stare, he realized he'd spoken a little too loud.

"Well, go on," she prompted.

Ever since he'd arrived, she'd been walking on eggshells around him, but apparently not anymore. She was asking for an argument, and he was all too happy to oblige.

"Fine. You want to know what I think?"

"As a matter of fact, I would," Grace challenged back.

Micah clenched his teeth, struggling against the urge to march down to the river and rebuild the bridge all by himself, plank by plank. "I think the only reason you're here at all is to convince me to sell. I'm not falling for this altruistic excuse of yours."

"We don't want your land," Grace cut in. "At least not all of it. We're only interested in purchasing some of the water rights. Nestlé did a similar thing in Chaffee County a few years back, and it was a win-win for everyone involved."

"Is that so?" He would be willing to bet half his flock not everyone had come away from that deal unscathed. "And what about Callie's new business?" he asked. "Do you plan to take over that project as well?"

"Does anyone want another scoop of peach crisp?" Callie interrupted. "Maybe some more tea?"

"No thanks. I was just leaving." Micah stood and reached for his empty plate and glass. He stomped toward the kitchen and plunged the plate under a stream of scalding water before turning to leave. Halfway across the dining room, he heard Caden's heavy footsteps behind him. A hand came down on his shoulder, but he shrugged it off. "I'm not going back out there.

So, if you came in here to convince me otherwise, you can save your breath."

Caden didn't say a word, only held his hands up in surrender.

Before Micah could receive an earful of witty comebacks or teasing remarks, he moved to the front door and crossed the rest of the yard to his truck. He'd apologize later. Another item to add to his growing list of transgressions.

He revved the engine and peeled out of the driveway. Windows down, he let the smell of pine and dirt soothe the tension from his body. Every mile he put behind him felt like a weight slowly lifting from his shoulders. As long as he and Grace stayed far away from each other, then maybe they could make it through the rest of this month in one piece.

CHAPTER

Ten

ITEMS NUMBERS TWELVE and thirteen on the list of things Grace was thankful for: *rain boots and leather gloves.*

She scribbled them down before folding the page and slipping it and the pencil back into her front pocket. Her therapist's idea of keeping a gratitude journal seemed as silly now as it had when she'd suggested it a few months ago. At this rate, she'd celebrate her fortieth birthday before reaching one thousand entries.

But for as much as Grace initially disliked the overalls, they had their useful moments. Her hands, however ... She flexed her sore muscles from yesterday's yard work and winced at the fresh blisters. And that had been with the gloves on. She didn't even want to imagine what sort of condition she'd have been in had she gone after those weeds bare-handed.

She'd hardly mentioned a word about it to Callie, but somehow, the woman had already known. Which explained today's slightly less demanding activity...

Callie had disappeared inside a few minutes ago—something about duct tape and a bee-keeper suit, neither of which sounded the least bit appealing to Grace. Just the thought of being swarmed by thousands of bees, suit or not, made her skin crawl.

Something tickled the back of her arm, and she swatted at it. Heart racing, she spun around, only to find one of the climbing vines had slipped from its lattice.

How in the world was she going to endure honey harvesting like this? She should be at the ranch, earning Micah's respect enough to convince him of her proposal. Not playing *Little House on the Prairie*, no matter how much she enjoyed Callie's quirky personality. And if last night's argument was any indication, she still had a long way to go.

"Hello? Anybody home?" A familiar deep voice echoed from the front driveway.

"Out back," she hollered, hoping Caden could hear her. Sure enough, he slipped through the gate, clad in a navy T-shirt and jeans, and greeted her with a wave.

"Thought I'd find you here." His teeth were white against his tanned skin, no doubt a fact Callie hadn't failed to notice, either.

"Where else would I be?"

He shrugged. "Dunno, but I'm glad I caught you. Is Callie here, too?" He leaned forward and peered through the open back door.

Grace didn't miss the way he swiped his palms against his legs and kept stealing glances at the house. He might as well have been wearing a sign around his neck that said: *I like Callie.* She wondered if her friend had picked up on his interest as well. Their behavior last night and the way they had talked the other morning by the pasture gate—she had no doubt something was there. And from where she stood, all they needed was a little push.

Grace smiled, knowing she'd found her solution. "What would you say to a trade? You stay here and help Callie, and I'll cover for you back at the ranch."

"Really?" The excitement in Caden's stance told her he was eager to jump at the offer, but his tone said he was trying hard to play it cool.

"Absolutely. I can handle whatever Micah throws at me."

"Hmm. You sure about that?" The humorous tilt to his smile said he thought otherwise. "And what makes you think I'd trade, anyway? Maybe I enjoy working with my cousin."

"Right," she scoffed. "Because he's such a ray of sunshine."

"He's not usually so bad. In fact, he's actually pretty great once you get to know him."

"So I've been told. I must bring out the worst in him, is that it?" she countered.

"Hey, you said it, not me."

Why couldn't Micah be more like his cousin? Caden was so much easier to talk with, and she didn't feel like a complete fraud when she was around him.

Peeling his gaze from the door, Caden seemed to relax, his arms crossing casually over his chest. He leaned against one of the lattice support beams with a natural ease. "You know, on second thought, I think I might take you up on that offer of yours."

"Really?"

He gave her a pointed look as if proving his earlier point. "Look who's backing out now."

Enough second-guessing. She'd wanted a way to show Micah what she could do, and she was messing up her chance. "Not backing out. Just making sure you're okay with the trade."

Caden laughed, a boisterous sound that seemed to echo across the patio. When he finally quieted, he sent her an approving smile. "I think my cousin may have met his match. I wouldn't want to stand in your way."

He reached out a hand to help her stand. Before Callie walked out the door and could stop her, Grace slipped through the garden and around the house, anxious to prove to Micah, and herself, just what she was capable of.

Caden had only meant to drop by and apologize for Micah's early exit last night. Never once had it crossed his mind he might end up spending the day with an army of honeybees. Another thing he could add to his extensive resume.

"What happened to Grace?" Callie asked the minute she walked out of the house. The sun on her copper braid made her freckles stand out more than usual. Despite her question, she didn't seem upset to find him there instead of Grace, so he took that as a good sign.

"She seemed a little green around the gills at the mention of bees, so I offered to step in."

"How noble of you." Callie dipped her head to the side, no doubt humoring him, and deposited her bundle of supplies on the grass.

He swooped his arm in a showy arc and bowed forward. "Always happy to be of service." She stifled a giggle, and a sense of satisfaction washed over him.

Callie propped her hands on her hips, flaming hair glowing around her face with a few loose curls. Even with the smudge of dirt across her cheek, she'd never looked prettier. "Do you even know anything about bees?"

"I worked a summer at a meadery in California, so I figure that's close enough." He tilted his head and smiled. So they'd purchased all the honey from a local vendor, but she didn't need to know that.

"Is there anything you haven't done?" Callie returned the smile and brushed the loose hair from her face.

She meant it as a joke—he knew that—yet something within him soured. A part of him wanted to prove her wrong. Or to prove to himself that he was capable of sticking with something. As it stood, he'd already been here longer than he'd intended—the itch to leave warring with the longing to stay. Bees hadn't been part of his life plan, but if anyone could convince him otherwise, it was Callie.

He'd kept his misgivings from everyone, including Micah, and he wasn't about to spill his soul now.

"Well, you may be in luck," Callie interrupted his heavy thoughts. If her friendly smile was any indication, she must not have been looking for an answer. He could spend half a lifetime basking in that warmth, but that would require a sacrifice he wasn't sure he was capable of.

"I ordered a new suit last spring but forgot to check the size. I can practically swim in it, it's so large. But it might fit you just fine."

He hiked an eyebrow. "Are you calling me fat?"

A nice flush crept over her sun-kissed skin. "What? No. I mean ... you're like what, six-two?"

"Six-three, but who's counting?" He shrugged, not bothering to hide his laughter.

After she'd swatted him with a pair of gloves, Callie visibly relaxed. "Like I was saying. The suit should fit you fine... But the hat might be a bit snug. You know, with how big your head is and all."

He laid a hand over his heart and pretended to stumble backward. "Ouch. That one hurt."

"I think you'll live." Her green eyes glittered under the partial canopy of aspens, as if part of the forest.

Five minutes later, they were suiting up on the lawn between the garden and a cluster of hives. Caden stepped into the white suit, the heavy cotton causing him to immediately start sweating. Once he was all set, he helped zip Callie into hers.

He glanced at their matching white jumpers and grinned. "I feel like we should be fighting off ghosts or something. All we need now are a couple of proton packs, and we'd be good to go."

She laughed. "Sorry, all I have are these beehive smokers." She held out two metal objects that looked like watering cans.

"As long as they ward off any unwanted attacks, I'm in." Caden held one of the cans while Callie ignited a wad of paper and placed a handful of dried pine needles inside. Once smoke began to rise from the nozzle, she clicked the door shut and demonstrated how to pump the smoke toward the hives.

"You want to move gently without startling the bees. Once there's enough smoke, they'll calm down, but it can take a few minutes."

"I think I can handle a few bees, Cal. What's the worst that could happen?" He flashed her the same grin he'd always given her and stepped toward the huddle of white boxes. Callie's footsteps followed behind, a second smoker in her hand. Together, they worked in tandem, sedating the bees in the first hive. Fascinated, he watched as the insects seemed to grow more drowsy every minute.

"The smoke doesn't harm them, does it? They look like a group of drunken college students after a night of partying."

"That's probably from all the honey they're eating." She angled her smoker in a smooth arc over the top of the hive. "The smoke tricks them into thinking there is a fire, so they retreat to the hive and feast on the honey as if preparing to relocate. But just like us, all that food can make them a bit sluggish."

"So, we're sending them all into food comas. Doesn't sound like a bad way to spend the day."

"I never thought about it that way, but I guess so." Callie raised the lid of the box and blew another puff of smoke into the hive. Once most of the bees seemed to be moving toward the bottom of the box, she used a wooden brush to coax the remaining stragglers to join the others. Handing her smoker to Caden, she pried at the edges of the first frame and, after a few tries, lifted out a panel encased in waxy honeycomb.

She propped the frame against the box and put back the lid. "I thought we'd take only one from each hive for now and leave the rest for another day. Even so, we'll have eight frames to extract honey from, which should be about sixty pounds, give or take."

"Wow. That's like..." He paused to do the math and gaped at the answer. "Five gallons?"

Callie nodded. "Now you see why I want to sell it. One girl can only eat so much honey." She winked at him and scooped up the heavy frame.

Once she'd carried it to the patio, they moved on to the second hive. Caden's smoke began to thin. He pumped the bellows to reignite the fuel, but only a trickle of smoke emerged. Not the plume he'd expected.

"Hey, Cal. I think something's wrong with this smoker. Do you have any more pine needles?" He turned into the sunlight and shielded his eyes. Blinking, he took another step and paused when something buzzed in front of him.

Caden zeroed in on a large honeybee crawling on the veil above his nose. Without thinking, he waved his hand with the smoker to shoo it away when he heard Callie's voice somewhere behind him.

"Don't provoke him. He's only curious."

The fixed hood made it difficult to see, but he could tell she was close. He tried to turn his head, but the hat and veil got in his way. "Sorry, reflex I guess."

Determined to prove her faith in him, he pumped the handle on the smoker a few more times, and to his surprise, a cloud of white smoke billowed out. He would have let out a whoop of excitement if it weren't for Callie's earlier warning to remain calm. With a thumbs up, which was rather difficult with the heavy gloves, he rejoined her at the next hive.

This time, Callie let Caden take the lead. Acting as if he'd done this a hundred times, he repeated the steps he'd seen her do earlier and lifted out his own honeyed frame. A couple of bees buzzed past his face, landing once more on the mesh veil. After Callie's earlier warning, he knew better than to swat at them. "Don't worry, we're not taking all your honey," he whispered to them.

He could almost feel Callie smiling beside him. Him talking to bees. What had the world come to?

With the frame in one hand, he moved to put the lid back on the hive when something brushed against his face. A second later, a searing pain shot through his cheek, and he dropped the wooden frame.

Caden couldn't get the hood off fast enough. Something stung him again, this time right on the nose, and he smacked a gloved hand against his face.

How had they gotten inside his suit? He clawed at the hood, but the thick gloves made it impossible to grab onto. Desperate to stop the attack, he ripped off the first glove and pulled at the hat as the bees gave him one final sting.

The moment the hood was off, the swarm seemed to dissipate, and Caden finally opened his eyes. Honey oozed from the broken frame onto the grass, and Callie stood speechless beside it.

It had all happened so fast. Caden could already feel the welts beginning to form on his face, but the warmth that washed over him was not from the bee stings.

"Callie, I'm so sorry." He reached for the frame and brushed bits of grass from the sticky coating, as if that could somehow fix everything.

Somewhere in the chaos, Callie had removed her gloves, and she laid her hand over his. He didn't want to look her in the eye but forced himself to do so.

"It's only honey," she said, concern written across her forehead. Her voice was soft, pitying even, which made him feel all the worse. "We should remove those stingers before your whole face swells." Her smile did little to lighten his mood, but he didn't argue when she brushed a cool finger against his cheek.

He'd played this moment countless times over in his head, but never had he envisioned making a fool out of himself to earn her attention.

She disappeared inside the house for a moment and returned with a cool washcloth and a pair of tweezers. "Now, this might sting." Her face contorted in a grimace. "Sorry, wrong choice of words."

His smile felt forced, but for Callie's sake, he'd play along. With their hoods and gloves removed, they sat off to the edge of the hives. Not a single bee seemed the least bit interested. Of course, *now* they left them alone.

Caden stifled a groan as she removed the barbs one by one, and then relief washed over him. He unclenched his fists and slowly coaxed the blood flow back into his limbs.

"Uh, thanks ... and I'm sorry about the, um ..." He motioned to the broken frame and then to his face, searching for the right words.

She set aside the washcloth and shrugged. "It was nothing."

For a moment, only the sound of thousands of bees buzzing nearby punctuated the silence. Nothing about today had gone as planned. He'd wanted to impress her with his honey-harvesting skills and sweep her off her feet in one go. But instead, he'd been swept away by a swarm of bees.

"I should probably get going," he finally said, wishing he could take back the last half hour.

"Are you sure?"

Caden nodded. "Lots to do on the ranch. Probably shouldn't have stayed so long, anyway."

Callie didn't appear convinced by his weak excuse. The skeptical tilt to her brow told him as much. Couldn't blame her, really. She always had been able to read his thoughts.

"Take this, at least." She held out a small jar of honey, an apology written across her worried wrinkles. "It should help with the swelling."

Caden didn't want to even think about bees or honey at the moment. He thanked her and tucked the jar in his pocket, assuring her once again that he was fine. He helped her salvage what honey they could from the busted frame and carried it inside. As soon as he was satisfied she had everything else under control, he stripped out of his cotton suit and draped it over one of the patio chairs.

He'd been running his whole life—from consequences and responsibility. So why did this feel so different?

With a final look over his shoulder, Caden passed through the gate, the metal latch echoing behind him like a gavel, and climbed into the truck.

CHAPTER

Eleven

WHERE WAS THAT slacker of a cousin of his?

"Caden, you here?" Micah called inside the barn, but the only answer was the neighing of Roper and Dune in their stalls. He exhaled a hot breath before stepping back into the blinding sunlight. In less than a minute, he was across the yard. His truck sat, ready and waiting to head down to Cranford's Gulch to continue working on the new fence line. All he needed now was his second pair of hands.

Micah dropped another roll of wire into the truck bed for good measure and scanned the nearby fields where the sheep grazed on the alfalfa. So much for that last harvest he was counting on.

He glanced once more at the clock on his dashboard. Had Caden already forgotten about their plans to work on the fence this afternoon? Based on the fluffy clouds overhead, they'd risk getting caught in another late afternoon storm if he waited around much longer. A little rain wouldn't hurt, but getting caught in an electrical storm while installing metal fence posts was another thing entirely.

He closed the tailgate with a click, rattling the stacks of metal rods and supplies in the bed. After another five minutes of waiting, he was about to head off alone when the sputter of an engine reached his ears. He walked around to the other side of the truck where Finn sat waiting, tongue out and tail thumping against the earth. Callie's old Chevy appeared around the corner of the house and pulled to a stop, a cloud of dust rolling over its blue and white exterior.

Relief washed over him. His harsh words of last night had disrupted his fitful sleep, but he'd been too embarrassed this morning to seek her out to apologize. That, and he'd been busy avoiding another run-in with Grace. Callie's presence now made his hopes rise. The fact she'd driven over must mean she wasn't as upset with him as he'd expected.

Shielding his eyes against the sun, he watched as Finn dashed ahead of him. Before the dog reached the truck, the door swung open and ... Out stepped Grace.

"What are *you* doing here?" he asked a little too forcefully.

Grace stopped scratching behind Finn's ears and looked up with a frown. "Contrary to what you might think, I'm true to my word." She closed the door and walked toward him. "I said I'd help out while I'm here, so here I am. If you want me gone, you'll have to carry me out yourself." She had a pair of gloves clasped in her hands, apparently ready to be put to work.

She was more stubborn than he'd given her credit for. If she was willing to come back here, the least he could do was try to be civil. He released a breath and started over. "What I meant to ask was, where's Caden? He was supposed to meet me here a half hour ago."

She blinked. "He's over at Callie's helping her out with something." Her manicured eyebrows drew together in another frown. "He didn't tell you?"

"Must have slipped his mind."

"I can go back and get him if you need—"

"It's fine." He'd give his cousin an earful when he next saw him. But Caden was Caden, and that wasn't Grace's fault. "The fences aren't going anywhere."

The nearby bleats of sheep punctuated the awkward silence.

"If it's any consolation," she finally spoke up. "I'd be willing to help."

"Really?" After the past couple of days, he'd thought she'd want to keep as much distance between them as possible.

Grace stood half an inch taller, the top of her blonde hair barely reaching his chin. "Why not?" she challenged back.

"What, and let you spy on me again?"

"It's either that or I follow you with my binoculars." She smiled, and the tension eased from his chest.

What was the saying about keeping your enemies close? He peered down at the woman in front of him—clad in Callie's baggy overalls and rubber boots—and tried not to laugh. She looked about as threatening as a newborn lamb.

"Hop on in."

Her eyes grew wide. "You mean it?"

He shrugged. "Why not? You're already here, and with any luck, we'll get most of these in before the skies open up."

"And what if they do?" One glance at the blue-and-white-streaked sky and her smile faltered.

He tracked her gaze to the billowing cumulus clouds. "We'll cross that bridge when we get there."

"You mean the one that's still a few feet below water?" Her mouth lifted at the corners, the flicker of concern gone.

Micah bit back a smile. When she wasn't trying to trick him, she wasn't all that bad. He still wasn't willing to concede friendship by any means, but like it or not, they were stuck with each other for the time being. Which meant declaring a truce. At least until they got the fence finished.

He inclined his head toward his truck. "We can stand here debating the issue all afternoon, or we can get a move on."

"What, and miss this?" She tipped her head to the side and planted her hands on her narrow hips. "I'm just taking it all in. Micah Prescott... almost smiling."

He scoffed. "Don't get used to it. I'm only thinking about the fence that needs repairing."

"Mm-hmm. Whatever you say."

Micah nearly rolled his eyes. "You won't be laughing once we get to the river. Just remember, you're the one who offered to help."

He led her to his truck, and after a final once-over of their supplies, they were off. A few minutes of bumpy driving later, Finn finally settled into the middle seat between them and laid his head across Grace's lap. They drove in silence, the house and barn shrinking in the rearview mirror as the truck dipped farther down the hill.

Gopher holes and erosion tracks made for a bumpy ride. Open fields stretched on either side, pockets of trees dotting the valley, and soon the sounds of the grazing sheep were replaced by the wind through the open windows. The radio had died years ago, as had the air conditioning and a dozen other things in the truck. Micah had stripped the thing bare and rebuilt it piece by piece over the years. All except for the radio. Normally he'd enjoyed the peaceful quiet—under the open sky, away from the world and its worries. But today, with Caden gone and Grace in his place, he found himself wishing for some music, or even a boring weather report, to distract his wandering thoughts.

He slid a glance to his passenger and found her watching him. The focused attention made him uneasy, as if she could read him like a book. He tilted his hat to better cover the scar and returned his focus to the road ahead.

Micah cleared his throat, buying a second to think of something to say. "Look, about last night..."

"Forget it." Grace waved his attempt at an apology aside. "I knew it was a sore subject and brought it up, anyway."

"I shouldn't have been so quick to judge." It wasn't necessarily an apology, but it was all he could manage at the moment. Again, he sensed her focus on the side of his face. She seemed to be thinking. Either that or he'd suddenly sprouted a third ear.

"For what it's worth, you're not what I expected," she finally said.

"Yeah, and what was that?"

"Mmm, I'm not falling for that one."

Based on her nervous laughter, it hadn't been pretty. Hiking an eyebrow, he sent her a humorous look. "You probably thought we all wore flannel, ten-gallon hats, and chewed on hay, didn't you?"

She smiled and peered down at his worn leather boots. "Don't forget the cowboy boots."

"Very funny."

She stroked behind Finn's ears and turned her attention to the fields before them. "Let's just say I had a less-than-flattering mental picture in mind."

He knew all too well what some people thought. Unless one grew up around a farm, it was hard to fully appreciate the lifestyle with all its sacrifices and blessings. People formed their own judgments, blaming ranchers for the world's problems while never stepping foot on a working property to see for themselves. He'd figured Grace would be the same way, but so far, she'd surprised him.

"You're not what I expected, either." Definitely not the same Francis G. Riley he'd imagined a week ago.

"Why? Because I'm not a man?" she supplied.

Among other things. He slid her a cautious glance, knowing better than to take the bait. "You said it, not me."

She leaned back against her seat and fluffed a hand through her wavy hair, the ends whipping in the warm breeze. "I'm used to it. Why do you think I prefer to go by Grace?" She tied her hair back with an elastic from her wrist and let the long tail spill over her shoulder. Propping her right arm against her door, she watched the fields give way to willows and aspens.

After a few long moments of silence, he got the sense their conversation had come to its natural end.

Micah eased the truck around a small grove of trees and over the rough terrain until their destination came into view. He studied the familiar landscape and tried to imagine what the place looked like through Grace's eyes. Could she see the natural beauty around them, the rugged landscape painted with tufts of orange-and-purple wildflowers? Or did she only see the sagging fence and fields of dirt and rocks? No doubt she'd been calculating the value of the land in her head as they drove, broken fence and all.

Micah parked the truck at the far corner of the field, beneath a cluster of cottonwoods that grew beside the river. He looked again at the old barbed wire fence sagging in its feeble welcome and sighed. Whatever she saw, they had their work cut out for them, that was for sure. Stealing one more glance at Grace, he killed the engine and prepared himself for what would surely be a long afternoon.

"Well, here we are."

From the tilted metal posts to the loose strands of barbed wire lying limp against the grass, it was a surprise the thing was standing at all.

"Looks like we came just in time," Grace said as she jumped down from the truck. Thick mud squished beneath her boots and clung to the rubber soles when she tried to walk. The river appeared to have overflowed its banks with the recent storm, soaking the surrounding area to the consistency of oatmeal.

Micah rounded the truck and popped open the rear door. Without waiting for her to join him, he set to work unloading the piles of wire and metal stakes onto the marshy grass. In one movement, he lifted a chord of heavy-duty wire from the back and dropped it with a thud beside the others.

Unsure how best to make herself useful, Grace slipped on her gloves and reached for the wire cutters and post-hole digger lying by her feet. Finn barely seemed to notice her as she wedged between him and the seat, so she kept the window down and closed the door.

When she looked back toward Micah, he'd already unloaded half the truck.

"How much of the fence were you planning to work on today?" she asked.

Setting aside his load, he peered toward the river and shielded his eyes from the sun. "You see that large oak tree?"

He pointed somewhere downriver, but for the life of her, Grace couldn't make out which oak he was talking about. A fact he didn't seem to notice or care about based on the tight set of his jaw. She'd known volunteering to help had been a bad idea the moment she mentioned it, but Micah was sorely mistaken if he thought he could run her off with a simple fence.

She nodded, not wanting to seem dense. "And how many yards would you say that is?" She hoped the question didn't betray her weary thoughts.

He shrugged. "Fifty. Maybe seventy-five yards."

Grace followed the length of the fence until it disappeared behind some trees in the distance. She inwardly groaned. She'd wanted to prove herself to Micah, but this? What had she signed up for?

"There are other sections that need tending, but they can wait." Micah glanced down at her as if gauging her response. "I did try to warn you."

At his flat tone, she turned back to him and paused. Was that a slight lift to the corner of his mouth? It wasn't exactly friendly, but she could sense his guard lowering in the slight gesture. "Obviously you didn't try hard enough."

He made a grunt that almost sounded like a laugh.

Almost.

"Tell you what. If we can get half that amount done today, I'll call it a success. Besides, there's always tomorrow." A gust of wind caught the brim of his hat, exposing the scar he'd tried to hide earlier. She only caught a small section of the jagged pale line, but again, it piqued her curiosity about the man beside her.

He must have noticed her staring. He angled his body toward the sunlit field, seeming to take in every last rock and blade of grass. His voice almost seemed loud when he finally spoke again into the uninterrupted stillness. "There's always something to be done here."

Before this week, Grace hadn't put much thought into the inner workings of a ranch. To her, it was only an obstacle to overcome on her way to the top. But after only a few days here, and earning her fair share of blisters pulling weeds the day before, she couldn't argue.

As if satisfied with what he saw, Micah returned to his task of unloading the truck. Eager to help, Grace jumped in, but she only felt in the way when he swung around with a large armload of steel wire. They sidestepped each other, doing a little dance before he finally dropped the bundle on the grass. His clenched jaw told her he was trying to hide his frustration. No doubt, he'd have been better off had she never volunteered to tag along. But like it or not, she had.

"So..." Grace hunted for something to say and settled on the safest topic she could think of. "What exactly did you have in mind for the fence? Can we somehow straighten the entire thing as is?"

He sent her a look that made her feel like a kid who'd asked the wrong question in class. How did she keep managing to put her rubber-soled foot in her mouth?

Expression relaxing, Micah cut two lengths of galvanized steel wire and hooked one around the other at an angle so she could see. "We're replacing this barbed wire with a woven mesh. We don't want to hurt the sheep, just keep them inside the fence." He then twisted two more sections until he'd formed a square. "See?" He pulled against the knots, and they tightened. "Much more difficult for a sheep to sneak through."

He offered it to her, and Grace pretended to inspect the foreign-looking mesh. In their close proximity, his arm accidentally brushed hers. She flinched, and he took a step back.

Numbers she could work with. They were concrete and absolute. Whereas Micah ... He was anything but predictable. Three days in, and she still hadn't been able to get a read on him. She didn't need another distraction from her goal. And Micah Prescott definitely classified as a distraction.

"So, where do we start?" she asked, trying her best to stuff down her confusing thoughts.

Tugging on his baseball cap, a habit she was quickly becoming familiar with, he turned toward the half-unloaded truck bed. The two shovels lying on the ground looked as if they were over a hundred years old, with rusted spades and splintered wood. He handed one to Grace, and she almost dropped it on her foot from the unexpected weight.

"You know we have a post-hole digger, right?" she asked.

He gave her a funny look and closed the back end. "We have to remove the old posts before we can put in new ones."

"Oh. Right." She dropped her free hand to her side. Obviously, she'd never installed a fence before, but she chastised herself for the slip-up all the same. *Use your common sense, Grace. Rule number one of talking with a prospective client: don't let them sense any weaknesses.*

Shovel in hand, Micah pivoted away from the truck and snatched the mesh sample from the grass, tossing it in the back.

Before she could say something to rectify the situation or make it worse, he was halfway to the fence. Picking up her shovel, she took off after him, intent on proving to Micah she had what it took to fit in here. Even if it was only for a few weeks. He'd respect her more for it, and for some reason, beyond the land and the contract, she valued his opinion.

CHAPTER

Twelve

MICAH HAD JUST started unloading the truck when Caden stalked through the yard and into the barn. His usually cheerful smile was gone, and in its place was a surly frown and a handful of angry-looking welts.

Micah dropped the discarded fence post behind the barn door and followed his cousin inside. "What happened to you?"

"Don't want to talk about it." Caden looked about as happy as a kid who'd dropped their ice cream cone. Stomping all the way to the makeshift kitchen in the far corner, he clicked on the single bare bulb, and the light bounced off something shiny slathered across his skin.

"Is that—" Micah squinted for a better look—"honey on your face?"

Caden's ears reddened to match the color of the welts. "Callie said it would help with the swelling."

Honey to treat honeybee stings. The irony was not lost on Micah. "Did she, now? You sure she wasn't messing with you?"

Caden glowered at the mini fridge plugged in beside the barn sink and muttered under his breath. "This is what I get for trying to help. Fat lot of good that did."

"Why *were* you helping Callie with her bees, if you don't mind my asking?"

"Actually, I *do* mind." Caden twisted open a bottle of soda but only stared at its contents.

Micah tried to hold back his laughter, but between the honey and Caden's expression, he couldn't help but smile. As long as it didn't involve the ranch, he had no problem pushing his cousin for more. "Someone's got a bee stuck in his bonnet."

Caden's frown deepened. "No, I don't. And you're not even using that right." As if suddenly remembering the drink in his hands, he lifted it to his lips and downed half its contents in one pull. Aside from the welts that appeared to be growing redder by the second, something else seemed to simmer below the surface. As far as Micah knew, nothing upset Caden. And he'd suffered far worse than a few stings working on the ranch this past year alone.

So what had happened to put him in such a sulky mood?

Caden finished off the soda like it was the first thing he'd drunk in days. Swiping a hand across his mouth, he winced when he accidentally brushed over a fresh welt. Acting more than a little frustrated, he capped the bottle and sent Micah another look of warning.

Micah raised his hands in surrender. "Don't worry, I'm done."

Caden's shoulders seemed to relax. He looked down at the crinkled plastic in his hands, suddenly sheepish. "Sorry about that." He let out a forceful breath and massaged a hand over the back of his neck. "It's just been a long day."

Micah could relate. Showing Grace the ropes hadn't been a walk in the park, either. "Couldn't have been as bad as trying to install a new fence with your sworn enemy."

Caden winced. "That bad, huh?"

Micah wanted to shoot back a retort about ruining the ranch in more ways than one, but a quiet voice in his head told him it would be a lie. Sure, she hadn't been the fastest ranch hand. She'd dropped more wires than he could count, nearly broke the post-hole digger with the way she'd thrown it against the dirt, and they'd barely set half the length of fencing he'd hoped for.

But the truth was, he also couldn't have done that much without her.

Now it was his turn to look sheepish. He gave a not-so-reluctant shrug, as if the admission didn't grate against his every belief. "I might not like the reason she's here, but I'll admit, she's a hard worker."

Caden whistled long and low. "Careful, that almost sounded like a compliment. Should I be worried about the competition for my job?"

"If you repeat this conversation to anyone, you very well might have to."

For the first time since his arrival, Caden cracked a smile. "I don't know. Seems to me that might be doing me a favor. Not that I don't mind the long days and coming home smelling like sheep manure and all."

This sounded more like the Caden he knew. "Careful. I hear The Gold Bar Café is looking for a new dish-boy."

"What, and have to cover this with a hair net all day?" He pointed to his mop of brown hair and grimaced. "I'll take roundups and bees to that any day."

Despite the teasing, his laughter lacked its usual bravado, and Micah wondered once again what had really happened. "Seriously, though. You sure you don't want an antihistamine or something? Those look pretty nasty."

Caden waved aside the offer despite his obvious physical discomfort. "Nah, I'm okay. It looks worse than it really is."

Micah hoped that was true, but based on earlier, he wasn't convinced. In his experience, people dealt with things in their own time and way, only he had no clue what that was for Caden. "Suit yourself. I'm going to finish unloading, if you'd like to help."

"Anything to keep my mind off these welts."

Micah chuckled and reached for an extra set of gloves. Caden chucked his bottle into the recycling bin and slipped them on, clapping the dust from the leather. "Well?" he asked, ready to jump right in. "Let's get a move on."

With that, he took off toward the open barn door, leaving Micah to follow behind.

Readjusting his cap, Micah joined him by the truck, and together, they stacked the rest of the old fencing in a neat pile behind the southern wall. They worked in relative silence, but Micah didn't mind the quiet. Caden would open up in time, or he wouldn't.

Micah, on the other hand, couldn't stop thinking back over his time with Grace. The very idea of her stepping foot on his property had made his toes curl the day before, so why had he been so ready to challenge her to help out?

Something told him he didn't want to know the answer.

Instead, he forced himself to turn his focus back to the fencing material and the shrinking number of days before the bank's deadline. He already had enough on his plate to worry about. The other question could wait for another day.

Grace had returned to the ranch the next day to help with the fence. And the day after that.

After the third day working side-by-side with Micah and Caden, she finally felt as if she'd found her stride. She wasn't considering a career change, but she was fairly certain, if given the chance, she could tie off fencing wire in her sleep.

Even Callie had joined them today, something about leaving honeycombs to drip and all that. Micah had almost seemed relieved when she'd showed up, leaving her and Grace to finish up their section of fencing while he and Caden moved on to the last stretch.

"What do you think that was all about today?" Grace stirred a dollop of honey into her second cup of tea and sipped at it, letting the warmth seep through the green ceramic mug and into her tired hands. All of today's interactions with Micah, and especially Caden, had seemed . . . odd.

Callie's knitting needles clacked away in the corner, the rhythmic sound blending with the cricket's melody floating in from the garden. Without looking up, she replied, "I think I'll need a little more information." Looping the white yarn over the blue, she referenced the pattern before moving to the next row.

Grace never understood how some people found the activity calming. All those threads and knots looked like a nightmare waiting to happen. She plucked at a few stray hairs from her own sweater and moved to join Callie by the fireplace.

"I don't know. Didn't the guys seem a bit ... off today?" She didn't know how else to put it. She'd thought she'd been making decent strides the last few days, but maybe that had been her own hopes talking. "Am I crazy?"

Callie lifted her eyes from her work long enough to give Grace a reassuring smile. "No, you're not crazy. If anything, I'd say it had more to do with me being there than you."

"What does that mean?"

Callie shrugged. "You know how Caden swapped places with you the other day?"

"Yeah." She said it like it was a question.

"Well, things didn't quite go according to plan." Returning to her pattern, Callie zipped out another few stitches of alternating blue and white. Did this woman ever sit still?

"Callie." Grace called her friend back out of her crafty trance.

A slow blink was her only reply.

Ugh. Sometimes it felt like she was living with a honeybee herself. Full attention one place, then another a second later. "You and Caden ... the beehives ..."

Only then did Callie seem to realize she'd left Grace hanging. "Oh, right. It wasn't anything big, per se, but I think I might have embarrassed him a little."

"A little, as in ..."

"As in a lot." Callie dropped the half-finished sweater to her lap, not caring that the end of her needle was close to unraveling. "It was all going so well before that bee got in his hood. I told him not to panic. That always gets the bees agitated."

Grace cringed. So that explained the redness she'd spotted on his face yesterday.

"And to top it off," Callie continued, "I treated him like an invalid. I mean, I wasn't going to leave him to deal with it on his own, but I should have given him a little more space instead of hovering the way I did." Her face suddenly grew pink, making her green eyes and red hair stand out even more against the beige-colored armchair.

"I'm sure it wasn't that bad," Grace offered.

Callie's curls bounced as she bobbed her head. "Oh, it was. Believe me. I might as well have been his mother." But what Grace had earlier mistaken for worry turned into something altogether different. Instead of a sob, out slipped a giggle. Then another. And a whole slew of them bubbled up from there.

Grace wasn't sure how to react. Either her friend had lost it, or she was missing something.

Callie drew in a stilted breath, no doubt catching Grace's concerned look in the process. "I'm sorry. I know it isn't funny." Another giggle escaped before she regained her composure. "I guess I've gotten so used to things, it just dawned on me how lost I must have seemed when I first moved back here."

Grace must have looked as confused as she felt, because Callie kept going. "I didn't always live here. I mean, I lived here with my family before the fire. But after that, they wanted nothing to do with this place. Too many bad memories. Too much loss."

Grace knew that feeling. Only she'd spent her entire adult life trying to run as far from her past as possible. "So, what made you move back?"

Callie sobered a little and sighed. "They may not have been able to forget the bad times, but I couldn't forget the good ones either. That, and the fact I couldn't afford to live anywhere else."

Again, Grace felt as if she were missing something. "I thought land was expensive up here?"

"Oh, it is, believe me. After the fire, my parents sold the property to Micah and his family. I know he paid far more than it was really worth, but he wouldn't take it for anything less. When he found out I wanted to come back, he offered to lease it to me for a ridiculously low price."

"And Caden?" she asked, curious to know how he fit into the equation.

A dreamy expression stole over Callie's features, one that resembled Caden's a few days ago. "Now *he* was a surprise."

Oh, she was a goner.

"And I take it he doesn't know how you feel?"

Callie's eyes grew wider than the mason jar lids stacked in the kitchen. "Of course not. And if the other day was any indication, I doubt he ever will."

Now it was Grace's turn to know something Callie didn't. Sipping her tea, she debated against spilling her own assessment of Caden. "I don't know. You might be surprised."

Callie shook her head, slower this time. "I've made my peace with it. We're friends—at least, I hope we still are. And besides, you're probably more his type than I am."

Grace held her hand against her mouth to avoid spitting her tea across the room. "I'm not the one who is starting her own business. I think *that's* pretty impressive."

"So what? Guys don't care about that sort of stuff. They like silky hair, skinny jeans, and skin that doesn't look like a tractor sprayed mud on it." Callie reached once more for her knitting and restrung the dropped stitches.

What did someone say to a person who'd already made up their mind? When nothing came, she turned her focus to Callie's flying needles and suppressed a sigh. Despite her earlier opinions, she voiced her next question, intent on removing the resigned expression from her friend's face by whatever means necessary.

"Callie, would you mind teaching me how to knit?"

Grace would have regretted the decision had her friend's face not lit with excitement. Diving into the box beside her chair, Callie pulled out a roll of yarn and thrust it into Grace's arms. The color reminded her of her aunt's pea soup, but if this was what it took to see her friend smile, then she'd knit a hundred dreadful scarves ... and donate them all to charity.

CHAPTER

Thirteen

AS FAR AS angry voicemails from one's boss went, it could have gone worse.

Grace tossed her cell on the quilted bed and sank into the blue-and-white-checkered coverlet. Katrina's words had been calm and measured, so very like the woman they belonged to, but there was a directness that warned Grace not to mess this up. It didn't matter that she had saved more than a month of vacation time. Apparently, she'd chosen the wrong week to go traipsing across the Rocky Mountains—Katrina's words, not hers.

The buzz around the office was that Prospect & Gould was looking at a potentially large new client. They expected every associate to work overtime to close the deal before one of their competitors scooped them up, and according to some—Katrina wouldn't say—the future of the firm, and its employees, rested on this contract.

Never mind that she was only here because they'd thought the same thing about this water project a few months ago. She'd wanted to prove herself, but to whom she now wasn't sure.

Grace rolled over and shoved her face into a flower-shaped pillow. She wouldn't scream, not with Callie asleep next door. But the soft pressure against her skin worked like a paper bag to slow her rapid breaths. When the moment seemed to pass, she righted herself and snuggled the warm pillow between the others against the headboard. Her arms felt like lead from the past few days, and she wondered yet again what exactly she was doing here.

Callie had already gone to bed, leaving Grace feeling alone in the house again. Despite the early morning hours, Grace still hadn't adjusted to the early evenings. She was used to staying up late and waking up to the sound of her alarm clock well past sunrise. This whole early-to-bed and early-to-rise thing was worse than jet lag. The sun had only set a little over an hour ago, and she was still wide awake.

Clicking on the lamp beside her bed, Grace swiveled toward the door and paused. Her attempt at a scarf mocked her from the spindle-backed chair in the corner, the putrescent green yarn a reminder that she didn't fit in here either. *Imposter*, it seemed to croak, like the toad it resembled.

Not that she'd really wanted to learn to knit, anyway. It had been in the service of a friend. It would, however, do her some good to feel as if she could do something right for a change.

"Enough with the self-pity, Grace." She whispered the admonition before reaching for the notepad and pencil sitting by her suitcase. Her gratitude list had grown since arriving, surprising even her. She flipped to a fresh page and scribbled under the light of the single bulb.

Things I'm grateful for: good tea and friends to share it with.

Speaking of tea, another cup couldn't hurt. Grace smiled and swapped the notepad for the empty mug.

Barefoot, she eased open her door and tip-toed past Callie's room and down the old staircase to the kitchen, careful not to make too much noise as she filled the metal teakettle at the sink. Using her nose as her guide, Grace selected a minty-scented box and scooped a spoonful of its contents into the kettle. Before the steam could make it whistle, she removed it from the hot burner and savored the tingly aroma as she slid into one of the empty chairs at the table.

Moonlight spilled through the windows, illuminating the stacks of boxes and jars piled along the length of the rustic slab. To say she'd grown accustomed to the clutter would be an overstatement, but even she could begin to see the vision for what Callie hoped to create. She could start local. Set up a little stand in town at farmer's markets and then switch to an online platform when the winter months settled in. Of course, she'd need a logo and a solid marketing strategy, but those would be easy enough to pin down later.

Something bittersweet settled in Grace's stomach. Reaching for the jar of honey, she spooned a generous dollop into her tea and tried to ignore the unwanted sensations. She was *not* jealous of Callie. She was happy for her—a single woman going after her dreams and making them a reality.

Between braving bees, a stubborn neighbor, and the isolation out here... really, she was an inspiration for all women.

The clock above the mantle chimed. Squinting into the dark, Grace sighed when she read it was only nine-thirty. She took another sip of her drink when an idea began to take shape. With nothing else to do, and at least another hour before the tea kicked in, she grabbed the nearest sheet of paper and scrawled across the top in the dark:

Among the Bees: Honey & Herbal Remedies by Callie ... Business Plan.

One hour flew by, and then two. By the time the clock chimed again, it was nearing eleven-thirty, and she'd already covered three pages front and back.

A slow smile spread across her face in the dark. She didn't need to reread her notes to know this could work.

Micah raised the ax above his head and brought it down in one fluid motion. The satisfying crack of wood met his ears as the log split in two on either side of the stump. Muscles sore, he stretched his back to work out the kinks and wiped a sleeve across his sweaty forehead.

Last night had been a particularly chilly evening, one where he'd regretted not getting around to that growing woodpile behind the house sooner. With so much to do, more than a few things had fallen to the wayside, but now they had piled up to the point Micah could ignore them no longer. It may only be September, but soon enough, winter would be upon them, and he'd be glad for the store of seasoned wood.

A ray of sun crested over the nearby granite ridge, the glow of pink and orange a stark contrast to the shadowed valley below.

Gathering the pieces of wood, Micah stacked them on top of the pile. He propped the ax against the side of the house and climbed the patio steps to the back door. Inside, the kitchen was empty and dark. Either Caden was still asleep, or he was out working somewhere on the ranch with Finn.

Sliding the door closed, he stepped inside, and the smell of coffee told him his cousin had already come and gone. In the pre-dawn darkness, he fumbled around in the cabinet for a clean mug and poured himself a cup. He didn't always add cream to his coffee, but after the morning he'd had, today felt like one of those days. Setting the lukewarm mug on the counter, he tugged open the fridge door and froze when cool darkness greeted him.

"What the?" Looking behind the appliance, he confirmed the plug was in the socket, but the appliance was eerily quiet. Micah reached a hand inside and tested the temperature. Cool, but not cold.

Not again.

He slammed the door closed, leaving the carton of cream on the top shelf, and tried the panel on the wall. He flipped the switch, and ... *nothing*.

Great. What else could go wrong? Micah pinched the bridge of his nose and squeezed his eyes shut. He didn't have time to fix the generator. Not today. Not this month.

There was a light knock on the front door, followed by a voice he hadn't hoped to hear for at least a few more hours. How was it she always happened to show up at the worst possible moment?

"Hello? Anybody home?" Grace's voice drifted into the room moments before her footsteps echoed across the hardwood floor.

Great. And now she was in his house ... again.

Micah braced himself for what was sure to be a trying day and faced the unwelcome guest. "I see you decided to let yourself in." He didn't attempt to cover the sarcasm in his tone. In fact, if it convinced her to leave, all the better.

Unfortunately, she didn't seem fazed by the terse greeting. Rather, she seemed almost excited to see him. Odd. He couldn't think why that would be.

"Good morning to you, too." Her smile seemed too bright, and her tone far too chipper. Something was up, and he wasn't about to get tricked by another one of her or Callie's schemes.

He stopped her before she could voice whatever she'd come here to say. "Grace, I don't have time for this. I have a lot on my plate today without keeping an eye on you, too." He hadn't meant for it to sound like he'd been watching her, but it was hard not to notice an unwelcome stranger working day in and day out on the ranch.

To her credit, her smile didn't falter after his rude comment. "Perfect. Sounds like you could use the extra help, then." Dropping her bag onto the counter, she crossed her arms and gave him the sweetest look of challenge he'd ever seen.

He held his groan in check. No use arguing with a stubborn sheep, let alone a woman on a mission. If he didn't get a move on and get that generator fixed, he'd be cleaning up more messes than he cared to think of. He might not have wanted a tagalong, but it appeared he had one, like it or not.

"I promise not to get in the way," Grace cut in. "And for what it's worth, I think I'm getting the hang of installing fences. You might even say we make a good team." She smiled once more, and she may have even batted an eyelash or two.

She was good. He'd give her that much. She could probably sweet-talk her way into most contracts with those expressive eyes and full smile. He wasn't about to fall for her charms, but that didn't mean he couldn't make use of her help while she was here.

"Fine. You can help. But we're not working the fence line this morning."

"Oh? Why not?" They still had forty yards left to repair, which, of course, she already knew.

"Don't worry, we'll get back to it later." He couldn't help but grin at the slight dip at the corners of her mouth. Before she could ask any more questions, he turned and pushed the sliding glass door open. When he looked back, she hadn't moved a step from where she stood in the kitchen.

"If we're not doing work with the fence, then where are we going?" Grace had that same look as the day he'd found her on the side of the road.

"What, afraid of a little adventure?" Maybe it was petty of him to goad her like this, but he couldn't seem to help himself. Not where Grace was concerned.

His challenge hit its mark. Without so much as a blink, Grace marched ahead of him through the door and down the steps. She was something else. He'd known girls like her growing up, all bravado and talk, but unlike them, Grace didn't seem afraid to get her hands dirty.

The door clicked shut behind him, and he joined her by his pickup. "Ready to go?" he asked, in case she'd changed her mind in the last few seconds.

Instead of answering him, Grace hopped into the passenger seat and clicked her seatbelt across her hips.

Micah chuckled and climbed in as well. As soon as he had the engine running, they pulled out of the yard and turned onto an overgrown trail. He stepped out of the truck twice to open and close the first and second gates, and then they were off. Grace clutched the handle on her door as they passed over gopher holes and rocks, so Micah eased up on the gas as they crossed a small runoff stream bisecting the road.

The road curved uphill, and less than a minute later, they reached their destination. Micah killed the engine and reached for the toolbox between his and Grace's feet. Looking over his shoulder, he caught her confused look and smiled.

"Know anything about hydroelectric pumps?"

CHAPTER

Fourteen

GRACE WATCHED WITH curiosity as Micah unlocked the brass padlock on the door of a small shed. The gray weathered wood and rusted hinges protested the movement, squeaking and groaning as he eased the door open to reveal a large pit filled with water.

Micah waved her closer. "Don't worry, you won't fall in."

Cautiously, she stepped up to the threshold and peered down at what resembled a green anaconda wrapped around a series of boxes and dials. It wasn't altogether unimpressive. Quite the opposite. She didn't know what she'd expected to find, but it hadn't been this. "This is your hydroelectric system?"

He wedged a rock beneath the door to keep it open and knelt toward the damp earth before reaching for one of the plastic hoses. "I helped my dad install it when I was in middle school, but I've made some changes over the years. It can be a finicky system at times, but it saves us the expense of connecting to the power grid all the way out here."

His hands worked as he talked, inspecting the numbers on the dials and tightening bolts as he went. Once he'd turned off the spinning turbine, he rolled up his sleeves and reached into the water, grabbing hold of the metal box and lifting it out. A plank of wood beneath the unit was enough to keep it propped up and out of the water while he worked.

Grace was wholly unqualified to offer any assistance, so she stood behind him like a statue and watched. It appeared complex, yet simple. Homemade, yet elegant. The mechanics were beyond her understanding, but Micah took his time to explain the ins and outs of the system.

And she loved it.

Micah checked an app on his phone before he unscrewed one of the nozzles and pulled out what almost looked like an airbrush.

He swapped the old nozzle for a new one from the toolbox and screwed it tightly back together. Water splashed his face with the close proximity to the bubbling stream, and he wiped his cheek against his shoulder before restarting the turbine. He checked the app once more and frowned.

"What are you looking for now?" More than a little curious, she inched closer, growing more and more comfortable around him by the minute.

"I thought there was a problem with the spear valve, but now I don't think that's the case."

Grace nodded as if she understood what he was talking about. "So that means ..." she prompted, hoping he'd continue.

He flipped another switch and waited as a series of digital dials quivered on the screen. Angling his body to face her, he indicated the app and handed her his phone. "See how it's hovering around four hundred watts?" He pointed to the center dial. "When I reattach the third and fourth nozzles, it should go up to about seven hundred, but something is causing a drop in pressure. Since this didn't fix it, there's probably a blockage in one of the pipes upstream."

"What does that mean?" Grace wished she'd paid more attention in her high school physics class, but even then, she doubted that would have offered much help.

Micah was silent for a minute before he released a long breath and pushed to standing. "It means we'll have to find the problem ourselves. Either the intake is sucking in air, or we'll have to run the pig down the penstock to clean out the entire pipe." Micah closed the door and replaced the padlock.

"Excuse me?" She had to have heard that wrong. "What does a pig have to do with a hydroelectric system?" Micah had taken a few steps down the slight hill toward the truck, and Grace had to scramble down the dirt slope to catch up with his long strides.

They reached the vehicle, where Micah withdrew what looked like a dumbbell-shaped cylinder.

"This—" he indicated the red-and-black object—"is the *pig*." He handed it to her before grabbing two radios from the truck. "It's like a giant pipe cleaner. As it slides down, it will clean out any debris or silt clinging to the walls. Hopefully, it will solve the issue, but I'll warn you, it can get a bit messy."

As if he could scare her off so easily. "Don't worry about me. I don't mind a little dirt."

Micah's raised eyebrows seemed to say, *suit yourself.* Without another word, he clipped the radios onto his belt and reached for the toolbox at his feet. "Ready when you are."

Grace followed Micah's lead, and together, they hiked a few dozen yards beyond the shed. They stopped beneath a short rocky cliff at a stretch of exposed PVC pipe barely wider than the six-inch pig she was carrying.

Based on the pipe's layout, it looked as if it traced all the way back to the shed. The other end, however, had been buried into the base of the hill, most likely following it up and over to the intake Micah kept referring to.

"We'll need the strap wrench to unscrew the fitted connector. Would you like to do the honors?" Micah was already standing beside the pipe with what appeared to be a belt of rubber looped through a clamp.

Grace jumped at the opportunity, even though she had no idea how to work the tool in his hands. With a little help, he showed her how to thread the rubber strap around the PVC and use it to loosen the cap. Once she had it, he stepped back and let her take over.

Grateful for something to do, she gave the strange rubber wrench a good twist and ... nothing. The PVC didn't budge. She tried again, leaning her body weight against the strap until she felt the cap loosen a smidge.

"You know, as much as I hate admitting it," Micah spoke while she worked, "I've actually appreciated having an extra set of hands around. Not that I needed it, but more hands make light work. Especially since you have nothing else to do until the bridge and your car are fixed."

Grace readjusted her grip and managed to turn the cap another quarter of a rotation. "I wouldn't exactly say nothing."

"And what does that mean?" He raised his eyebrows beneath his baseball cap.

Grace shrugged. It wasn't like it was a secret or anything. "I'm helping Callie with her business."

"Really? I didn't realize you were serious about that." His tone wasn't judgmental, only curious.

"Of course. She's already done a lot for me, and it's the least I can do. And business marketing is what I'm good at."

"When you're not busy knocking down people's doors, you mean?" It was as close to a joke she'd heard from him all day, and based on his relaxed stance, it wasn't meant as an attack.

"Yeah. Something like that." A hint of a smile touched her lips. After a few breaths, she tried twisting on the belt again and managed another rotation of the PVC cap before taking another break. "Actually, I'm in awe of Callie and what she's trying to accomplish."

"Thinking of changing jobs and raising bees now?" He teased.

Wouldn't that be something? "Of course not. It's just impressive, that's all. Starting a new business is risky, especially when you don't have a safety net to fall back on."

"It's definitely not for the faint of heart." She could sense his probing gaze on her and, undoubtedly, the pipe she'd yet to unfasten, but he didn't step in to take over. "Is that something you'd be interested in doing? Running your own business, I mean."

"Maybe. One day, when things are more stable." With a final twist, she finished unscrewing the connector, and water began to leak from the seams. "Um, are you sure this is right?"

"Perfect. Now we just need to unhook the two pipes and we'll be good to go." He reached his arms around her in the tight space to help, an intimate position if it weren't for the mud squishing beneath their boots. Grace tried to tell herself it was the sun making her neck grow warm, but with the morning temperatures still in the fifties, that wasn't likely.

"There," Micah interrupted her embarrassing thoughts. "Now we're ready. I'll hike up real quick to the intake and let you know when I release the pig."

"Sounds like an ominous warning."

Micah chuckled. "Yeah, well, whether it's the mechanical kind or the ones you find on the farm, they both can make a mess." He unclipped one of the two radios from his belt and handed it to her. "I'll drop it in up by the intake, and all you'll need to do is wait at the bottom for it to pass through."

When Grace nodded, Micah took off up the hill through the trees, eating up the ground with his long legs before disappearing through the trees. Less than five minutes later, a crackly voice came over the radio's speaker.

"Okay, Grace. I've got the intake screen removed, and I'm about to drop in the pig—"

"Can we stop calling it that?" Although Micah couldn't see her smile, she knew he could hear the humor in her voice.

"What else would you like me to call it?" She could imagine him rolling his eyes at her. "How about Fred?" he offered. "Or Agatha?"

"Okay, okay." Grace couldn't hold back her laughter. "Never mind. Just send it down already, will you?"

"Whatever you say." The radio went silent, which meant Micah was most likely busy getting the device in place.

Grace watched the gentle stream of water, wondering what exactly she was supposed to see. A handful of seconds went by, and when she was about ready to radio Micah back to see if he'd released it yet, water began to spurt in all directions. The flow seemed to intensify, and with it came an increasing amount of silt and dirt.

Grace took a few steps back as brown water gurgled forth like an angry geyser. A few breaths later, it returned to its original flow rate before reducing to a trickle.

"That was it?" From Micah's warnings, she'd expected a little more, but he was the supposed expert. Picking up the connector, she took a step toward the exposed pipe to reconnect it when the odd gurgling noise started up again. It was coming from the section above her. She couldn't pinpoint the source, but as soon as she realized it was moving down the pipe, it was too late.

All at once, mud and debris launched from the end of the pipe right at Grace like a cannon.

Grace screamed as she fell onto her backside, mud splattering across her overalls and her face. She scrambled to stand, but her feet only slipped on the slick embankment as sludge continued to burst out from the exposed pipe. Eyes closed, she crawled toward what she hoped was solid ground. She tried again to regain her footing and yelped as she landed hard on her tailbone.

Suddenly, strong arms wrapped around her waist, pulling her up and away from the spray. Her eyes snapped open as she looked up into the face of her rescuer.

Amused, Micah scanned her from head to toe, taking in the splatters of dark mud clinging to her clothes and skin. "Are you alright?"

"I'm fine. Just a bit embarrassed." More like mortified by her clumsiness.

He didn't seem convinced, but the tension between his brows had relaxed. His hands, however, remained firmly on her waist, doing all sorts of funny things to Grace's head and heart.

In hopes of putting some distance between them, she stepped back. Her heel slipped out from under her, and in one fell swoop, she careened backward, pulling Micah down with her.

They fell with an audible *oomph*, murky water splattering in all directions as they landed on top of each other in the mud.

Although his front seat might say otherwise, Micah had to admit that Grace handled the sticky situation like a champ. He'd have to scrub the dark stains from the fabric later, but he didn't mind. Nor had he minded the feel of her against him as they lay sprawled in the mud.

He parked the truck and looked over at Grace. "Would you mind getting the gate?"

"Is that your not-so-subtle way of telling me I stink?" Bits of mud and a few stray leaves streaked her blonde hair, but the rosy glow of her face was far from unappealing.

"If you smell, then so do I." Micah laughed. They probably both smelled like sour mud and something else he didn't care to identify.

Grace opened the door, and her laughter followed her outside.

Nothing about today had gone as planned. Between the malfunctioning power system and Grace showing up unannounced, Micah shouldn't feel so content. Although, the incident a half hour ago might account for the lessened tension in his shoulders.

When Grace finally had the gate open, he inched the truck forward and waited for her to close it behind him.

She climbed back into the truck and collapsed against the damp seat. "Wow, I felt like Houdini trying to figure that thing out."

Micah laughed at her overdramatized complaints. "All you have to do is lift the two pins at the same time and swing the gate open."

"Don't forget the chain you have wrapped around the post as well," she shot back.

How could he? After all the fancy gate locks he'd installed over the years, there was always one sheep who figured out how to get through. But not a good old-fashioned steel chain. Those, oddly enough, were impenetrable, even if they were simple. "Got to make sure the sheep don't get out."

"Hm-mm." She hummed beside him. "I think you succeeded."

They drove the short distance through the upper pasture while sheep grazed contentedly in the distance. Dozens of lambs scampered between their mothers, uncoordinated and awkward on their spindly legs. The sight never failed to lift Micah's spirits, even if it did bring with it a weight of responsibility.

A few four-legged onlookers watched as the truck made its way through the pasture and up to the second gate. Micah parked the truck once again, and Grace hopped out, appearing more comfortable with their new routine. She made it halfway to the gate before the first group of wooly spectators cut her off. He watched with amusement as she struggled to weave between the masses.

"How do I get them to leave me alone?" she called out from the edge of the pasture. Between the mud-stained overalls, the leaves in her hair, and the flock of sheep surrounding her, she looked like a flustered version of Little Bo Peep.

"Could you stop laughing for a second and help me?" she yelled over the rumble of the engine.

"Looks like you've got things pretty well under control." A small lamb had taken a particular interest in the hem of her overalls and appeared to be nibbling at the loose threads. Micah would have taken a picture of the scene if he thought he'd survive Grace's wrath.

"Micah!"

At the panic in her voice, he swung his legs out of the truck and calmly walked toward where she stood, trying to shoo the lamb and its friends away. It took all his willpower not to laugh. Instead, he eased his way through the sheep until he stood beside her.

He nudged her shoulder with his until she looked up from the lamb licking her boots.

"Follow my lead." Micah spread his arms to the side for Grace to see. She seemed to relax in his presence and mirrored his movements. "Good. Now we're going to walk slowly toward them, herding them away from the truck and gate. Think you can handle that?"

Tentatively, she nodded.

"Okay, just keep walking forward, and I'll draw them together from the side."

They walked forward, increasing the distance between them until they were on two sides of the flock. Grace kept her focus ahead, moving the sheep forward despite her obvious discomfort.

"Perfect. Now keep pushing them away from the gate and I'll drive the truck through."

"You're leaving me to handle this on my own?" she shouted across the field.

"Don't worry. You've got this, and I'll be back before you know it."

Before Grace could protest, he ran back to the gate, unlatched the lock, and drove through. Making sure there were no stragglers nearby, he left the gate open enough to slip back into the pasture and retrieve Grace.

"Thanks for the help." She blew a loose strand of hair from her face and slumped against the seat.

Micah had the strangest urge to capture that lock of hair behind her ear, but he shook away the thought. He didn't need any distractions, least of all Grace. It was better if they kept things simple. She was here to do a job, as was he, but that didn't stop his teasing remark. "I might be wrong, but I think that counts as three, now."

"Three what?" Grace sulked in the passenger seat beside him, looking as if the day's adventures had taken their toll. With no heater on, and wearing wet clothes, she had to be cold. As much as he found her excitement over the sheep comical, it had obviously distressed her enough to ask for his help.

He almost thought better of answering.

Almost.

"That's three times now that I've rescued you."

Grace swiveled to face him, mouth open as if winding up for an argument. "You did not—"

"I'm only saying," he cut in. "First it was the car, then the mud, and now the sheep. I may be only a country rancher, but even I can count to three." He smiled, despite her look of dismay.

When he thought she was about to chew him out, she surprised him with a burst of laughter. Micah couldn't hold his back either, nor did he want to. He hadn't felt this relaxed since before he'd received that letter from the bank. Odd, that it was with Grace.

After a few moments, they finally caught their breaths, Grace wiping a few tears from her eyes. "I think we can agree that neither of us won against the mud." Smiling, she indicated their ruined clothes as she hiccuped on one last laugh.

Micah looked down at his shirt and jeans and grinned. "Fair enough. But that still puts me at two."

"So it would seem." Grace made no attempt to argue, and he found he quite enjoyed it when they got along.

"Either way" —Micah peeled his gaze from her long enough to shift the truck back into drive— "I think we've earned ourselves some hot coffee and one of Callie's scones."

"Now that the power is working again?" she asked.

"Exactly."

Looking forward to the promise of dry clothes, they passed through the second gate and rounded the barn, stopping short of running into a group of sheep grazing in the yard beside the parked tractor.

"What the?" Micah put the truck in park and jumped out, Grace close on his heels. Pushing past the huddle of sheep blocking the truck, they rounded the barn, and he froze at the sight that greeted them.

Sheep. Everywhere.

A low groan escaped him. And all the morning's levity evaporated in a single breath.

CHAPTER

Fifteen

SOMETHING GRACE WAS *not* thankful for: mud.

She knew so many women back home who swore by their clay masks and the benefits of mud spas. Well, they could keep their mud. If she never saw another puddle, it would be too soon.

The last bits of dirt lifted under the now-soiled terry washcloth, exposing her red, chapped skin beneath. Grace reached for the jar of Callie's *bee-balm* and scooped the thick cream onto her fingertips. Instantly, her skin felt more like itself and not like it had been scrubbed raw.

Stacking her dirty clothes on the edge of the bathroom vanity, she frowned at the frayed hem where a lamb had tried to eat the cotton.

The second thing on her list she could do without ... *sheep*.

Sure, they were cute—from a distance. And she didn't mind the warmth of her wool socks back home. But she was not cut out to care for them.

The moment she and Micah had pulled up to the ranch house, it had been a mad dash to round up every last ewe and lamb from the yard. Three hours of sheep-rustling later, she'd been cold and achy, wanting nothing more than a hot soak and one of those cinnamon vanilla lattes from her favorite café down the street from her apartment. Instead, she'd settled for a moderately warm shower and a cup of one of Callie's teas.

The sweet scent of honey enveloped her in the tiny bathroom as Grace pulled on her pink sweater.

What had she been thinking? That she could actually prove herself out here?

Everywhere she went, it seemed disaster followed. First, her car, then the whole not-revealing-who-she-was thing. That had been a *huge* mistake. And now today. She wouldn't blame Micah if he dismissed her as nothing but a city girl who couldn't be taken seriously. She'd had a lifetime of experience dealing with people's low expectations. Their pity. And now that someone was finally giving her a chance to prove herself, she didn't want to blow it.

With Micah or with Callie.

She left her damp hair to hang limp against the soft fabric of her sweater, twin trails of water dribbling down the front, and descended the stairs to join Callie. Two mugs of tea sat waiting on the table, one for Grace and the other for Callie, sitting forgotten beside her as she clicked away on her knitting needles.

"How's the sweater coming along?" Grace pulled out a chair and plopped down on the other side of the table. She'd intentionally left her own knitting project upstairs, hidden beneath a throw pillow for good measure. Really, she was doing the world a favor by not finishing it.

"See for yourself." With a flourish, Callie spread the bundle of light blue and white yarn on the wood for Grace to see. The body was now finished with one sleeve already complete and the other not far behind. The Nordic-looking pattern stitched into the sweater looked like something out of a fairytale.

That is, if Cinderella lived in Norway and spent her time at a ski lodge.

"What?" Callie asked. "It's not that bad, is it?" She reached for the pattern and compared it to the lacey rosettes beneath the collar.

Grace stifled a laugh. "There's absolutely nothing wrong with it. It looks amazing, actually." With a teacher like Callie, she might be able to make something of her scarf-hat-thing upstairs after all.

"You think so?" Callie asked, voice raised in hope. "Then what's so funny?"

Grace shrugged. Wrapping her hands around her mug, she inhaled the scents of chamomile and lavender before taking a sip. "It just reminded me of something, that's all."

Callie studied her for a moment as a knowing look spread over her face. "Must be something good. Whatever it is has you smiling."

Grace couldn't deny it, nor did she feel the need to. "It reminds me of a book I had when I was a kid. My mom used to read from it every night before bed." She could still remember turning the silver-gilded pages as her mom lulled her to sleep with story after story. "Cinderella was her favorite," Grace mused aloud, "though I never could understand why until I was older."

"And why is that?" Setting her work-in-progress aside, Callie leaned her elbows against the table and propped her head against her hands. A captive audience.

Despite the bittersweet memory, Grace smiled. "She said it takes bravery to face life's challenges, and not to lose heart when the world around seems to grow dim. Whenever we finished reading it, she'd remind me that, unlike the girl in the story, we are never truly alone. That God is always walking beside us, ready to wrap us in His arms." Grace furrowed her brow to fight the sudden burning in her eyes.

"Hmm. Sounds like a wise woman."

Over twenty years had passed, an entire lifetime to a kid of only eight. Grace hadn't thought about that silver-and-blue hardbound book in years. Even now, she was surprised she still remembered it.

"She was. Or, what I remember of her, at least." Something about being here, alone in the mountains without all the distractions, the memories had begun to flood back. They left her feeling raw yet loved at the same time. For so long, she'd wanted a friend to share them with, and as unlikely as it seemed, she'd found that in Callie. "I was only a kid when my parents died and my aunt took me in," she began. "We were driving to my aunt's house after church when it started to rain. I don't remember much of what happened after the accident, only a bright light and waking up in the hospital with my aunt sitting beside me."

To this day, she still hated driving in the rain. Hated the reminder of that awful day and the realization that life could change in an instant. All it took was a little extra water on the road to steal the people she loved most. There'd been no one to blame other than her and God, and she'd spent most of her childhood convincing herself of that.

"For years, I resented the fact that God spared me and not them. I think that's the farthest thing from bravery." She still didn't really know why she was spilling her deepest fears to a near-stranger. But then again, Callie had never felt like a stranger.

Callie reached across the table and wrapped her fingers around Grace's with a gentle strength. There was no way she could know how much the small gesture meant to Grace, but already her friendship was invaluable.

"You might not believe me, but I know what that's like." There was a pause, as if every plant and piece of furniture waited with Grace to hear what Callie would say next. Even the buzzing of insects outside seemed to dim.

Grace had been on the receiving end of enough pity over the years. People meant well, or at least that's what her aunt always said, but none of it ever made the loss feel any less painful. Once people knew her story, they tended to treat her differently. Like she was a fragile thing ready to break at any moment.

"Do you remember the fire I mentioned before? The one that made my parents decide to leave and start over?" Callie asked, surprising Grace with the sudden shift in conversation.

Grace nodded. For the first time since they'd met, Callie seemed to grow pensive, as if weighing her words before speaking. However, it didn't take long for her to keep going. "What I didn't tell you is that the fire started at the Prescott ranch."

Grace tried not to choke on her tea. "What happened?"

Callie grew unusually still. She pushed aside her knitting before speaking again. "It was an accident, a spark inside the hayloft. By the time we got the call, we could already see a tower of smoke on the other side of the hill. My dad and uncle were the first to respond, and they, Micah, his brother, and their dad all fought to contain it."

Grace couldn't imagine what that must have been like.

"They worked as fast as they could, but the winds were too strong, and the embers carried down the valley for miles. Dozens of families lost their farms. Their livelihoods. But Micah and Tye lost so much more. As did we."

At Callie's somber tone, Grace's stomach dropped. "The ranch?"

Callie shook her head. "Somehow, by God's mercy, most of it survived. The fields, the sheep. Even the house. But Micah's dad and my uncle ..." Callie's sniff cut her off short.

"Oh, Callie. I'm so sorry." Grace squeezed her fingers around hers. She knew how empty the words had seemed all the years she'd heard them growing up, but she couldn't think of anything else to say to her friend.

"Thank you, Grace. It was a hard time for both our families. My parents decided to leave it all behind—start over—and Micah's family stayed. After high school, his brother Tye went off to college, and while their mom stayed here with Micah, her heart always seemed elsewhere. I suspect that was why she eventually left as well to live with her sister-in-law and her husband in Florida." Callie's grip was soft, yet firm. Despite all the loss, she appeared the embodiment of peaceful strength, something Grace had been searching for all her life.

"Why come back here after so much loss, then?" After finishing high school, Grace had moved as far away as she could from her hometown and all its reminders. So had her aunt, leaving her with no other reason to return other than to entertain ghosts.

Callie smiled. "Because I have faith that God can do so much more than we can ever imagine. No matter how far gone we think something, or someone, is, beauty can still come from ashes."

The conviction with which Callie spoke made it all sound so simple.

Faith.

The word beckoned to Grace like an open embrace. How she longed to put the past behind her and live with that kind of hope. But it also meant being willing to risk everything as well. And she wasn't sure she was ready to do that yet.

But there was something she *could* do. And to do that, she needed to find Micah.

How could he have forgotten to lock the first gate?

Micah kicked his boot against the dirt, launching a cloud of dust into the air at his feet. He was distracted, that's why. If Grace hadn't insisted on coming along, he never would have missed such a simple detail. His grip tightened around the reins in his hand. The stiff leather bit into his palm until he finally released it with a long sigh.

He was being unfair. The fact Grace stayed when she didn't have to spoke volumes. As did her help with the generator. If he were being honest with himself, he'd expected her to camp out at Callie's or attempt to persuade him further of her company's offer. Not to actually try and help.

Leading Roper into the barn, he grabbed a brush and got to work brushing down the bay's reddish-brown coat. Long, gentle strokes, like his dad taught him when he was a kid. Before everything had changed.

Normally, the simple act soothed both him and his horse, but even Roper seemed to sense his frustration.

Who was he kidding? He'd already lost the crop from the upper pasture he'd been counting on to cover the loan. The fence repairs, while necessary, would put him back a few grand. And now he'd lost another day to rounding up the sheep. Again.

Having finished, Micah set the brush back on the shelf and did one final inspection around the barn. His body ached from the day's activities, but that didn't stop him from checking to ensure the horses had fresh hay and clean water for the evening. If anything, he'd hoped the familiar routine would help clear his mind, but it only served to provide a blank canvas for his thoughts to wander back over the day.

It wasn't enough for Grace to have intruded on his home and his livelihood. She had to take up residence in his thoughts now as well? Micah swiped off his hat, ran his fingers through his hair, and shoved the cap back in place. Grace may not have been to blame for him leaving the gate open, but she was most definitely a distraction. And one he couldn't very well afford.

Ready to go inside and crash onto his bed, Micah rounded the barn when he spotted Grace by the woodpile. "Of all the ..." He shoved down the surge of warmth at seeing her again and marched across the yard as she hefted the old ax onto her shoulder.

She raised the tool above her head before he reached her, and dropped it with a thunk on the stump. Any other time, he might have found the feeble attempt comical, but he was tired and wanted nothing more than to be left in peace.

"Would you mind telling me why you're trespassing again?" he asked.

At his voice, Grace bolted upright and swiveled to face him.

"Caden told me you were outside." She sounded a little out of breath. He couldn't be certain, but her eyes seemed a little red around the edges. Either from allergies or something else, he wasn't sure.

"So naturally, you decided to chop some wood while you waited?" He eyed her expensive-looking sweater and leggings, wondering what had possessed her to do such a thing.

Standing upright, she propped her left hand on her hip. As if the act alone explained why she was there doing yard work. "Not at first, no. But when I couldn't find you, I decided to do something useful."

He looked down at the in-tact log at her feet to the meager pile of splintered branches and wood chips around them. "How long have you been out here?"

She shrugged, a sheepish look on her face. "Twenty minutes or so?" Delicate brows furrowing, she raised the ax and hefted it back onto her shoulder.

Twenty minutes? Had he been so dense not to have heard her all that time? Micah slid another glance at the pathetic pile. "Wait 'til tomorrow morning. You'll be feeling it for sure. Just watch your—"

Grace turned toward the stump and swung, nearly missing him on the backswing. Micah jumped to his right, not wanting another scar to match the one he already had,

Gasping, Grace immediately dropped the ax, which landed with a thud on the grass. "I'm so sorry! Are you okay?" Her face reddened to match the faded barn exterior.

Something of a laugh threatened to escape, but Micah held it in check. "You're as deadly with that thing as you are with that umbrella of yours." He massaged the faded bruise beneath his baseball cap, her eyes tracking his fingers with a wince.

She ducked her head and seemed to study the patchy grass at her feet. "About that. I really am sorry."

"What, for nearly taking my head off twice in one week?" He should feel an ounce of remorse for thinking her discomfort amusing. His mom would surely agree, but she wasn't here. Micah found he quite enjoyed these unexpected encounters with Grace.

"No. Of course, you're right. I mean ... about the umbrella and ..." A blush crept down her neck as she stumbled over her words. She peered at the ax lying between them and back at him. "I'm sorry about everything. The car, not telling you who I was from the beginning, making myself the unwanted houseguest. I should have taken your unanswered emails as a hint, but I thought if I came out here and talked with you, things would be different." Her apology tumbled out in a single stream, as if she couldn't contain it any longer.

For the first time, he caught a glimpse of the vulnerability beneath her tough exterior, and he felt an unexplainable desire to calm her worries.

"To be fair, you're Callie's houseguest, not mine." Why was he defending her? She was finally admitting to all the things he'd blamed her for. He should be letting her tank her case, prove her guilt, and walk away quietly. Not that he could get much of a defense in with how fast Grace was speaking. She was almost as bad as Callie when she got upset.

"And then when I found out about the fire and everything your families have been through—"

"Whoa. Back it up." He stared at her, his mind processing what she'd said. "What are you talking about—?"

"Callie told me. I had no idea what you'd been through."

So, he'd heard correctly. And based on her pained expression, he could only imagine what all Callie had said. He didn't like being tricked, but even more so he hated people's pity. "And would that have changed your mind about coming here?"

"Yes. Maybe ..." Grace tilted her head back toward the sky, the first stars emerging from the darkness, and released a defeated sigh. "I don't know. But it changes things —"

"What exactly did she say?" Micah didn't care that he'd cut Grace off. Callie had no right sharing his family's secrets with a near stranger. Especially one who could use it against them. Sure, everyone had their suspicions. He saw the way people still looked at him in town, the way they'd always looked at him and his family after the fire that lost them their livelihoods. But if they really knew the whole story ...

"I'm so sorry about your dad, Micah. I didn't know."

"Know what? That he's the reason this town hates us? That I've been working all these years to rebuild what he destroyed?" That he still carried the physical scars from that fateful night? As if on cue, the jagged line above his temple began to throb. If she knew the whole story, she wouldn't be looking at him with that infuriating mix of sympathy and pity.

"Callie said the fire was an accident. Besides, how can you accuse your dad of something when he's not here to defend himself?" She'd raised her voice to match his. No doubt the neighbors a mile down the road would be able to hear them soon enough, but Micah didn't care.

Upon reflex, he massaged his forehead against the pounding headache. He wanted to take back all the positive thoughts he'd had about Grace moments before and throw them aside. What right did she have to come here and use his family's past against him? She was exactly like he'd imagined she'd be—stubborn, nosy, intrusive, and for Pete's sake, she didn't know when to stop talking.

"You don't know the whole story," he ground out. Each passing second, the vice around his chest seemed to intensify until he felt it might squeeze all the air from his lungs. His gaze dropped to her lips, and the rest of his argument vanished like the morning mist.

"Then enlighten me." Grace propped her hands on her hips once again and took a step closer. He could feel her breath against his neck, the gentle warmth doing funny things to his brain. The fast-growing darkness seemed to wrap itself around them, drawing them closer until their toes were nearly touching.

"He's the reason we nearly lost the ranch. The reason all the ranchers in this valley had to start over." The conviction in his voice wavered. He tried to tell himself it was the strain of the day catching up with him, but that didn't explain the way his heart was nearly galloping. She was too close. He could make out the flecks of silvery blue in her irises, the way they almost shimmered like the stars above her.

Her boot bumped into his as she stepped closer. "I'm trying to apologize here. But don't yell at me for trying to—"

Before Grace could say another word, Micah pulled her in, silencing her with his lips over hers. For a split second, he was sure she would push him away, knock him over the head once more for good measure like he deserved.

Instead, her arms found their way around him, and she drew closer. Micah deepened the kiss as if he couldn't get enough. For the first time since the fire, he felt completely and utterly alive. Every instinct told him to stop. To run away before things could get complicated. But, by goodness, they were already way past complicated.

At some point, his hat came off. Grace's fingers traced freely through his hair, sending a trail of goosebumps down his skin until she brushed over the old scar. The innocent touch slammed him back to reality, shattering the sense of invincibility from moments before.

He pulled back, but his hands remained at her side, afraid to let go, yet afraid of what was happening as well. Grace gasped in surprise. Neither of them moved. It was as if time stood still, the future yet undecided within a single fragment of time.

In that rush of adrenaline, all his previous arguments seemed to fade away, and another terrifying memory rose in its place. The fire, the barn, the accident ... He could almost feel the heat of the flames licking over his skin, the crash of glass as the windows burst with the force of the explosion over the fields.

Micah couldn't stand to look Grace in the eyes, but neither did he want to let her go. He needed an anchor, and he feared what would happen if he were to let go. Somehow, he didn't care if she knew his family's darkest secrets. But beyond that, he needed someone to confide in, and who better than the person who would be out of his life in a matter of weeks?

His voice came out in a raspy whisper, and what he said shocked even him.

"I'm the reason they're both dead."

CHAPTER

Sixteen

"THERE'S NO NEED to run away, little one. I won't hurt you." Caden inched toward the lamb, arms outstretched. "That's it. Stay right there." Caden motioned for Finn to stay put as he moved forward. Just a little further. Careful of the mud puddle between him and the lamb, he leaned down, fingertips brushing the creamy wool seconds before he lunged.

The creature bolted. With nothing to hold on to, Caden splashed headlong into the mud. Finn barked from the sidelines as if laughing at the failed attempt, and Caden soon joined in.

"You may have won this time. But I'm not leaving until you're back safe with the others."

Undaunted, the lamb watched from a few feet away, teasing him with another round of bleats.

"Hey, I'm not the enemy here." Caden kept his voice even. If stealth wouldn't be on his side, then maybe reason would. Trusting brown eyes stared back at him. "You see all those other sheep on the other side of the fence?" He pointed across the field toward where the edge of the flock grazed in the upper pasture. "I'm only trying to reunite you with your family."

He, Micah, Callie, and Grace had spent the better part of the previous afternoon rounding up the escapees. By nightfall, they'd nearly found them all, save for a few stragglers such as the lamb before him now. The small animal couldn't be over six weeks old. Nowhere old enough to have already been weaned. And to find it all by itself and not with its mother was more than a little worrisome.

The animal stared back at him, its long lashes fanned over its eyes in a slow blink.

"Great." Caden laughed. "I'm actually talking to a sheep. First bees, and now this." He stood and rolled up his sleeves, exposing the compass tattoo wrapped around his right forearm. Every day, the symbol inked into his skin reminded him how far he was from finding his direction in life. He hadn't had much of a plan a year ago when he'd skipped out on helping his friend Austin and came to the ranch instead. In fact, he still wasn't any closer to a plan, but today, he was determined to see this lamb returned to the flock.

Shielding his eyes from the intense morning sun, he looked back toward the sea of white and again at the stubborn animal. Something rustled behind him, and he turned to see Finn rooting through the bushes, nose trained on the ground.

Micah would kill him if he let the dog roll in another pile of manure. Last month, Finn had come into the house smelling like rotting sewage. The acrid scent had lingered for hours, even after they'd washed him twice and thrown open the windows. Caden wasn't sure what the dog had found this time, but the fact he wasn't rolling in it was a good enough sign.

Pacing a few yards away, Finn ducked his head into a thicket of sagebrush and pawed at the dirt. Normally, Caden wouldn't think twice about the dog's behavior, but Finn's high-pitched whine made him grow tense.

Caden looked back over his shoulder to see the lamb hadn't moved from its spot. He really should focus on getting the lost sheep back. The clock was ticking for him to reunite it with its mother, and the little creature had proven trickier to catch than expected.

Finn's whining stopped, replaced by a series of rapid barks.

Caden was torn between leaving the lamb and investigating what had obviously upset Finn. But the fact that Finn rarely barked had him on edge.

With slow steps, Caden moved away from the calm lamb, praying it would stay put while he went to investigate.

Finn wagged his tail at Caden's approach, but his ears remained alert and rigid as he circled a cluster of bushes.

"What is it, boy?" He lowered his hand to the dog's back and stroked its bristled coat. He pushed aside the silvery mound of sagebrush, releasing the plant's oils in a cloud of pollen. Choking back the overpowering scent of sage, he clamped his mouth shut and peered at the ground.

A footprint, not much smaller than his, was cast into the dry mud.

He stepped farther into the thicket and knelt beside the imprint. From the rounded toe and raised heel, he'd say it was from some kind of dress shoe. But what it was doing all the way out here was beyond him. The recent rainstorm would have washed away any old marking, which meant this could only be a few days old. Something white caught his attention, and he pried a used cigarette butt from the dried mud—coffin nails, as his mother called them. Despite the charred end, the paper appeared fresh, and the scent of burnt tobacco still emanated from it.

Before Caden could investigate further, Finn lowered his nose to the unfamiliar footprint and took off toward the upper pasture, stopping at the edge of the fence. Slipping the cigarette into his pocket, Caden went after the dog and froze when he spotted the hole in the wire mesh.

"What the...?" He lifted the limp piece of wire as something soft nudged his hand, and he looked down to see the lamb nibbling at the grass and mud stuck to his pants.

"Now you choose to cooperate."

The animal wagged its bushy tail, and he couldn't help but run his fingers through the wooly topknot. At least he'd solved one problem this morning. "I'm not letting you out of my sight until I know you're safe."

Not about to let it loose in a pasture it could easily escape from again, Caden unrolled a wad of string from his other pocket and looped it around the animal's neck like a leash. After a few encouraging tugs, the lamb followed, and the three of them made their way toward the barn.

Oil and water, Micah. Oil and water.

More like water and acid, according to his high school chemistry class. And when those two mixed, they tended to explode.

That's exactly what kissing Grace had felt like. An explosion of every emotion he'd stuffed down for years—frustration, guilt, uncertainty for the future, and a touch of recklessness—all colliding in one singular moment. And that confession. Micah kneaded the knots at the back of his neck. What had he been thinking? Had he really admitted his deepest fear, and to her of all people? He almost didn't want to step out into the daylight for fear of what unexpected consequences might await him. He had enough to worry about without adding an umbrella-wielding, ax-throwing, drive-a-man-crazy-kind-of-attractive city-dweller into the mix.

"Morning."

Micah lurched like a startled lamb and spun on Caden, who stepped into the office. Dark mud stains marred his white T-shirt, and knowing Caden, there would be a story to go with it.

"Catch you at a bad time?" Caden asked. The pitter-patter of claws echoed through the cavernous barn as Finn came trotting into the small room at the back.

Embarrassed to have been so easily surprised, Micah stood to his full height and tried to tamp down the unease slicing through him. "To be honest, I'd love nothing more than a distraction right about now."

"Is that so?" Caden hiked an eyebrow as if he could read the thoughts going through Micah's head. The playful guise faded, and his expression suddenly grew serious. "In that case, I think I need to show you something."

"I don't like the sound of that." How was it he kept on trading one unpleasant situation for another?

"Then you'll like what you see a lot less." Caden tilted his head toward the door for Micah to follow him and strode outside.

A few steps past the door, Micah paused when he spotted a lamb with a muddy handprint on its otherwise clean wool. "What happened there?"

The little animal nuzzled its wooly head against Micah's hand, earning him an audible huff from Caden. "Seems to like you. It took me nearly an hour to catch her. And how does she reward me? By going straight to you without so much as a handful of hay as a bribe."

Micah wove his fingers through the fine curls and smiled. "Guess she likes me better."

"Funny." Caden's annoyed expression didn't fool Micah for a second. "She may be cute, but that's not why I brought you out here." Caden grabbed the end of a rope looped around the lamb's neck and led the way toward the upper pasture.

Curious as to what had his cousin in such a mood, Micah followed. Neither of them spoke as they walked, which suited him fine. He had enough problems bucking around in his mind to worry about making small talk.

The closer they got to the pasture, the louder the sounds of bleating sheep became. Micah eyed the once pristine alfalfa, noting how much of a dent the few hundred sheep had already created. He'd known when he'd decided to move them there the crop wouldn't be good for another harvest. But a tiny bit of him had hoped for some kind of break.

Once through the gate, Caden held the end of the rope while Micah removed the makeshift leash from the wriggling lamb's neck so it could join the others. But for all the trouble Caden mentioned about trying to catch it, the animal didn't seem to want to leave Micah's side.

"Figures. And after all I did to rescue her." Caden gave the little animal a gentle push from behind, but she dug in her hooves.

"How about we start walking?" Micah suggested. "Sooner or later, she'll figure it out. She must be starving after being out all night. Surely that will motivate her to find her mom."

"I hope so." Concern laced Caden's tone. If the lamb had been out since yesterday afternoon, who knew when it had last been fed?

With Finn and the lamb close behind them, Micah followed Caden toward the fence that spanned the southern border between the upper pasture and the adjacent field. In the distance, something swayed in the breeze between a section of posts. From where they stood, Micah couldn't make out if it were an old branch caught in the wire, but the closer they got, the more the band around his chest tightened.

At the end of the field, Caden knelt beside the fence line and pulled back a dry tumbleweed to reveal a gap large enough for a medium-sized sheep to pass through. He tugged on the loose mesh, revealing the broken wires.

Micah stepped forward and frowned at the smooth metallic edge. Not snapped. Cut.

"Who would have done something like this?"

Caden shook his head. "I don't know, but I don't like it." Dropping the limp wire, Caden rose and took his time brushing the dirt from his pants. When he finally looked up, Micah couldn't help but notice the worry edging the corners of his eyes. "I should have mentioned it earlier, but I'm pretty sure I saw footprints this morning, too. I wouldn't normally think much of it, but with this..."

Micah didn't like where this was going. "You sure they weren't from Grace or Callie?" Both had spent a lot of time at the ranch lately. Especially Grace. It wasn't beyond the realm of possibility one of them had wandered up here on their own.

Caden shook his head. "Definitely a man's shoe. And last I checked, neither of us has picked up smoking." He fished around in his pocket and withdrew a crumpled white cigarette butt with blue wings stamped on the tip.

Even after fifteen years, Micah would recognize the old label anywhere. It had to be specially ordered from out of state, and only a few people in town smoked that brand, one of which used to be his father.

"So, what are you saying?" Dozens of scenarios swam through his mind, and he prayed they were all wrong.

"I don't know, exactly. But this looks intentional to me."

So, that meant he hadn't left the gate open after all. The thought brought little comfort, knowing something far more sinister was going on. "Do the girls know?"

Caden shook his head once more. "I thought I'd let you know first. Besides, I didn't want to alarm them. Especially if it was nothing."

He'd love it if that were the case, but based on the state of the wire and all that had transpired the past couple of weeks, Micah knew better than to ignore the facts. "Thanks for showing me."

"Sure thing. And as far as I could tell, this is the only section. A single patch should be enough to fix it."

Micah nodded, all the while raking his brain for an answer. A simple prank was one thing. They'd had their fair share of them over the years—usually bored teenagers looking for some fun—but this time felt different. This had been deliberate. For the life of him, he couldn't think of why someone would do such a thing.

And that's what scared him the most.

Something soft brushed against his hand. Micah looked down to see the lamb sniffing his pockets and released a pent-up breath. These sheep were his responsibility. Despite his fondness for the wooly animals, they were not the smartest of God's creatures—much like people. He figured that was why Jesus referred to himself as the Good Shepherd and people as His sheep. If God hadn't given up on him fifteen years ago, he could trust He wouldn't start now.

Okay, God. I'm counting on you to get us through this.

Nothing but the wind through the distant trees answered his plea. He hadn't really expected a reply, but the empty silence felt deafening.

Micah was about to head back toward the barn for some tools when a loud bleating stopped him in his tracks. The lamb still hadn't moved from his side. It looked up at him with its soulful brown eyes, as if he held all the answers. Innocent. Trusting. Alone.

Well, not exactly alone. There was an entire flock on the other side of the pasture, no doubt wondering where this one had gotten off to.

The lamb nudged his leg and baaed once more.

"I know you're hungry, little one." Micah lifted his eyes to the fence once more and back to the baby lamb. Caden could handle the repairs. After all, it was only a small patch job.

"Let's go find your mom."

Before he could stop her, the lamb wriggled ahead of him through the opening and took off down the hill.

"Wait. Come back here!" Micah took off after the lamb, stumbling in his attempt to jump over the fence. The hem of his jeans snagged on the exposed wire before ripping free as he crashed onto the hard earth. Without so much as brushing himself off, he hopped back to his feet in time to glimpse a white tail disappearing behind a grove of trees.

Caden's hurried footsteps echoed behind him as he dodged gopher holes and shrubs. A few seconds later, Micah rounded the pine thicket and paused as Finn raced ahead of him. Caden bumped into him a few seconds later, and they both nearly tumbled into the empty clearing.

Micah threw a hand out to steady them and tried to focus on the sounds of rustling leaves and crunching gravel, any sign of movement.

"Which way did she go?" Caden breathed heavily from the unexpected sprint, punctuating the tense silence. Micah swatted his cousin in the stomach to remain quiet, and he tried listening again.

A few seconds later, a high-pitched cry and Finn's bark carried over the breeze, raising the hairs on the back of Micah's neck.

Caden took off first, heading downslope in the direction of the river.

If anything happened to that lamb ... If it made its way to the water's edge and got swept away by the current, he'd never forgive himself. Of course, they'd lost livestock before, and this wouldn't be the last, but it was another thing when he literally let a lamb slip through his fingers.

"This way," Caden shouted as he pivoted south, parallel to the river.

Micah remained hot on his heels, ducking beneath low branches as they made their way through willow brambles and oak brush. The feeble cries grew more urgent, quickening their pace. They had to be close. Movement to Micah's left made him pause, and he gestured to his cousin to move toward the break of sunlight.

A branch swept the backs of their heels as they emerged from the thicket. At the base of a large cottonwood stood Finn with the lamb a few feet away, spindly legs shaking as it greeted them with another short baa. Relieved to find the animal physically unscathed, Micah took a step forward. He gave the dog a well-deserved scratch behind the ears but paused when he spotted another mound of white buried in the tall grass. Caden halted behind him, having seen it too.

Sensing his cousin had gone as far as comfortable, Micah steeled himself and waded through the grass. The lamb nudged its nose against his boot as he knelt toward the other sheep.

Its neck was twisted back at an unnatural angle, and a dark red stain marred the snowy wool. Flies already buzzed around the area, revealing exactly what he feared before even touching the lifeless form.

"Is it...?" The rest of Caden's question died on his lips. He'd been around the ranch long enough to see his fair share of loss, but he seemed unsure how to handle something like this.

"I'm afraid so. Looks like a coyote or maybe a wolf. Although there hasn't been a sighting in over ten years." Hands on his knees, Micah then stood and walked back to his cousin.

Caden reached down and brushed his hand over the lamb's back. The gentle touch seemed to calm its shivering for the time being. "No wonder she wouldn't go to the other sheep. She knew her mother wasn't there." He peered up at Micah. "What now?"

Micah felt the weight of a mountain settle over him. "We take her home and hope another ewe will accept her as her own. If not, she won't last much longer on her own." It was a harsh reality, and one he'd never gotten used to. No matter the fact he'd spent his entire life on this ranch. Like the story of the shepherd who leaves the ninety-nine sheep to go after the one, he'd wanted to save every animal, even when his dad told them it was a lost cause.

"Saving one sheep won't make much of a difference, son."

Well, it might not change things on a large scale, but if it meant the difference in survival for that one animal, it was worth a try.

"I'm not taking any more chances with you." He spoke in his most soothing tone to the lamb, and the animal stared back at him with all the trust in the world. Careful not to traumatize it any more than necessary, Micah carefully scooped it up and draped its willowy body across the width of his shoulders. It felt like hardly any weight at all as it relaxed against him. So fragile. Innocent ... And entirely his responsibility.

"All right, you. Let's go home."

CHAPTER

Seventeen

CALLIE RAISED HER old DSLR camera and brought the bright pink blooms into focus. Holding her breath, she waited for the honeybee to land on the large coneflower before snapping another picture.

"Gotcha." She took a couple more before the bee flew away and then stood to stretch her back. She couldn't remember the last time she'd taken so many photos. However, it felt good to be using her old camera once again. Callie made a mental note to mail her mom a few prints once she and Grace had them developed.

"You really think we'll be able to use all these photos?" She'd known a website would eventually be a necessity if she ever got the business up and running. But with the time she'd put into fine-tuning her recipes, she hadn't put much thought into its design until now. And seeing as the bridge to town had yet to be repaired, she could forget those dreams of setting up a stall at next week's farmer's market.

Grace lifted her eyes from the stack of notes she'd been scribbling on for the past hour and looked at Callie. "Absolutely. The first thing for any new startup is to establish your brand. Customers want to connect with a story, to see what goes on behind the scenes of a product. What better way to do that than by inviting them into your garden?"

They'd been at it all morning. Going over marketing strategies, branding, and something about KPIs. *Key Performance Indicators,* as Grace put it. As if Callie knew what those even were. If she could help others with her products, she'd be happy. She much preferred spending her time tinkering with new tea blends and tending the hives to talking about finances or the benefits of an LLC over a sole proprietorship. That was Grace's strength, not hers. Which was why she was even more grateful for the help.

And speaking of helping others …

"You can't avoid it forever, you know," Callie said.

Grace's head shot up from her stack of notes, ponytail swishing wildly from the sudden movement. "What are you talking about?"

Callie wasn't born yesterday. Grace had been acting strange ever since she'd come back from the ranch yesterday evening. Sensing her friend's discomfort, she hadn't pushed at the time, but it had taken an insurmountable amount of self-control on her part not to butt in before now.

"Don't get me wrong, I'm stoked to have my own personal marketing specialist for the day, but something tells me you're hiding out here for a reason. Not that a beautiful fall day and a yard of flowers aren't enough to get someone out of bed. It's only that normally by this time, you'd be out the door and off to the ranch."

"It's nothing. Really." Grace shrugged and shoved her nose back into her pages of notes.

As if that could fool Callie. "Whatever you say. But I've seen that expression enough times on Micah's face over the years to know what I'm talking about."

A blush crept over Grace's neck at the mention of Micah. So that's what this was about. "I don't want to talk about it," she said a little too forcefully.

Now they were getting somewhere. Callie plopped into the chair beside Grace and leaned against the table. "I think something happened between you and Micah, and you've been dying to talk about it ever since."

"Nothing happened!" Grace stammered.

"Which means something definitely did." Callie could hardly contain her excitement, but for Grace's sake, she tried. Really, she should be awarded a medal for how long she'd held out before now.

"I'm not going to dignify that with an answer." Grace didn't seem to share in her enthusiasm. As if to prove her point, she buried her nose to the stack of papers, pretending to get back to work.

If Grace was this worked up, she could only imagine what Micah was like. What Callie wouldn't give to see the man loosen up for once. He seemed set on carrying the weight of the world on his shoulders. It would do him good to let someone else in. And even though they'd only known each other a little over a week, she had a good feeling about Grace.

Beside her, Grace sniffled and retrieved a wadded-up tissue from her pocket.

"Allergies?"

Grace blew her nose and nodded. "I ran out of antihistamine a few days ago, and I've been a wreck ever since."

"You sure it has nothing to do with a certain rancher?" she teased, earning her a frown from Grace. "Okay, fine." Callie raised her hands in surrender. "But speaking of allergies, I have just the thing." She disappeared into the house and pulled down a jar of honey from the shelf above the stove. Once back outside, she spooned a hefty dollop into Grace's tea. "Local honey is great for treating allergies, and this is the most local you're gonna get."

"You sure that's not an old wives' tale?" Grace took a sip and visibly relaxed. "Not that I'm complaining. This is delicious."

Callie beamed under her friend's praise. "If it works, it works. Sometimes the simplest answers are often the best."

"Hmm. I can get on board with a honey diet." Grace closed her eyes and took another long sip.

"Speaking of honey ... Are you ready to brave the beehives today?" Callie didn't miss Grace's frown as she lowered the tea she'd been enjoying. "Either you help me with the bees or tell me what's turned you into a super-businesswoman all of a sudden." She'd get Grace to face one of her fears if it was the last thing she did. And if it wasn't talking about what had obviously happened between her and Micah, then it would have to be the bees.

"As ready as I'll ever be, I guess," Grace mumbled. She shuddered, and Callie snorted back a laugh, earning her a comedic eye roll from Grace.

"Joking aside, I really think you'll enjoy it."

"What? Getting stung or dressing up like an astronaut?" Grace finally cracked a smile, a good enough sign for Callie to continue.

"I promise you won't get stung. And just think of all the honey we'll have afterwards. You'll be allergy-free in no time."

Grace took another sip of her tea and hummed in thought. "Mmm-hmm. Right, so Caden just chose to stick his head in a beehive, then?"

Callie waved her hand. "That was a freak accident. I'll make sure you're perfectly sealed and bubble-wrapped."

"Don't even think of taking a picture of me in that thing." She pointed at the camera dangling from Callie's neck and grimaced.

Callie couldn't hold back her growing smile. "I can't make any promises. After all, you're the one who said, and I quote, 'Customers want to connect with a story, to see what goes on behind the scenes.'"

Grace laughed, the sudden sound startling a hummingbird zipping through the honeysuckle behind her. "I meant you, not me. Your business. Your garden."

"Tomayto, tomahto." Callie tilted her hand back and forth and grinned.

Grace shook her head. "You and your tomatoes." Pushing her empty mug aside, she gathered the papers in front of her and shuffled them into a neat stack. Stalling, more like.

Callie waited for Grace to finish before they headed toward the hives. She'd already laid out their suits, hats, and gloves earlier, confident in her friend's ability to see this activity through. At the edge of the garden, they slipped into their gear as Callie explained what they were about to do.

"And Grace" —she handed Grace the smoker and paused, willing her friend to look at her— "just so you know, I'm always here if you ever want to talk. Or if you want someone to drink tea in silence with. I'm not going anywhere."

Grace raised an eyebrow, or at least it looked like she did through the mesh beekeeper hood. "Silence? Really?" she teased.

So maybe that had been a bit of an overstatement. "Okay, fine. But you know what I meant."

Grace nodded. "I do. And thanks, Callie. That means a lot."

As much as Grace appreciated Callie's offer, she wasn't ready to bare her heart. Not when she couldn't understand her own emotions. It had been less than twenty-four hours since her run-in with Micah, and her head was still spinning with unanswered questions.

The spruce boughs creaked and swayed above her. She'd mentioned something about wanting to take a walk to clear her head, and Callie had pointed her in the direction of this trail. Animal trail, more like. If it weren't for the few strings of yarn tied to the branches every now and again, she'd have gotten lost the first five minutes. But as much as the trail demanded her attention, it wasn't enough to distract her thoughts.

Like that kiss, for starters. It had been completely out of the blue. Yet the moment Micah pulled her into his arms, nothing had felt more right. All thoughts of the contract and the ranch vanished, and she was wholly consumed by the explosion of sensations ricocheting throughout her body. When he'd started to pull back, all she'd wanted was for that moment to last forever.

But then there'd been that confession and the haunted look in his dark eyes. Nothing could have prepared her for that kind of whiplash—flying one moment and crashing back to earth the next. She'd hardly recovered from her past traumas; she didn't know if she could handle another person's baggage on top of it all.

Grace followed the curve of the trail through the trees, faint as it was, the silent forest providing the perfect canvas for her mind to wander.

What exactly had he meant when he said he was the reason his father and Callie's uncle had died in the fire? Based on what Callie had told her, it had all been an unfortunate accident. But as soon as Micah had whispered that confession, he'd retreated into the house. She'd known it wasn't the best time to ask him questions. She wasn't sure if she was capable of speaking coherency after his kiss, so she'd gone back to Callie's. As much as she wanted answers, she wasn't about to rip open that old wound again. Not if she could help her friend move forward with her life.

Which was precisely what she'd decided this morning. She'd even braved thousands of bees for her. If that didn't speak to their friendship, she didn't know what would. It most certainly had nothing to do with the fact she didn't know how to face Micah. Callie had been right about a lot of things, but even Grace didn't fully understand what had changed last night.

Nor did she want to overanalyze it now.

She ducked beneath a low branch and closed her eyes against the blinding sun. Immediately, an image of Micah flashed before her, and she snapped her eyes back open. She didn't want or need an explanation. It would only complicate things further, and that was the last thing she could handle. She was here to do a job. The fact that she was already developing feelings for him only made it that much more difficult.

After a few minutes, the trees opened into a private meadow. Tall grasses swayed in the breeze, and a smattering of purple and yellow flowers dotted the landscape. She paused at the edge of the field and marveled at the beauty of God's creation.

Here, alone, and surrounded by nothing but nature and her own thoughts, her world felt louder than ever. A voice she almost didn't recognize seemed to be drawing her closer, and she knew she didn't want to merely survive anymore. Last night had awakened something in her she'd thought long gone, leaving her feeling both vulnerable and alive all at once.

And the realization terrified her.

Grace remained where she stood, her feet unwilling to carry her out into the open. One step. That's all it would take to leave her sense of security behind.

Birds chattered in the branches above as if they, too, sensed her dilemma. It wasn't until a few sharp chirps came from the field that, one by one, they flew from the branches to join the other winged creatures.

Who was she kidding? Things were already beyond complicated. Had been ever since Micah had picked her up on the side of the road ten days ago.

Goodness, was that all it had been? Ten days to make her question everything.

At a familiar bark, she turned to see Finn bounding toward her. His head nearly disappeared between leaps as he sank below the tall arched blades of grass until he was at her feet.

"Hey, there, boy. What are you doing all the way out here?"

Finn gazed up at her with those mismatched eyes of his, and she scratched behind the dog's ears, earning her a few affectionate licks. Peeling her gaze from the warm welcome, she scanned the corner of the field from where the dog had come and saw the faint outline of a building through the sparse cluster of aspens.

So that's why Callie had directed her this way. She'd been leading her right to Micah's place all along.

Finn nudged her with his nose as if encouraging her to take the next step.

She released a steadying breath. Callie was right. She couldn't hide forever. And if there was going to be a future with Micah, professional or otherwise, she'd eventually have to see him again.

With another fortifying breath, she stepped toward the building and lifted a rusty prayer heavenward.

Micah nodded as he listened to his brother's advice over the phone. It had taken a few tries to get ahold of Tye amidst his busy work schedule, but when it came to animals, he trusted his brother's professional opinion above anyone else.

"Okay, will do. Thanks. And say hi to Beth for me." Micah hung up the phone and turned to leave when a voice startled him from behind.

"Who was that?"

He spun on his heels and spotted Grace near the workbench. She was wearing a light yellow T-shirt and a fresh pair of overalls that had been rolled at the ankles. The boots still looked to be half a size too large for her small frame, but in an odd sort of way, she looked like she belonged.

"Eavesdropping?" He pinned her with a questioning look and started to walk outside. After last night, he didn't trust himself to be in the same room with her.

"What? N-no," she stammered. Despite more than a half-foot difference in height, she managed to catch up with him by the barn door. She made a show of marching after him, only to nearly trip over her own shoes at the threshold. Gracefully managing to avoid falling face-first on the barn floor, she grabbed hold of the doorframe to steady herself and drew in a lungful of air.

"Okay, technically, yes. I did overhear a little of your conversation. But it's not like I followed you in here or anything." Her face flushed, and she shuffled backward a step. "I heard someone talking, so I came in here before I realized you were on the phone."

Micah raised his hand to stop her rambling and the memories of last night, steeling himself not to pull her in for another kiss. "Relax. I was only kidding."

"Oh." She paused, seemingly at a loss for words. There was a long, awkward silence before either of them spoke again. Grace fidgeted with the splintered edge of the door. "You might want to work on that next time. The joking, I mean."

"Duly noted," he said with a soft laugh.

He knew it was his turn to fill the quiet when she went silent again. Anything to stop the thoughts from last night flooding his brain when she looked at him like that. "To answer your question, I was on the phone with my brother. He's a veterinarian in Loveland." Good. Animals seemed like a safe enough topic. "I know these sheep better than anyone, but I respect Tye's training and wanted to get his input on a few things."

While Tye was busy studying and getting A's in school, Micah had spent his free time in the fields, the sheep and horses his daily companions. It was no wonder he'd been the one to stay and manage the family ranch after their dad passed. A tough decision for a kid of eighteen, but someone had to step up. And his brother's current happiness was enough to convince himself he'd made the right decision.

Micah indicated the bottle of freshly mixed sheep formula in his hand and inclined his head out the door. "Care to join me?" he asked.

When Grace didn't object, he led the way outside and toward the old stables out back. At the small round pen, they stopped, and Micah lifted the latch. Quietly, he entered so as not to startle the lamb and secured the gate behind him, acutely aware of Grace's presence the entire time.

Grace watched from behind the fence, elbows propped against the wooden frame as if she were afraid to come any closer. Afraid of him or the lamb, he wasn't sure.

"Listen, about yesterday..." he started, wanting to clear the air between them.

"Don't."

Her single word stopped his unrehearsed speech. A sense of relief washed over him, mixed with a niggling doubt he hadn't been able to shake since last night. He didn't know what he'd been about to say. That he was sorry? That he shouldn't have kissed her and then promptly dumped his personal garbage at her feet?

Grace shifted, but her gaze never wavered from his. "I'm sorry. What I meant to say is you don't have to explain. We were both emotional, and things happened from there." She gave him a partial smile, but he could tell there was more she'd wanted to say.

Another awkward silence settled over them, but the fact Grace was still here and hadn't run away yet somehow eased the knot in his stomach. What was it about her that made him feel so exposed yet understood at the same time? Perhaps it was the effect of spending so much time together in such a short period. It blurred the line between stranger and friend, a middle ground he didn't know what to do with.

"So, why's this one here and not with the others?" she finally asked, abruptly changing the subject. Her grip loosened a smidge on the rough wood, but she remained rooted where she stood. At this rate, it'd take an hour for her to get inside the pen.

"Caden found her this morning outside the fence. Must've been out all night. The poor thing was nearly starving by the time we brought her back."

Something between sympathy and regret passed over Grace's features. She released her hold on the fence and crossed her arms over her stomach. "I'm sorry."

"Don't be. It wasn't your fault." A small comfort, despite the fact that someone else had deliberately sabotaged the ranch. He withdrew the used cigarette from his pocket and held it up for her to see. "It looks like someone cut a hole in the fence in the upper pasture. That's most likely how all the sheep got out yesterday. Caden and I fixed the damage, but we still lost a few good sheep to either coyotes or wolves, including this one's mother."

Grace's gaze dipped from the crumpled cigarette to the lamb at his side, her face contorting with unspoken emotion. He thought he saw a shimmer of moisture, but she blinked it back a moment later.

"What's going to happen to her now?"

"Without her mother, she'll starve. I could try to match her with another ewe, but there's no guarantee they won't reject her, which would land us right back here in another few days. Our best bet is bottle-feeding her until she's old enough to rejoin the flock. However, that requires time Caden and I don't have."

As he spoke, a plan began to take shape. Maybe it was a bad idea, but for some reason, he didn't seem to care. "Why don't you take care of her?"

"Me?" Grace squeaked.

"Why not? She needs round-the-clock care, and you're right next door."

"And I know absolutely nothing about sheep. You saw how I acted yesterday when they started nibbling at my shoes." Her blue-green eyes went wide, and she took a step away from the enclosure.

How could he forget? It had been the highlight of his day before rounding up the strays. "Neither did Caden when he first came here and look at him how. Besides, it'll only be one lamb this time. I'm not asking you to watch over the whole flock."

Based on her silence, he assumed she'd run out of excuses. Opening the gate, he held out a hand, and after a few long seconds, she hesitantly placed her free one in his. Micah tried to ignore the smoothness of her palm against his rough, work-hardened one. He tugged her hand toward the animal's back, her hand between his and the tightly coiled wool. "See? Harmless."

Grace's nervous laugh came unexpectedly, and he found he quite liked its soft lilt.

He picked up the bottle from the ground and offered it to Grace, who took it without pause.

"You're not making this easy on me," she said, her mouth tilting at the corners.

He grinned, liking this softer version of her. "I never said I would."

The low purr of an engine announced Caden's arrival. Now that he was back from the neighbor's, hopefully they'd be able to get out and check the rest of the fence line for any more unexpected surprises. That, and maybe the distance from Grace, would prevent Micah from blurting out any more rash ideas. Releasing her hand, he stood and took a step toward the gate.

"Where are you going?" Grace asked, eyes wide. She'd turned her back to the lamb, who was sniffing at the bottle in her hands. "You're not going to leave me here, are you?"

He tamed his grin. "You'll be fine. And if she doesn't drink it all at first, that's okay. I'll show you later how to measure out the formula later."

Confident the two of them would be alright on their own, he turned his back and stepped out of the pen. A moment later, a loud bleat and Grace's startled cry called him back. Micah spun to see Grace dripping with formula in the middle of the pen, bottle on the ground, the rest of the contents leaking into the dirt.

He covered the space in a few quick strides, trying not to laugh at the mess before him. "What in the world happened?"

Grace's eyes widened at the innocent-looking lamb. "She tried to pull the bottle from my hands and ... and the lid exploded."

Micah couldn't help but chuckle. "Is that so?"

Her face flushed a pretty pink, and in an instant, she pinned him with a frown. "Are you saying I'm a liar?" The irony of her words hung heavy in the air, pulling them right back to that first day.

A week or so ago, he would have dug into that open wound. But in this moment, milk stains dripping down her pants and a newborn lamb bleating at her feet, he couldn't summon the same resentment.

Retracing his steps to the pen, he knelt to the earth and scooped up the half-empty bottle and lid, all the while feeling the intensity of her gaze on his back. "I guess she's still not sure about you. Can't blame her, though. It took me more than a few tries to warm up to you as well."

Grace brushed at the wet stains on her clothes but kept her attention on the lamb.

"Just be yourself," he said. "She's a sheep. All she cares about is that you feed her and keep her safe. You can manage that."

As if noticing the formula dripping from Grace's clothes, the sheep inched toward her and licked the hem of her pants. The pink tongue went after the drenched cotton as if it were covered in honey, and Grace finally smiled. "If I can get along with troublesome cowboys, I guess I can handle a little lamb."

Micah chuckled. "Fair enough. Now let's see about another bottle. And this time," he added, pausing as the gate swung open, "the formula is for the lamb, not the ground."

Grace tossed him a playful scowl. "Remind me to spill it on *you* next time."

He'd like to see her try. But for all their differences, he couldn't help but smile. "It's a deal."

CHAPTER

Eighteen

"NO. ABSOLUTELY NOT." Micah swiveled his gaze from Caden to the two animals nibbling the grass behind his truck. If Caden thought this was the solution to their problems, he was sorely mistaken.

"Awe, come on. You haven't even heard my plan yet." Caden was practically bouncing on his toes as if he'd downed an entire carafe of coffee.

"If it involves llamas, I don't want to hear it."

"Alpacas," Caden corrected, a wide grin spread across his face. "And yes, you do. Until we know the sheep are safe, we can use all the help we can get. Say hello to Violet and Fiona."

"You've got to be joking." Nothing about the animals appeared even remotely intimidating, right down to their fluffy tails and large eyes.

Unfazed by Micah's reaction, Caden continued. "I've been doing some research, and it turns out alpacas are the perfect shepherds. They'll even fight off a wolf if it tries to attack their herd, which, as it stands, is exactly what we need right now. Even Ted Landry had a few on his ranch before... you know."

Yeah, he did know. But a few alpacas still hadn't been enough to keep the man from being forced to sell a few months later. Not that it was the animals' fault, of course.

"And where did you happen to find Fiona and Violet?" Micah couldn't believe he was even considering this crazy plan.

"I didn't steal them, if that's what you're wondering," Caden said. "And I know how tight finances are. I made a few calls, and it turns out Mr. and Mrs. Jensen were looking to cut back some of their work around the farm after his last hip replacement. They were more than happy to give me these two, knowing they'd only be two properties down the road."

The curly brown and white pom-pom heads reminded Micah of a pair of poodles. Their long lashes and spindly legs seemed about as sturdy as a puppy's, yet he'd heard the same stories as Caden. They *were* known to be a valuable asset on a ranch. "What if they don't bond with the herd? I won't have another animal terrorizing the sheep any more than they've already been."

"Have I ever steered you wrong?" asked Caden.

Micah could think of more than a few examples. "Do you really want me to answer that question?"

Caden shook his head good-naturedly and laughed. "Fine, but this is different. Mr. Jensen told me everything I needed to know, and he even offered to stop by and help if we have any issues." He reached out a hand to pat Fiona's head and looked back at Micah. His expression turned serious. "You know it's a good idea. And we can't afford to lose any more sheep."

Micah hated that Caden was right. What he hated more was that the flock was at risk in the first place. "Fine. They can stay, but at the first sign of trouble, they go back to the Jensens."

Caden patted the head of the nearest alpaca—Fiona—and smiled. "You hear that, you two?" he cooed to the animals. "I told you he'd say yes."

Micah rolled his eyes but couldn't stop the smile that crept up his face. He could always count on his youngest cousin for the unexpected.

Grace eased open the gate to the corral and closed it with a quiet click. The cool evening air seeped through her light sweater despite the simple space heater someone had plugged in near the barn wall. Micah, most likely, although she'd seen little of him since yesterday morning. No doubt he'd been busy introducing the alpacas to the rest of the flock. As much as he griped about them, she hadn't missed the faint smile on his face when he thought no one was looking.

"Here, little lamb." She lowered the bag from the shoulder and pulled out a bottle. "I've brought you dinner."

A wooly head popped up from behind a bale of hay, the animal's dark eyes watching her with caution. The other times had started off the same and ended with her chasing the animal around the pen for half an hour before finally giving up. She'd hoped the lamb's earlier interest in the formula meant they were in the clear, but so far, Grace had failed with every attempt to get it to eat.

This time, she managed to get within a foot of the animal before it bolted. The same concerns from earlier gnawed at her. She didn't know much about sheep, but Micah had told her enough to know these first few days would be crucial to the lamb's survival.

"I'm sure you miss your family, but you have to eat something."

She felt a strange kinship with this lamb. Both of them had lost their parents, and while Grace loved her aunt and all the sacrifices she'd made to help raise her, it still hadn't filled the void of loss.

"I know it won't bring back your mom, but you need to be strong. For her. Just because she's gone doesn't mean you're allowed to give up." Grace swiped the back of her hand beneath her nose, telling herself her allergies were acting up again.

Dropping into the chair she'd ransacked from the barn, she reached into her bag and exchanged the bottle for her knitting needles and ball of yarn. The lamb might be stubborn, but so was she. With another look toward the tiny animal, she leaned back and began to knit, ready to wait it out all night if need be.

"You're going to have to trust me, eventually," she said in a huff to her unresponsive audience.

With clumsy fingers, Grace worked her way through the rows. Knit. Purl. Knit. Purl. Row after row, the piece grew until the sun was well below the horizon. Darkness crept over the yard until she had to squint to see her pattern in the olive-colored yarn. Not that she needed a light to know how laughable it must look.

Joints stiff from the metal chair, Grace stretched her arms and instinctively looked toward the ground. One glimpse told her the bottle was still untouched. She laid aside the hopeless scarf and drew her knees to her chest. With her chin resting on her forearms, she let her eyes grow heavy.

Just a few more minutes. That's how much longer she'd stay before trying again tomorrow.

Her blinking slowed, and she tugged her sweater tight against the night breeze.

Just a few more minutes ...

Grace awoke some time later as something warm draped over her shoulders. Opening her eyes, she tilted her head back to see Micah standing beside her. She hadn't heard the gate open, but something about his presence soothed her wariness. She accepted the offering with a smile.

"You looked cold." His voice was deep, yet soft. Void of the harshness she'd grown accustomed to. He rocked back on the heels of his cowboy boots, one hand casually resting in his pocket and the other wrapped around a ceramic mug. "How's it going so far?"

Grace knew how to handle the standoffish version of Micah, but this softer side of him left her feeling off-kilter. Like the day he'd rescued her from the side of the road. He'd been nothing but helpful and charming until she'd ruined that, too.

"I can't do it. No matter what I try, I can't get her to eat."

She didn't know him well enough to know what his silence meant, but the tension from before was nowhere in sight.

"Have you decided on a name for her yet?" he finally asked.

Grace shook her head and stared at the lamb bedded down in the straw. "I might if she ever responded to me. She's so stubborn, but she must be starving. She doesn't know what's good for her, and she refuses to listen."

"You could call her Francis, then. I happen to know someone by that name who fits the description nicely."

"This is serious," she said as she felt the fight drain out of her.

Micah's expression softened into one of understanding. "I know. All I'm saying is don't write her off yet. She may surprise you, still."

As if sensing they were talking about her, the lamb lifted its head and looked their way. She stood on spindly legs and approached them at an agonizingly slow pace. Both Grace and Micah held their breaths as it stopped a few feet from them and dropped its head to nibble the edge of Grace's scarf poking out from the bag.

"Great," Grace whispered. "I bring her perfectly good formula, and all she wants to eat is Callie's yarn."

"It must smell familiar to her," Micah suggested, the warmth of his breath tickling the hair at her neck. "After all, Callie does get her wool from our sheep."

The lamb tugged at the loose end of the olive-colored fiber when an idea came to Grace. "What about ... Olive?" She whispered the name. The lamb raised its eyes to meet hers.

Grace slowly reached for the bottle at her feet and extended her arm toward the young animal. It took a moment to coax the lamb away from the yarn, but soon, little Olive was licking the tip of the bottle. Once she'd tasted the milk, she quickly latched onto the rubber end and hungrily downed half the bottle.

Micah's low laughter rumbled beside Grace. "Well, would you look at that? I think she likes it. Maybe she just needed time to figure out who you were before deciding if she could trust you or not."

"As if sitting out in the cold all night wasn't proof enough?" Grace shook her head as the lamb finished off the bottle. Relaxing her grip, she leaned back in her chair, suddenly exhausted as the stress of the past two days lifted from her shoulders.

"You're doing a great job. It takes a certain kind of fearlessness to care for these animals, and from where I stand, you're doing just fine."

She eyed his seated position beside her and raised an eyebrow.

"Standing, sitting..." A soft smile curved the edges of his mouth as he leaned an inch closer, his shoulder brushing hers.

"Here, you look like you could use this more than me." He offered her his mug, and she gladly accepted it.

The spicy scents of ginger and cinnamon tickled her nose as she cupped her hands around the ceramic, the warm liquid bringing a welcome relief to her parched throat. After a few sips, she looked over to see Micah watching her with a curious expression. "What? Do I have mud on my face again?"

Chuckling, he shook his head. "I was only thinking … she's not the only one you've impressed lately."

A different kind of warmth washed over her, and she waited in silence as he held her gaze.

"You've more than proved yourself. I only wish I hadn't been so hard on you earlier. Callie says I can be a bear. And, well, you caught me by surprise." He readjusted his ball cap and turned his attention back to Olive and the bag of yarn.

Hands still wrapped around the mug, Grace bumped her blanketed shoulder against his. "I'm sorry, too." She'd never planned to upend this man's life by dropping in, but she wasn't sorry for how things were turning out so far. "I'm just glad you finally came to your senses."

Micah laughed. "Me? What about you?"

Grace hummed her response and smiled. "I think I've known for a while what kind of man you are."

"And what would that be?" he asked, suddenly serious.

He had a past, and like her, it'd shaped him into the man he was today. He might not be the most open of people, but neither was she. His steady gaze never left hers, and she knew—despite his secrets and the fact she'd only known the man for a few weeks—he was different from anybody she'd ever met.

Grace smiled. "Someone I can trust."

CHAPTER

Nineteen

"WHAT DO YOU think? Would it be so bad if I stayed a bit longer?" Grace worked the needles back and forth over the green yarn, half-focused on the scarf-turned-lamb-sweater in front of her. "I know I told Katrina I'd get the contract signed and be back as soon as the bridge was fixed. But that was before I'd gotten to know this place. I get the sense Micah could really use the extra hands. And then there's Callie's business I promised to help with."

It wasn't as if Grace really thought the lamb would give her advice like her therapist, but she didn't know who else to talk to. If she mentioned anything to Callie, she'd risk hurting the best friend she'd had in years, and if she told Micah ...

No way was she bringing this up with him. She wasn't afraid of his temper so much as what she might accidentally say.

She knew her therapist would advise her to trust her friends with her worries, but she was afraid the relationships were too new. Untested. There was no telling what would break them.

Not to mention the ghosts in Micah's closet. After carrying around her own past traumas most of her life, she knew what that was like. If she could somehow ease that sense of guilt he'd placed upon himself, then it was worth it to try, however problematic that might turn out.

"Hey, stop eating my yarn." Grace tugged the loose end from Olive's mouth and frowned at the soggy spun wool. The lamb who'd contentedly laid at her feet all afternoon had suddenly decided it had an insatiable appetite for craft yarn. "First, I can't get you to eat at all, and now you eat everything in sight."

Sighing, Grace teased the yarn back out of the animal's mouth and grimaced at the mushy end. Now it really did look like her aunt's pea soup.

"What am I supposed to do with you? Huh?"

Dark brown eyes stared back at her, fanned by the creature's delicate white lashes. The picture of innocence.

"Grace, is that you?" Callie's singsong voice drifted around the barn.

"Back here." Grace stood, swiping hay dust from her overalls, when Callie skipped around the corner. She checked the time on her phone, surprised to see it was already close to noon. She'd promised to help Callie run some numbers for the business and had completely lost track of time.

"Thought I'd find you back here." Opening the gate, Callie stepped into the pen and bent to stroke Olive's curly head. When Callie finally straightened, she spotted the yarn and beamed. "Oh, did you finish it already?"

Embarrassed to show off her poor knitting skills, Grace picked up the lumpy mess and held it out for inspection.

"That turned out fantastic!" Callie exclaimed.

"Really?" Grace thought it looked more like a tube scarf with four holes in it than a sweater.

"Truly. My mom used to make something similar for Micah's mother to use on the newborns whenever there was an early frost. Gave her a chance to use up all her scraps, and let me tell you, she came up with some *very* colorful striped jumpers." She tilted her head, studying the simple yet finished piece. "The important thing is that it will keep Olive warm as the temperatures dip."

That fact alone was what had driven Grace to finish this project in the first place. She could add *caretaker of orphaned sheep and knitter of lamb sweaters* to her resume. No doubt she'd need it once she updated Katrina on the latest developments.

"I'm just finishing up here. We can head back any time now and get started on those calculations." Gathering the remainder of her supplies, she stuffed them into a canvas bag and slung it over her shoulder.

"Oh, there's no rush. We can get to those later."

Grace looked at her friend who seemed in no hurry to crunch numbers or talk strategy. "You're not changing your mind, are you? Callie, the last thing I want to do is take over. I only want to help."

"And I love you for that. I wish I had a better head for business and marketing, but I'd much prefer to just create. Isn't there a way that I can do what I love and people somehow magically buy it? Or better yet, you could manage the business side." Her expression was that of a kid pleading for a slice of cake before dinner.

"I'd love to, but I already have a job." At least, she hoped she did. But the idea of working with Callie in her garden oasis, flowers bobbing in the alpine breeze, and fresh honey available daily, tugged at her more than she wanted to admit.

"Tell you what." Grace exited the pen and closed the gate behind them. "We'll work together on the financial side of things this afternoon, and I promise to help with the next honey harvest." If that meant driving up here next spring to don a beekeeper suit with her friend, then so be it.

"I'll hold you to that," Callie said with a smile.

"I wouldn't expect anything less."

Micah walked by the open barn door as the phone inside started to ring. The sun was beginning to dip toward the mountains as the afternoon wore on, but there were still more than half a day's chores left to be done. Since Caden had taken Finn to check on the sheep, Micah ducked into the shadowed interior and picked up on the third ring.

"Micah speaking."

"Micah, hey! It's Tony."

"Tony, how's it going?" He could do with a friendly voice right about now. He'd be lying if he said he hadn't been hoping to catch a glimpse of Grace around the barn, but seeing she wasn't there, the distraction couldn't have come at a better time.

"Can't complain. Listen, I've got some good news and some bad news." Tony's Texan accent carried over the phone's speakers. Despite having lived there most of his life, he still sounded like all the other southern tourists that breezed through during the height of summer. The hum of an engine faded into the background as Tony must have stepped away from his shop for the call. "Bridge is fixed. And just in time, too. My dad's been worried about getting his steers to the auction next month. Been drivin' my mom crazy with all the projects he's been creating around the house."

Micah chuckled. "He's more than welcome to come over here. I've got a few things I could put him to work on."

"Oh, he'd love that. Mom, too. At least the bridge was only out a couple of weeks this time."

"No kidding. That's gotta be some sort of record. You're sure the bridge is passable?" Micah couldn't remember the last time the county had acted so quickly to restore access to the valley.

"Sturdy enough to drive a herd of cattle across, or so my dad says. Honestly, I was a little surprised, too, but I've learned not to look a gift horse in the mouth."

"Suppose that's a fair point. So, what's the bad news?" On one hand, having the bridge up and running again meant they had a way to sell their wool and sheep, but it also meant Grace was free to leave as well. He knew she couldn't stay forever, had counted on that fact to get himself through the last couple of weeks, but knowing she could leave at any time made his pulse quicken.

"That car you brought me the other week ..." His friend whistled on the other end.

"That bad?" Micah's stomach sank. He'd hoped for Grace's sake that Tony could fix it up without it costing her an arm and a leg.

"Yeah. I tried calling that number you gave me for your friend but it must have been in a dead zone. I'm hoping you can pass on the information?"

"Of course."

There was a pause on the other end of the line as if Tony were thinking about how best to share his diagnosis. "Well, between the busted engine block, a couple major leaks, and an electrical system hanging on by a few wires, I'd say it's a miracle it made it this far in one piece. I'll try to fix it up as best I can, but it's gonna take some time to track down all the parts. Not to mention my dad's keeping me pretty busy around here at the moment."

Micah didn't know what to think of the flood of mixed emotions washing over him, but he definitely knew he shouldn't feel so happy to hear about Grace's car.

"I'm sure he has. And thanks for the update, Tony. I'll let Grace know."

"Thanks, man."

"Not a problem. And keep me posted about any further updates."

"Will do." Micah lowered the wireless phone back into its cradle.

Much like the broken radio in his truck, he'd never much minded the quiet solitude of the ranch, but today, the silence of the cavernous barn felt oppressive—mocking, even, as he contemplated what Tony's news would mean for him and Grace.

He'd been content with his life before she entered it. Seeing the ranch survive was reward enough for all the years of hard work he'd devoted to this place. Even with the threat of the bank's deadline closing in, he'd have found a way. He always did. Anything to preserve what little sense of control he had left. Then Grace had to go and overturn all that with her stubborn determination and annoyingly refreshing smiles.

Voices floated in from outside, and Micah stopped to listen.

"Hey Callie, I'll catch up with you in a minute. I think I left one of the knitting needles in Olive's pen." Within seconds, footsteps were crunching outside the barn door. Grace's wistful humming drifted in, soft and carefree as a summer breeze.

Micah's spirits lifted a fraction but soon crashed back down as he remembered Tony's news about the bridge. At least when it had been out, Grace had a reason to stay. But even with her car out of commission, she could choose to hop on the first bus out of town and never look back.

Which is exactly what you wanted, a little voice inside him whispered.

Shoving the reminder aside, he stepped outside into the bright sunshine and nearly stumbled over Grace and the long needle clutched in her hands.

"Whoa, there." Micah's hands settled on her shoulders, rough calluses snagging on the soft cotton. The familiarity of this scene caused him to flashback to that night when he'd found Grace chopping wood. The near miss. Him steadying her. The kiss.

"Someone's in a hurry," he found himself saying through the haze of his thoughts.

A rosy glow crept up her neck as she shoved the dangerous-looking instrument into her bag. "Sorry about that. I really need to learn to be more careful."

He chuckled. "That's okay. So far, I've managed to survive an umbrella and an ax. I'd say a knitting needle is an improvement."

Grace crossed her arms in front of her chest. "You're never going to let me live that down, are you?"

"Hard to forget a woman attacking you on the side of the road. Good thing I have a thick skull." He rubbed the spot where the bruise had faded, and her eyes seemed to sparkle at the memory. Micah cleared his throat, suddenly self-conscious under her gaze. "Tony just called. It sounds like the bridge is all fixed."

Those delicate eyebrows rose as her eyes grew wide. "Really? That's wonderful!"

He kept his cringe in check at her excitement. Was she that eager to leave? Maybe he'd been imagining things the last few days. After all, they'd only recently gone from enemies to ... what exactly? Friends? Micah couldn't think of any friends who made his heart race the same way Grace did. Not even Callie. And the way he had to fight back the urge to pull her close every time he saw her ...

"Was there anything else?" The way the breeze played with her hair as she looked up at him made something in his chest constrict. He was half tempted to reach out and run his fingers through those honey waves. Last time, he'd dived right in like a man starved for air.

Shoving his hands into his pockets, Micah took a discrete half-step back, providing a breath of space between them. She was waiting for his reply, and he only wished he had better news to share. "Looks like your car is going to take longer than expected to repair."

"Oh." Her face fell a fraction, and Micah felt his chest tighten.

Blast it. He hated being the one to give bad news, but there was no point in lying. "Tony said it needs a lot of work, but he's doing the best he can with what he's got."

Grace responded to the news with hardly a blink and shrugged. "I understand. Tell him I appreciate him taking the time to look at it."

Micah answered with a small nod, curious as to her ready acceptance. Not sure where to go from there, he looked back toward the barn for a quick escape if need be.

"Listen, I've got some things I still need to take care of—stalls to clean, fences to check on." She didn't move to walk away, so he continued. "Would you … I don't know. Would you like to help?" He wasn't exactly sure why he asked—probably to see some other expression on her face other than disappointment—nor did he fully understand why he held his breath as he waited for her reply. But the simple answer was that he wasn't ready for her to leave yet. Not the ranch, not this valley. Even if it meant spending the afternoon mucking out stables or stringing fences.

Grace nibbled her bottom lip and looked toward the field that stretched between his place and Callie's. Maybe she was looking for an easy way out. Couldn't blame her, really. He didn't have much experience with women, but he was certain mucking out a barn didn't rank too highly on the list of acceptable topics of conversation.

He was about to take back the ill-planned invitation when Grace beat him to it. "I told Callie I'd help her with something this afternoon, but I could swing back around once we're done."

"Really?"

She smiled, revealing a pair of dimples that would be any man's undoing. "You sound surprised."

"I just thought ..." He massaged the back of his neck and gave her a sheepish grin. "Doesn't matter. I'll make sure to leave a few uncleaned stalls just for you."

"How very thoughtful," she teased.

He shrugged, relaxing his shoulders with their easy banter. "It's been known to happen on occasion."

"Well, then. How can a girl pass up an invitation like that?"

Maybe she wasn't in as big a hurry to leave as he'd thought. "Crazier things have been known to happen."

"Like showing up unannounced only for the bridge to wash out?"

"Exactly." Looked like his afternoon was shaping up to be something good after all. "So, I guess that means I'll see you later, then?"

Another breath of wind caused her hair to dance before her face, and she tucked it behind her ear with a smile. "Definitely."

She turned and took a few steps into the tall grasses toward the trail when Micah called after her.

"And don't forget to bring some gloves."

Grace chuckled, the sound dancing on the breeze. "It's a date."

Caden fought the afternoon winds that rolled off the San Juan Mountains as he set off from the house. He high stepped over a clump of sagebrush blocking his path and hiked the rest of the way up the short hill to the upper pasture.

Once there, he propped his arms across the metal gate and gazed out over the flock. Patches of white dotted the landscape. In the distance, lambs frolicked through the tall grass while their mothers grazed in peace. Everything appeared as it should, a fact that eased the knot in his stomach after the whole ordeal with the fence the other day.

Nearby, a few of the flock's newest arrivals lay huddled under the shelter of one of the alpacas. Near five feet tall, Fiona towered over the fragile creatures, scanning the fields on high alert for any sign of trouble. When all seemed clear, her demeanor softened, and she lowered her head to nuzzle one of the newborns. The lamb's mother didn't seem to mind, and Caden marveled at the affection between the wooly cousins.

And Micah had been worried the alpacas would terrorize the flock.

Pride swelled within him. He'd tried his best not to let it show, but he'd been equally concerned about how the sheep would take to the newcomers as Micah had been. Although, based on what he saw so far, he had nothing left to worry about. They now had their own little Peruvian Protection Squad.

He'd watch for a couple more minutes before carrying on with the chores. For just a moment, he wanted to slow down and take a breather. Life had been nonstop since setting foot on the ranch over a year ago. If he were being completely honest with himself, he'd been running at full speed since he left home for college. Always onto the next adventure, the new exciting thing. He'd never taken much time to pause and evaluate where he was, but from this vantage point, standing on this windswept hill with the ranch below him, he felt that same echo within himself calling for him to stay.

God, is that you? He'd never been very good at listening for guidance. That was his cousin Abigail's area, not his. She'd given up everything, her life in the city, her job, her future, and moved back home all based on what she said was God's call. Now she was happily married and running an antique shop with their great-aunt. And then there was his sister, Tess. God had overturned her entire world with an injury, but she couldn't seem happier with how her life had turned out.

Him, on the other hand … Caden wasn't sure if he was ready for God to overturn his life like that. However, he could think of worse places to end up than here.

With a slight nod toward Heaven, he released his tight grip on the gate and took a step back. A decision for another day. He was much better suited to the present, and what he wanted most right now was to see Callie's business succeed. He wasn't sure how—what with the mess he'd already made with her beehives—but he'd find a way. He owed her that much.

With long strides, he wove his way back down the hill toward the house, his pocket burning with the long list of items he'd yet to check off for the day: feed the horses, order new posts to finish the rest of the fencing, check on the sheep …

By the time he reached the yard, he was so focused on his own thoughts he nearly ran straight into Callie.

"Someone's in a hurry." Her smile went to her eyes, the color of aspen leaves in spring. She shifted her grip around the empty wooden crate she'd been carrying, balancing it on her hip. Based on the stacks of empty boxes in the back of her truck, he must have caught her in the middle of loading up.

"What are all those for?" he asked, curious to know what she was up to next.

"Oh, these?" Callie hefted the crate onto the others. "Didn't you hear? The bridge is fixed. I know it's short notice and all, but I had this idea about setting up a booth at the farmer's market this weekend, so I'm sort of rushing to get things together."

"How can I help?" The offer was out before he even realized it, but Callie waved him off.

"Grace and I have it covered for now. But if you and Micah wouldn't mind, I could use the extra hands on Saturday to load the truck and set everything up in town."

"Done."

Callie laughed at his eager reply. "You're that sure Micah won't mind?"

Caden shrugged. If there was anything he was good at, it was talking people into things. "I know he'd love to help out. What do you have left to do?"

"Well ..." Callie tipped her eyes to the clouds as if reading an invisible checklist. "There's the honey left to be jarred and labeled, teas to be bagged, I need to set up a payment system for customers, and I still haven't decided on a logo or any kind of signage, for that matter."

"What about a booth? Do you have that covered?"

Her copper curls bounced when she shook her head. "I'm still working on that, but I'm sure I'll figure something out. Grace has been a godsend. If it wasn't for her, there's no way I'd be ready enough for this."

Like that, the answer to his earlier question clicked into place.

"Let me build it for you."

Her eyes widened in surprise. "Really? But you're so busy here. How would you have the time?"

Now it was Caden's turn to wave aside her question. He knew her too well to build anything too fancy—that wasn't her style—but he already had a few ideas to make it special. No way was she going to talk him out of this. "Consider it as good as done."

"Caden, you're a lifesaver!" Before he knew what hit him, Callie threw open her arms and wrapped him in a tight hug.

It was a spur-of-the-moment thing, no doubt unplanned and entirely platonic on her end. But the moment she was in his arms, Caden knew he never wanted to let go. He might have imagined it, but she seemed to linger a moment—tucked into his chest like she belonged there—before she finally stepped back.

Unusually quiet, she pushed a wayward curl from her sun-kissed face and tucked it behind her ear. Her gaze seemed to focus anywhere but on him, and he knew she'd felt something, too.

Caden coughed to clear his throat as if that could clear his mind as well. "How about you meet us here and then we can load up Micah's truck to drive into town. What time were you hoping to set up?"

Callie's hand relaxed from her ear, and she winced. "Is seven too early? It's an hour's drive, so that means we'd have to leave around six."

"Sounds perfect. I'll let Micah know, and we'll be waiting for you and Grace." He was used to getting up early to tend the sheep. And he had a feeling he wouldn't be getting much sleep with thoughts of Callie flooding his brain.

Body still humming, he helped her load the remaining crates and waved goodbye as she eventually reversed out of the yard and drove off.

With a plan in mind, and fueled with renewed energy, Caden set out for the barn and rummaged around for some wood and a couple old cans of paint. With any luck, he'd finish the project in time. Even if he had to stay up all night to do it.

CHAPTER

Twenty

THIS WAS THE moment Callie had been waiting for. Today would be the first trial run of her new business. To some, a stall at the local farmer's market was little more than a step up from a lemonade stand, but to her, it was the start of a whole new chapter. She marveled at the handmade booth Caden had built for her, painted a golden yellow with her company name inscribed across the front.

Among the Bees: Honey and Herbal Remedies by Callie.

Any lingering fears that her booth would be overlooked at the farmer's market vanished, and she pinched herself to make sure this wasn't a dream.

"What was that for?" The man himself appeared at her side and looked down at her with that crooked smile of his that made her legs turn to the consistency of whipped honey.

Callie feigned composure and shrugged. "What? Never seen a grown woman pinch herself?"

His laugh rumbled in his chest. "Can't say I have. Although, you're not most women, Callie Spencer."

Warmth flooded her cheeks at the compliment. Suddenly feeling incredibly self-conscious, she pried her gaze from his and toed a line in the dirt with her boot. What was one to say in response to that? Before she could formulate a response, Caden spoke again, saving her from her own inevitable awkwardness.

"Hey." His hand rested on her shoulder, and she tilted her head back to see his soft smile. He must have mistaken her delayed response for worry. "It's going to be great. Once people get a taste of your products, they'll be coming back for more. I mean, look at Micah. If you can convince him to drink something other than coffee, then you can sell your recipes to anyone."

That made her laugh, and the rest of her concerns faded. "Thanks, Caden. That means a lot."

"What are friends for?"

The look in his eyes seemed to say so much more. He didn't come right out and say it, but she got the sense that things were already changing between them, and it excited yet terrified her at the same time. She wasn't naive. If something more grew between them and he left, she'd be heartbroken. But she'd long ago learned that was the price one paid to love someone. And it was a price she'd willingly pay if it meant exploring something new with her dear friend.

Caden bent to grab the box at his feet, flexing his tattooed muscles with the weight of a few dozen jars of honey. Callie reached for the back door to the truck, but Finn raced forward the moment it was open and launched himself onto the cushioned seat. Ready for an adventure, he smiled at her while his pink tongue lolled to the side.

"What, you decided you want to help, too?" She giggled at the animal's enthusiasm and spied a similar smile on Caden's face.

Micah gave a short whistle to call the dog down. Finn's ears drooped, and he slowly climbed out of the truck.

"He looks so sad. I'm sure he'd be fine in town if we brought him," Caden offered as he turned to put the box in the truck bed.

Despite the dog's pleading looks, Micah shook his head. "Someone's got to look after the sheep while we're gone." Kneeling beside the dog, he brushed his hand over the smooth coat and spoke in an assured tone. "Think you can do that, buddy?"

Finn barked in agreement, then bounded back toward the barn. Callie and the others laughed at the cattle dog's response.

Once Grace and Micah had left to do a final check, Caden leaned in and whispered to Callie. "Ready?"

The way he asked the question made her feel both safe and cherished, and she nodded—to both his spoken question and the one hidden behind his eyes. "Absolutely."

Caden's smile grew. His body seemed to shift closer, and if Micah and Grace hadn't been nearby, she'd have tilted her head back a little further, lifted onto her toes, and given in to her desire to kiss him—right then and there. But seeing as they weren't alone, she'd settle for the knowledge that this time, she wasn't imagining things.

By the time they reached town, the sun had barely crested the surrounding mountains, illuminating the valley with a warm and inviting glow. Grace hadn't paid much attention to the historic storefronts when she'd driven through the first time, but as they slowed on Main Street, she took in everything from the old mining town's colorfully faced facades to the spacious park where parents watched as their children played.

They drove past a crowded-looking café, and a whiff of something sweet made her stomach rumble. They'd been so busy carting supplies over to Micah's and loading up the truck, she'd forgotten to grab something to eat on her way out.

At the end of the block, they turned off the main drag and into a large dirt parking lot where posters for the farmer's market hung in swags around the short fence. Already, the lot was nearly half full, a good sign for the farmer's market starting in less than two hours. After waiting for a family to finish unloading their bikes onto the dirt, Micah eased their truck forward and parked in the back corner. "First up, breakfast and something hot to drink."

Callie stirred beside Grace in the backseat, rifling through the burlap sack at her feet. "I've got a thermos of tea and a few leftover dandelion root muffins, if anyone's interested." She lifted a crumpled canvas bag in triumph.

Grace was a sucker for a good pastry, but as much as she loved Callie and even her alternative teas, a muffin named after a weed didn't sound the most appetizing.

Micah grunted from behind the wheel, no doubt thinking the same thing. "No offense, Callie, but I need something with a little more substance to get me through the morning."

"Suit yourself." Callie replaced the bag and leaned back in her seat, but not before tossing Grace a conspiratorial wink that made them both laugh.

Ignoring them, he pushed open his door and climbed out.

A tiny bell chimed above the doorway as they entered The Gold Bar Café. Grace was immediately welcomed by the scent of fresh coffee and hash browns. Micah went straight for the single empty booth in the back, and the four of them piled in. Before long, a young waitress with pink and blonde hair skipped up to their table and took their orders back to the kitchen.

"Wow, this must be a popular place." Grace looked around, and nearly every table was full, including the long, polished bar top at the back.

Micah thanked the waitress as she handed them their drinks and waited for her to leave before he sipped his coffee. "Tourists, mainly. Every year they come up from Texas to escape the heat with their four-wheelers and campers. It's a lot quieter in the winter, though."

Grace wrapped her palms around the warm mug and inhaled the rich aroma. One taste, and she knew why Micah had suggested they come here. Not that she minded Callie's teas and odd concoctions, but nothing compared to a properly brewed cup of coffee.

"So, what's the plan for today?" she asked between sips. She'd been the one to suggest setting up a booth at the farmer's market, but she'd left the rest of the planning up to Callie.

"Well, I was thinking we'd set up where the Jensens used to sell their alpaca wool, near the vegetable stands and food trucks. Once we get everything unloaded, it's just a matter of arranging the booth and talking with customers."

"Do you think you'll need me the entire time?" Micah asked. "I've got a few people I'd like to talk with about some sheep before we head back."

"Not a problem. We only need one or two people manning the booth at any given time, and Grace has already volunteered."

The kitchen door swung open behind them, and an older woman with salt-and-pepper hair bustled through, waving at their table as she approached. Before Micah had lifted his hand in return, she was already making her way over. She wore a crisp red-and-white checkered apron tied around her waist, and the name tag pinned to her shirt read *Pauline*.

"Micah, what a pleasant surprise seeing you here." Her short hair bobbed as she talked. "When Sarah told me you were here, I had to come out and say hello."

Micah smiled at the woman before whispering to Grace, "There's life in a small town for you."

"Oh, stop your whining." Pauline playfully swatted him on the shoulder. "I know full well how much you love this place. And you brought friends this time. How nice to see you two again." She smiled at Caden and Callie, who returned the gesture. Before anyone else could get a word in, she pinpointed Grace and beamed. "And who might this be?"

All eyes turned toward Grace, but Micah cut in before she could respond.

"This is our friend Grace. She's visiting from out of town."

Warmth wrapped around her at the way he said *friend*. One look at his relaxed smile and she knew he meant it.

"Wonderful to meet you, Grace. I hope you've been enjoying your stay."

Grace slid a knowing smile toward the others and nodded. "It's been an adventure, to say the least."

"Wonderful!" Pauline's energetic response drew a few stares. "Well, I'd better get back to the kitchen. This crowd's not going to feed itself. Lovely seeing you all." With another wave, she disappeared through the swinging door just as the rest of their food was brought out—a stack of banana oat pancakes for Callie, hash browns and eggs for Caden, a rancher's skillet for Micah, and a tomato feta quiche for Grace.

Following Micah's lead, they all bowed their heads as he murmured a quiet prayer of thanks over the meal. Once he'd finished, the four of them dug in, and silence draped over the table.

A half hour later, and with a few extra cups of coffee to go, they made their way back to the truck to begin setting up.

Callie flitted back and forth between Micah, who'd been tasked with unloading the boxes from the truck to their station on the spacious lawn, and the rest of them, who were busy staging rows of items across the booth's counter. "Herbal teas go next to the soaps, between the honey and lotions. And samples should be laid out in front."

Around them, the city park buzzed with people focused on organizing the other dozens of booths for the weekend market. From what Callie had told her, this event only happened once a month, so vendors put everything they had into the affair.

Grace wiped the back of her hand across her brow, already warm despite the cool morning chill. Needing a short break, she stepped back and surveyed the setup with satisfaction. The black-and-yellow sign perfectly complemented the handmade labels she and Callie had spent the past day making. Every jar, tin, and bag had been meticulously labeled with ingredients and instructions, complete with a flower stamp, which read, "Made with Love."

Grace's chest swelled. This had been Callie's vision, and the fact that she got to play a small part in it made her all the more grateful. Reaching for her nearly empty coffee cup, she took a final sip as Callie and Caden put the finishing touches on the display.

Micah had disappeared a few minutes ago to retrieve the last few boxes from the truck. Between boxes, her gaze wandered in the direction she'd seen him go until something else caught her attention.

On the edge of the lawn stood a middle-aged man dressed in slacks, dress shoes, and a crisp button-up shirt.

Now she understood just how out of place she'd looked when she'd first arrived. Not a single other person in attendance had ironed their clothing, yet his shirt looked as crisp as a newly pressed dollar bill.

Something about his rigid posture put her on edge—why, she wasn't sure. She could only see the man's profile, and he appeared deep in conversation with Pauline from The Gold Bar Café. Grace hadn't spoken with the woman for long, but she got the sense she could read a person like a book. And the tight purse to the woman's lips said she didn't like what she was seeing.

Grace caught up to Callie and elbowed her in the arm. "Who's Pauline talking with?"

Callie looked up from her flower display and frowned as the man released a puff of cigarette smoke into the air. "That's Jack Flanagan."

"You say that like it's a bad thing." Grace had never seen Callie look so put out before, which only piqued her curiosity more.

"He's another local rancher, but ever since he joined the Planning Commission three years back, he's been trying to make some big changes. I've heard talk of him trying to negotiate a deal with a big city developer, and that's the last thing this place needs."

The sound of footsteps approached, and Micah appeared beside them. His forehead dipped in a stern expression. "Jack Flanagan has been a blight on this valley since the day his uncle died and gave him that ranch."

Callie spun toward him, apparently not having heard his approach. "I know he's not your favorite person and all, but he came through for us with the bridge, didn't he?"

Micah grunted and set down the box he'd been carrying. "More like he was avoiding an angry mob if he let it drag on as long as the last time."

Jack finished his conversation with the café owner and walked down the street, but the wake of unease he left behind was palpable. Grace watched in silence, trying to ignore the chills pricking the back of her neck.

She'd never met the man before, so why did his name sound so familiar? "I feel like I'm missing something here," she finally said when he was well out of earshot. "I thought small communities usually worked together."

"Generally, yes. But every town has its exceptions." Micah fixed the tilt of his baseball cap before opening the box at his feet. He handed a few jars of honey to Grace before continuing. "For years, he's been trying to force his will on those of us that share a boundary line with his ranch. The morning of the fire, I saw him arguing with my dad about a piece of property along the river. I'd never seen my old man so worked up when that man finally left. Who knows, if Jack hadn't come by that day, maybe my dad wouldn't have been stress-smoking in the hayloft. Maybe the fire never would have happened."

Callie stopped what she was doing and faced him, hands on her hips. "Micah, you can't blame the man for that."

"Yeah, well, I wouldn't lose any sleep over it if I did." Micah unpacked the last of the jars and stood. "Looks like that's the last of them. Need any more help while I'm here?"

Callie paused before shaking her head. "I think Grace, Caden, and I have it covered from here."

Micah nodded and turned to leave. Grace watched his retreating form until he disappeared behind a row of white tents.

Despite his sharp tone, Grace couldn't help but feel sympathy for Micah. He'd shown her his deepest fears—had confessed the very thing that must have eaten at him for years—and buried them once again. Much like him, she'd searched for someone to blame for her parents' deaths, including herself. Callie hadn't been wrong to speak up to him about it, but if there was anything Grace knew, it was that a person who's hurting will look for any way to ease the pain. Truth or not.

"I'm sorry. I didn't mean to stir things up." Grace reached toward a tea bag that had slipped from its neat row and aligned it with the others. A small consolation for all the things she'd put her foot in lately.

"Don't worry, it's not your fault." Callie's tone was soft yet unyielding. Finishing with the display, she arranged a few more sachets of lavender around the table before stepping back to survey their work. Hands on her hips, she gave a nod of approval before looking back at Grace. "To be completely honest, Jack isn't my favorite, either. But if I ever want to have my own shop in town, I can't afford to make enemies. Especially with someone as powerful as him."

Grace understood what that was like. That was the same kind of thinking that had landed her here in the first place. For years, she'd worked to impress first her classmates, then her college professors, and finally her bosses at Prospect & Gould. They'd all had the power to decide her future at some point in her life, and the fear of losing control once again had driven her to excel.

She'd always thought that was her greatest asset, her drive, but maybe that wasn't a strength at all.

Callie returned to the table and began fanning out the bags of loose-leaf tea from their orderly rows, brimming with nervous energy. "What do you think?" Her nose scrunched in thought.

Grace smiled at the informal-yet-inviting display, so much a reflection of the woman next to her. "Everything looks perfect. Now, how about you stop fussing and enjoy the moment? People are going to love these no matter how you arrange them."

Grace spied an elderly woman weaving her way toward Callie's booth, a large empty basket dangling from her crooked elbow. "Speaking of which." Grace nudged Callie with her shoulder and pointed. "I think you might have your first customer."

CHAPTER

Twenty-One

IF THERE WAS anyone people secretly hated in this town more than Micah, it was Jack Flanagan.

Much like a deer tick caught on a sheep's fleece, the man was nothing more than a parasite out to make a name for himself off the backs of others. Nobody got that rich that fast without having greased more than a few palms on his way up the social ladder. Despite Callie's chastisement, he knew she felt the same. He didn't trust the man to look out for the valley's best interests, even if he had come through with the bridge repair.

The scents of kettle corn and roasted poblano chilies tickled his nose as he weaved through the crowded street, bypassing local produce stalls and food vendors on his way to the other end of the park.

"Micah, wait up!"

Micah turned as Tony emerged from one of the tented booths, a half-eaten doughnut in one hand and a paper bag in the other. The man lifted his chin in greeting and cut across the crowded street. Micah waited beside a table stacked with handmade baskets until they were within earshot of each other.

"Any news about the car?" he asked as his friend joined him.

Tony shook his head as he took another bite of pastry, causing a dusting of powdered sugar to spill onto the smooth front of his John Deere T-shirt. He brushed off the crumbs with the back of his hand as he spoke. "Still waiting to hear back on a couple of parts. Who knew a VW-1200 engine would be so difficult to track down these days? They sure don't make cars like they used to." He finished off the doughnut and drew another from the bag. "Hey, do you remember that summer after senior year we worked on your dad's '89 Dodge Ram? Good thing that truck was built like a tank. Otherwise, we probably would have destroyed it."

"You mean before your dad stepped in to help?" Micah chuckled at the memory, grateful for his friend's timely presence to lighten his mood now and back then. For two eighteen-year-olds who'd grown up in the country, they'd been surprisingly inept when it came to fixing up a truck, and it had been the perfect distraction after all that everyone had lost that year.

"Hey, Tony. You wouldn't happen to know if Frank Johnson is here, would you? As much as I'd love to catch up, I'm in a bit of a time crunch."

"Say no more. Last I saw, he was headin' toward the petting zoo with his granddaughter."

"Thanks, man."

"Any time." Tony slapped him on the shoulder and turned to leave. He didn't make it far, though, before he stopped at a table of jarred fruit spreads and pickled vegetables for a sample. Smiling, Micah left his friend to his shopping and headed in the direction Tony had indicated.

In his pursuit, Micah sidestepped two bakery stands, a face painting booth, several more tables selling the last of their summer produce, and an entire row of tables stacked high with boxes of Palisade peaches. The fruity scent followed him long after he'd passed the gingham tablecloths and mingled with that of hay dust as he approached the fenced enclosure.

Small children raced about the circular pen, tottering between ducks, piglets, and other four-legged animals that scurried about. Their screeches of laughter punctuated the air, and parents shuffled after them, often bumping into each other in their attempts to capture as many pictures as possible.

Feeling a bit out of place as the only childless adult, Micah kept to the fringe until he spotted Frank on the opposite side of the ring. The man waved at a little girl who must have been his granddaughter and smiled as she chased after a row of ducks.

Careful not to step on anyone's toes, Micah worked his way through the throng of parents. A few yards away, he caught Frank's attention and tipped his hat in greeting.

"Micah. Good to see you, son." Frank gave him a hearty pat on the back. The man's signature black Stetson covered most of his silvery hair. Although he was in his mid-sixties, the man didn't look a day over fifty. "What brings you out here? Can't imagine it's for the pony rides." He grinned, and Micah couldn't help but laugh.

"No, but I've got two alpacas at home who'd fit right in." Perhaps next time, he could bring them.

Frank raised his bushy eyebrows and blew out a whistle. "Sounds like there's a good story there, but I know better than to ask."

A screech of laughter drew the man's attention toward his granddaughter, who was currently feeding dried corn to the chickens, which gave Micah time to find the right words.

"Actually, that's part of the reason I wanted to talk to you," he said over the animal noises and nearby chatter.

Frank sobered and trained his steely eyes on Micah as if he could somehow read his thoughts. "Alright, son. You've got my attention."

Among the valley's first settlers back in the 1800s, the man's ancestors had ranched this land for over a century, commanding the respect of most people this side of the San Juan mountains. That kind of legacy didn't come without its challenges, which was why he'd understand Micah's struggles better than most.

"It's no surprise that a lot of properties have struggled the past few years, and the drought hasn't helped." Micah paused, questioning how much he should tell the man.

Frank dipped his head in understanding. "A lot of people have suffered. It broke my heart when I heard Ted Landry was forced to sell his ranch. His grandparents came here not long after mine, and his family will be missed." His normally sunny disposition dimmed, no doubt remembering all those who'd already been forced to leave. "We do what we can to help, but at the end of the day, we have to trust God to handle the rest."

Micah knew some of the hardships Frank and his own family had faced. And yet they'd never wavered in their faith. As often as he made it to church, which was far less often in recent months than he cared to admit, Frank and his wife Eileen were always there, ministering to others in ways he could only dream.

Yes, he could confide in Frank.

"I know times are tough, but you wouldn't happen to know anyone who's looking to buy some sheep, would you?"

Frank gave a decisive nod. "Say no more. Tell me how many you wish to sell, and I'll see what I can do."

A weight he hadn't realized he'd been carrying seemed to lift from his shoulders. There was hope yet. "Thank you, Frank. That means a lot."

The man's discerning gaze seemed to read between the lines of Micah's relief. Stepping closer, he rested a work-hardened hand on his shoulder. "You've done an admirable job, son. A lesser man would've sold the place years ago, but I've always respected you for sticking it out all these years. Your father would've been proud."

Micah squirmed under the man's praise. He'd craved such validation for so long, he wasn't sure how to receive it. "I don't know about that, but I appreciate the vote of confidence. Most of the time, I feel like I'm holding onto the place by a thread, then something like this happens, or a few sheep get out, and I'm right back where I started."

"Funny you should mention that." Frank readjusted his Stetson and turned his back to the animal enclosure and crowds of families inside. Arms crossed over his chest, his expression turned serious. "Last week, we lost a couple head of cattle that managed to get through the fence onto national forest land. Figured it must've been wolves that got to them, but what I don't get is how they got out in the first place."

"Did you report it?" An image of the attacked ewe came to mind, and Micah wondered again about the hole in the fence.

"Sure did. After I spoke with Parks and Wildlife, I went straight to Jack's. One of my ranch hands found the slaughtered cattle not too far from his place, so I thought it best to warn him, but he brushed it off without concern."

Micah kept a close-lipped expression. Any rancher worth their salt knew the animals came first. As stubborn as the man could be, he was still trying to run a business like the rest of them. Unless the rumors were true, and he really was thinking about selling off to some big-city developer.

"I trust your instincts, Frank. If you think there's reason for concern, then so do I."

The sound of tiny footsteps approached, interrupting their conversation, as Frank's granddaughter ran up to them. Pieces of hay clung to her ruffled skirt, and a rosy grin stretched from ear to ear.

"I'll keep you posted if I hear anything," Frank said as he lifted the girl over the latched gate and onto their side of the fence. "Until then, better safe than sorry. I'm keeping a close eye on things, and I suggest you do the same."

"Will do."

The little girl was already pulling her grandpa away from the petting zoo and toward the cotton candy machine when he stopped for one more parting comment. "When I get home, I'll check with Eileen and see if we know anyone who's looking for some sheep. A few names come to mind, but I'll call you with the details this afternoon."

"Thanks, Frank. I appreciate it."

The man tipped his hat at Micah and gave in to his granddaughter's pleas, leaving Micah with the ponies and chickens.

"That'll be seventeen-fifty for the honey, tea, and bundle of lavender." Grace typed the order into the accounting app she'd helped Callie download yesterday and carefully packaged the items for their new home. Smiling, she handed the paper bag to the young mother of three and watched as the four of them disappeared into the crowds.

"Looks like we're the hit of the farmer's market." Caden joined her and Callie at the table, having taken a break from counting their inventory, and lazily draped an arm across Callie's shoulders. He gave her a lopsided grin, and her deep blush told the rest of the story.

Grace smiled to herself. She couldn't be happier for her two new friends, and a part of her celebrated the knowledge that she'd been able to play a small part in making it happen. It wasn't her place to pry. At least, not yet. This evening, on the other hand, was another matter entirely.

Fiddling with a sprig of lavender, Callie dismissed Grace's knowing look. "It's only one farmer's market, but it's been an exciting one."

"You can say that again," Grace said with a chuckle. Two hours left to go, and they were already on the last box of salves and creams. They'd had to go digging to find the bag of *Tension Tamer* tea Grace had sold moments before.

"And a great idea to use the leftover lavender to make flower sachets. Who would have thought they'd be so popular?" With his free hand, Caden took a bite of one of the dandelion root muffins Callie had packed with only a slight grimace and washed it down with a gulp of her homemade tea. When he offered her a bite, she gladly took it.

"It was a last-minute inspiration, but based on today's sales, I'll be sure to add them to the permanent list."

"Flowers are always a good idea." With his free hand, Caden plucked the sprig of lavender from between Callie's fingers and slipped it behind her ear.

Grace had to work extra hard to keep her growing smile in check. Based on this morning, Callie and Caden appeared to be getting along like a house on fire. The last thing they needed was her hanging around like a third wheel.

"Seeing as things are starting to slow down," she began to say, eyeing the pair as well as the quickly dispersing crowds, "maybe I'll slip out for a few minutes and look around a bit. Buy some heirloom tomatoes or maybe a pie. I even heard someone say there's a vendor selling homemade candles."

Not that she needed any candles. And they all knew Callie's garden had more tomato plants than beehives, which was saying something.

Callie gave Grace a knowing smile.

"That's a great idea." Caden beamed at the suggestion. "No one does a summer market like Lake City. Be sure to stop by Sal's Soda stand. Despite the name, he makes the best kombucha."

Grace reached under the table for her purse and slung it over her shoulder. "Do you want me to grab you guys anything while I'm out?"

Callie shook her head. "Just have some fun. You deserve it for all the help you've been. Caden and I can hold down the fort, right?" She angled her head toward Caden, who nodded his approval.

"Okay. If you need anything, give me a call. Otherwise, I'll be back in about an hour or so." Grace turned to Callie and mouthed a 'good luck' before slipping out the back and into the flow of pedestrians.

For the size of the town, Grace couldn't believe the number of people who'd turned out for a country farmer's market. Families meandered the dirt streets, ice cream cones in hand, while the older generations sat watching contentedly from the benches circling the park. Groups of college students and kids darted from stall to stall, their lively discussions over the day's upcoming adventures filling the square.

Grace soaked it all in—the noise, the crowds, the buzz of chatter and excitement ...

It reminded her of home. A slight comfort amidst the strangeness of the past few weeks.

In the distance, there were the unmistakable sounds of childlike laughter and the bleating of sheep—the latter something she was quickly becoming familiar with, as well as the earthy smell of hay that seemed to follow the creatures wherever they went.

She took her time weaving from stall to stall, sampling everything from kettle corn to locally roasted coffee and something called fire cider that practically cleared her sinuses of her seasonal allergies.

In hopes of cooling the burning sensation still lingering in her throat, she made her way to Sal's Soda stand, and after half-a-dozen samples, selected a bottle of hibiscus raspberry and another flavored with coconut and lime.

Market haul in hand, and still with another twenty minutes to spare, Grace slipped past the park crowds and found her way toward the row of shops lining the historic Main Street.

Lake City was more of a small mountain town than what the name implied. Raised boardwalks lined the road, where dozens of painted Victorian storefronts seemed to defy the test of time. The stone-faced arts building towered over the two-storied wooden facades, their elaborate corniced tops still impressive even after a hundred years.

Even the old-style creamery looked like something right out of a western movie. Not that she'd seen many to know. She'd always been too busy with school and then work, but everything about this place made her want to slow down and soak it all in.

Up ahead, Grace spotted a sign that read *Treeline Mercantile*.

An open sign hung in the window, inviting her into the quaintly furnished shop. Rustic knick-knacks and souvenirs lined the walls along with rows of shelves packed with artisanal trinkets one would expect to find in a small mountain town like this.

Making her way deeper into the store, she perused the rows of artwork and beetle-kill furniture until she spotted a couple of clothing racks in the far corner. Grace looked down at her worn overalls, stains and all, and made a beeline for the stack of jeans.

It wasn't that she didn't appreciate Callie lending her clothes—she'd even been surprised by how comfortable the casual work attire had been—but it was time she found something of her own. And her high-end clothes she'd packed were definitely not suited for life on a ranch.

After trying on a few pairs of jeans, she settled on a slim straight cut that skimmed her hips. From there, she browsed the shop a little further until she found a pair of used boots and a colorful headband to keep her out of her face while she worked.

Looking at her selection, Grace couldn't help but chuckle. If she'd known three weeks ago that she'd be working on a ranch dressed like this, she'd have called herself crazy. Back home, it was always business attire and dress shoes. Rarely did she ever have a chance to wear something so casual.

If only Katrina could see her now.

Katrina. The reminder brought a bitter taste to her mouth more pungent than that from the fire cider. She'd put off calling her back as long as possible. Long enough, in fact, to fall in love with this valley, the ranch, and its people.

She distracted herself for a few minutes more before making her way to the checkout counter. While waiting in line, Grace studied the display of handmade car accessories and selected a rather brightly colored potted air plant that made her think of Callie—fun and whimsical, so very much like the woman herself. It would go perfectly with the solar-powered daisy stuck to her truck's dashboard. And the llama-shaped pot was sure to make her and Caden laugh.

Grace added a few more items to her shopping bag before paying. Back outside, she let the warmth of the sun wash over her as she started back toward the park and its dwindling crowds. In that moment, everything seemed right. She didn't know when the change had first begun, but this place began to feel more and more like home every day.

The high of retail therapy lasted all but one block before Grace remembered the call she still needed to make.

"The sooner you get it done, the better," she whispered under her breath. Before losing her nerve, she reached in her bag for her phone and hit the redial button beside the last number on her recent calls list. The call went to voicemail, and Grace expelled a sigh of relief.

"Hi, Katrina. I'm sorry for not getting back to you sooner, but a lot has happened since I first got here." A massive understatement of where the past few weeks had led. So much had changed since then, and she hoped her boss would understand and respect what she was about to tell her. "I'm calling to let you know I won't be able to close that contract after all. I still have another week of vacation left, but I promise I'll be back in the office after that to help with the new project."

That was, if Katrina didn't fire her before then. She knew she was taking a huge risk choosing the ranch over her job, but for all the nervous energy pulsing through her, she knew this was the right decision. It had been so long since she'd felt like she truly belonged somewhere, she wasn't about to forget it all and leave. Surely Katrina could respect her for that.

"Anyway. I just wanted to call and keep you updated. I'll see you in another week. Bye."

Grace hung up and pocketed her phone, glad she'd only reached Katrina's voicemail and not her directly. She couldn't handle the censure that would've been in her boss's voice had she picked up.

As long as Grace was here, tucked away in this peaceful world, she could pretend that her life was perfect. Mess-free. The complete opposite of her reality.

The rest of the farmer's market had been such a hit that, aside from a few jars of honey, there'd been hardly anything left to pack up and haul home. Pauline had surprised them all with a piece of pie each to take home—leftovers from the lunch rush—which made the perfect ending to a successful day.

Micah was almost finished stacking the empty boxes inside the barn when the phone rang.

"Micah, it's Frank. Got a second?"

"For you, I've got two." Micah shifted the receiver to his other ear and whispered a silent prayer. He had a little over a week left to raise the money he needed, which left him counting on Frank's contacts to come through.

"I spoke with Eileen, and as luck would have it, her brother is in the market for some good wool-bearing sheep. I told him yours are the best in the valley, and he's already keen on the idea."

Thank you Lord. Micah clamped his mouth to keep from shouting with joy. His mind was spinning so fast he almost missed Frank's next question.

"Think you can have them ready by Tuesday?"

Micah almost choked. "This Tuesday, as in three days from now?"

"Yessir. I know it's short notice, but like I said, he's keen to get moving. Plus, I figured you'd appreciate the quick response."

He'd have to shear them all before then if he still wanted to sell the wool. Between him and Caden, they'd be hard-pressed to make such a quick deadline, but if he could convince Callie and Grace to help ...

"We'll be ready. Thank you, Frank."

The man's gravelly chuckle sounded over the speaker. "Don't thank me yet, son. You've got your work cut out for you, but I have faith you'll be just fine."

Micah ended the call, believing for the first time in weeks that there might be a way through all this. Though the sale would only account for part of the money he owed, it would make a significant dent. And if he could somehow prove to the bank managers that he wasn't a liability, maybe they'd extend the loan a little longer.

CHAPTER

Twenty-Two

GRACE SMOOTHED THE front of her pink shirt and studied herself in the full-length mirror of Callie's bathroom. In the past few weeks, her hair had turned noticeably lighter, a couple of shades more than the painted highlights her stylist usually gave her. A few more freckles also dotted the bridge of her nose, further evidence of her recent time in the sun.

Her new and gently used boots nearly shone under the incandescent bulbs after Callie had shown her how to oil them last night. They weren't the heels she was used to, but the soft leather and solid rubber soles made her feel oddly grounded—present—far more so than she was used to.

Without the makeup, straightened hair, and designer clothes, the reflection staring back at her was a striking difference from the crisp, business-savvy woman from before.

"Grace, you almost ready?" Callie called up the stairs. She'd woken her earlier than usual to help Micah and Caden with the sheep and was no doubt busy prepping a basket of goodies to take with them as she spoke.

"Be down in a minute." Grace gathered her hair into a messy braid before joining Callie in the kitchen.

Wrapped in their sweaters to ward off the morning chill, the two hauled everything to the truck and set off toward the ranch. They didn't pass a single car on their way there, and when they pulled up behind the house, everything seemed quiet.

"Are you sure they're expecting us?" Grace asked as she stepped out onto the dirt. Not even Finn raced out to greet them.

"Oh, I'll bet they've been busy for at least an hour getting the place ready. Let's go find them." Callie slipped her camera from the back seat and looped the strap over her head. She shrugged at Grace's curious expression. "Thought I might take some pictures while we're at it. You know, for the website or something."

Grace smiled, unconvinced. "Of course." Because shearing sheep had so much in common with herbal teas and honey.

Before she could say as much, Caden came sauntering up to them from the open barn, Finn close at his heels. "Morning, ladies." He flashed them a grin before lifting out the box of food from the truck bed. For six in the morning, he seemed far too awake, much like Callie, who'd been nearly buzzing with energy the entire drive over.

Grace was happy to give the two of them a moment to themselves and decided to go in search of Micah. She hadn't gone a few feet across the yard when the sliding glass door to the house swished open. Turning, she raised a hand to block out the rising sun and saw Micah descend the steps, a blue ceramic mug in each hand. Dressed in jeans, a blue-and-gray flannel shirt, and leather boots, he looked every bit the country cowboy.

He stopped a few feet from her and offered her one of the mugs, which she gladly took, the coffee's aroma enough to wake her sleepy mind. "Ready for a busy day?" he asked between sips.

She tasted the bold brew and smiled. "Why does that sound more like a warning than a question?"

His laugh seemed to warm her more than the hot drink. "Fair enough. I guess when you've been doing this as long as I have, you forget how daunting it can seem at first."

"You can say that again." She didn't know the first thing about shearing, but the moment Micah had asked, she'd found herself saying *yes* to today's project.

"Come on, I'll show you around."

Side by side, they walked the short distance toward the barn while Caden and Callie continued to talk by the truck. The bleating of sheep drew Grace's attention as they rounded the large red structure. Then the stench of manure hit her. The yard looked as if all five-hundred sheep had been funneled into a temporary pen of sorts, their collective baas like a noisy crowd at a football game.

"Caden and I spent yesterday afternoon driving the flock down from the upper pasture to the paddocks. Makes it a lot easier to shave the wool if we don't have to go back and forth each time."

Grace peered up at him, surprised at her disappointment that he hadn't asked her to join them. "You should have told us. We'd have been happy to help."

"I appreciate the offer, but between the two of us and Finn, it didn't take too long. Besides," he said, bumping his shoulder against hers, "today is when the real fun begins."

With that cryptic remark, he led her toward the nearest gate and walked into the barn through a small back door.

The last time she'd been inside the place, it had been nearly empty, save for a stack of hay along the back wall and a couple of horses in their stalls. Wooden ramps and temporary fencing now took up a large section of the square space, with a long table set up in the middle.

"We use the chutes to direct the sheep into the barn. It helps keep things moving at an orderly pace. Although, sometimes we'll still get a runner and one of us has to chase it down."

Grace frowned. The very idea of running through the mud to catch the wooly creatures made her stomach sour. A twinge of doubt crept into her mind at the size of the task before them. If she'd known what exactly she'd been getting herself into, she might have thought twice about volunteering. She cast a quick glance toward Micah, and his steady smile calmed her worries.

He leaned over, and she picked up a faint scent of his pine-scented soap. "Don't worry." His low baritone voice was smooth and reassuring. "Caden usually volunteers to go after those."

As if hearing his name, Caden appeared in the open doorway with Callie by his side.

"Everyone ready to get started?" He clapped his hands together, and Finn came bolting into the barn behind them.

"Grace and I can handle cleanup duty." Callie turned to Grace and linked an arm through her limp one. "I'll show you everything you need to know about collecting and skirting the wool while those two get started shearing." Her enthusiastic smile softened, and she gave Grace's arm another squeeze, infusing her with a little courage. A chorus of bleats and baas ricocheted through the rafters from outside as if cheering her onward.

"Works for me." Caden shrugged and sauntered over toward the far end of the ramp.

There was no backing out now. "I'm sure I'll catch on once we get started."

Callie squealed with excitement beside her, but she could only stare at Micah, who still held her gaze.

She wasn't here to sabotage his ranch or even just as a passerby. She wanted him to succeed, and she prayed he could see that. Already, she cared deeply for this place and these people. It broke her heart to know she'd have to leave soon, that she didn't truly belong here, but all the same, she wanted to do something to thank them for all they'd done.

After a moment, the corner of Micah's mouth curved, and the entire atmosphere inside the barn seemed to shift. Somehow, and Grace wasn't exactly sure how, she knew he understood.

"Are we shearing sheep today, or just going to talk about it?" Caden called from where he waited beside the ramp. When Micah gave the go-ahead, Caden reached up and unlatched a small door. With a little encouragement, the first sheep trotted inside, dense wool hanging like a rug over its back. As soon as it was in the barn, Caden slid the door closed and latched it shut.

Grace stood off to the side with Callie as Micah coaxed the animal toward the shearing stall. It put up a bit of a fight when he grasped onto the wool but calmed just as quickly as he spoke in tones only the animal could hear. With a flick of a button, the low hum of the shears filled the cavernous space, and he began to run the combed machine through the wool. He worked his way around the animal's back before readjusting its position and continuing.

To Grace's dismay, Micah lifted the ewe by its front legs until it was sitting in a reclined position. But despite the awkward-looking arrangement, the animal seemed perfectly content to lounge against Micah's legs as he took the shears to the wool.

Grace couldn't blame her.

Moving to the smooth underbelly, he ran the mechanical shears in short strokes across the skin, freeing the matted wool in clumps to the wood floor. He moved with quick precision, his strong arms holding the animal in a secure yet gentle embrace as he worked. Despite being manhandled, the ewe remained calm, straining only slightly when he trimmed the last patch of wool from around her neck. The moment Micah finished, he released her, and she skipped away, newly freed of her heavy coat.

"Wow, she looks like a different animal. It's like half a sheep is gone." Grace looked down at the pile of wool on the floor, surprised to see it had remained relatively intact.

"Just watch what I do, and before you know it, you'll be skirting wool with your eyes closed." Callie reached down and gathered the wool. Arms wrapped around the pelt, she carried it to the table and proceeded to roll it out flat. She cut away the loose and muddy tendrils with a pair of rounded scissors before fluffing and then rolling it into a tight bundle. "See? Easy as pie." Callie stuffed the final roll into a large white bag with a flourish.

Grace chuckled. "Apparently you've never seen me try to bake."

Once Micah finished with the next sheep, Callie stepped aside for Grace to have a go. Without the same ease, she swept up the scattered wool and clutched it to her chest. To her surprise, the wool was greasy and stiff, nothing compared to the finished product she was used to wearing. "Is this normal?"

Callie trailed behind her, picking up the felted clumps that dropped to the floor. "The more hair the sheep has, the stiffer and itchier the wool will be. These sheep here are Rambouillets, which means they'll produce softer wool once cleaned and brushed, perfect for textiles and your more delicate uses."

Grace dropped the heavy bundle onto the table, where she worked to wrestle it into submission. Once or twice, she caught Micah watching her as he worked silently on the next sheep.

A few mats and clumps of dirt clung to the edges of the wool, proving more difficult than anticipated to cut away from the fleece. Callie stood off to the side while Grace worked, checking in every now and again when she got stuck. Once Grace was finished, the two of them worked together to roll it back up like a sleeping bag and packed it in with the other cleaned fleece.

"Nicely done." Callie clapped her hands together once they'd tied off the full bag. "Two down, only four-hundred-ninety-eight more to go. But don't worry," she slipped in as Grace bit back a groan. "It'll go much faster once we get into a groove."

For all their sakes, she sure hoped so.

After an hour of gathering and skirting wool, Grace had already begun to work up a sweat. Callie suggested they take a short water break, and she couldn't have been more grateful. A few minutes later, Micah and Caden joined them.

"That's about forty sheep so far," Caden said before he gulped down some water. He wiped the back of his hand across a trail of moisture on his chin and turned to Micah. "If we keep this pace up, we might actually be able to get through them all by this evening."

Micah nodded and swallowed. "Sounds about right."

He stood so close, Grace had to tilt her head back to look up at him. At some point in the past hour, he'd stripped out of his flannel shirt, exposing tanned biceps beneath his gray T-shirt. Having tossed his hat on top of the folded sweater, his light brown hair flopped over his forehead, giving him a boyish charm she hadn't noticed beneath the hat he always wore. Even the scar he'd always kept covered seemed softer in the filtered light of the barn.

Her gaze dropped to his lips, and he smiled.

"What?" Her face warmed at his amused expression.

His grin deepened. "You were staring."

Grace's mouth dropped open, and she had the sudden urge to slap that silly grin right off his too-handsome face. She scrambled for something to say, but instead of a witty comeback, her mind went embarrassingly blank.

Micah's deep laugh reverberated through her, somehow soothing her discomfort and making her heart race at the same time. "Looks like there's more than one way to get you to stop talking." He chuckled.

The memory of their kiss flashed before her, and she tried not to blush.

Scooping up his hat from the floor, he stepped forward and placed it on her head, those honey-brown eyes never wavering from hers.

"Hey, Micah," shouted Caden over the sounds of bleating sheep. He'd finished his water and was already waiting by the shearing stalls. "Stop your woolgathering and come help me with these sheep."

Draining the last of his drink, Micah set his cup down and cast her a wink. "Duty calls."

Blushing, Grace couldn't help but watch as he walked away. She only remembered she wasn't alone when Callie chuckled beside her.

"It appears I *was* right, after all." Callie's pleased grin was like that of a cat who'd caught a canary.

"What about you and Caden?" Grace asked, trying to find a way to change the subject.

"What about us?" Callie darted a glance toward the men as she straightening the water bottles and cups.

Grace's face relaxed into a smile. "So, there's an *us* now?"

Callie screwed the lid onto the last bottle and dropped it back in the cooler. "I don't know. I mean, nothing's really changed. We already saw each other every day, but now it feels different. Better." There was no mistaking the sappy grin pulling at the edges of her mouth.

"I'm so happy for you, Callie." Grace pulled her friend in for a side hug, genuinely pleased.

"Hey, what are you two talking about over there?" Caden called over the sounds of twin shears going at once. "It better not be who's the better shearer."

"And what if we were?" Callie shot back with a grin.

Micah reached for the next ewe and paused to look at Caden. "I think we all know who'd win that debate."

Grace smiled as the two cousins bantered back and forth with Callie. Nothing about this moment was glamorous or world-shaking. In fact, shearing sheep in a barn in the middle of nowhere was one of the least glamorous things she'd ever done. Yet, somehow, between the fleece-lined floors and the constant laughter, it felt oddly comfortable.

As if she'd rediscovered a piece of her soul that had gone missing long ago.

God is in the details, her aunt always used to say. At the time, newly orphaned and uprooted from her normal life, she couldn't help but be angry at God. Instead of clinging to that truth like her aunt, she'd devoted her life to being as self-sufficient and independent as possible.

Now, looking back, she couldn't help but wonder if her loneliness had been of her own making.

Something soft bounced against her head, and Grace turned to see Micah, arm raised with a handful of wool raised above his head. Beside her, Callie tossed another clump toward the men, hitting Caden square in the chest.

Their laughter mingled with that of the ewes in their stalls, and Grace knew—she'd finally found the family she'd been searching for.

The muscles in Micah's back protested as he stood to release the freshly shorn ewe back to the rest of the flock. Rolling his shoulders, he tried to work out the knots that had formed and winced.

They'd been at this for well over seven hours. He knew they were all tired, which was why he hadn't said a word when Caden and Callie had slipped out for a break a few minutes ago.

With only a few dozen sheep left, the day was nearly done, and despite the pain and all the doubts that had plagued him through the night, by God's grace, it looked as if they were actually going to make it.

A welcome breeze drifted through the open barn doors, lifting a few loose clumps of wool from the wooden floorboards to dance across his feet. Taking a breather, Micah stripped off a glove and ran his fingers through the hair that had flopped over his forehead.

As he stood there, he couldn't help but watch as Grace moved with ease around the fleeces, her long braid swishing back and forth while she worked. All day, he'd felt his attention drifting back to her. Only a blind man wouldn't have noticed the way her new jeans hugged every curve, or how the shafts of sunlight made her hair glow like a field of wheat. She still wore his hat—a new life breathed into the tattered canvas—which warmed him more than the afternoon heat of the barn.

In that moment, had he walked in as a complete stranger, he'd have thought she'd been doing this all her life—that she belonged there.

Grace tied off the last remaining bag and looked up, catching Micah's gaze. With the sun behind her, he couldn't make out her shadowed expression. But unlike the other times, he didn't look away or pretend to count the bags of wool beside her. There was a magnetic pull between them, something he couldn't quite explain. Reason told him to be cautious, to keep her at arm's length until she eventually left, but the longer she stayed, the more he didn't want to fight it.

"I've got something in my hair again, haven't I?" Grace pulled her braid forward and rubbed a gloved hand down the golden plait. Never mind that she did, in fact, have a fuzz of wool clinging to the hair behind her ear. She'd never looked prettier.

Micah didn't know what to say, so he did the only thing he could think of. "Care to give it a try?" he asked, pointing to the shears in his hand.

Her eyes rounded as if he'd asked her to drive the combine. "Me?"

Micah chuckled, both at his offer and at her reaction. "Well, I sure wasn't talking to Finn." He looked over to where the dog sat happily monitoring the sheep and grinned. "What do you say?"

Despite her reticence, he could tell she wanted to learn. The same way she'd jumped at the chance to work on the fences or fix the hydroelectric system. Even though he was sure she'd never done either before, she never failed to impress him with her willingness to try.

Grace walked toward him and stopped once she was a foot outside the stall. In the two days since the farmer's market, he'd missed the smell of her shampoo—jasmine with a hint of vanilla—and he breathed in the refreshing scent as she stood beside him.

With his prompting, she stepped inside and planted her feet in the same place Micah had been standing all day. "If I can brave a few thousand bees to harvest honey, I think I can handle one sheep," she said with a determined edge to her voice.

"That's the spirit." There was no stopping Grace once she set her mind to something, that he know all too well. Convinced she was ready, Micah opened the small door above the chute and guided a seemingly docile ewe down the ramp toward Grace.

Frank's brother-in-law would be by tomorrow to load up the sheep, and they were nearly ready. There was more than enough time to let Grace try. He flicked the switch, and the shears whirred to life.

"So, how exactly do I do this?" she asked.

"First, you want to grab onto the wool and pull it taut, like this." Micah gathered a handful of the long, shaggy fleece and motioned for her to run the shears through it.

Cautious, she buzzed the clippers over the surface, and the fibers fell to the ground.

"That's it, keep it up," Micah encouraged.

As if moving through molasses, Grace ran her fingers through the long, coarse wool and took hold of another small section. She drew the shears close to the hair and hesitated only a moment before cutting it loose.

She made her way through most of the thick mat of wool covering the ewe's back. With increasing speed, she ran the shears in short strokes down its back, but the animal flinched as she neared its tail. She squealed at the unexpected movement, dropping the shears.

"Don't be afraid to manhandle her a bit to keep her from kicking."

Grace picked the shears up off the floor, her delicate eyebrows dipping in concern. "Won't that hurt her, though?"

Micah shook his head. "They're tougher than they look. And if they give you any trouble, just keep a firm hold on them, and they'll relax. Like this." He reached his arms around Grace from behind and steadied the animal enough for her to continue.

"Hmm. Is this how you teach all your ranch hands?" Grace's airy voice muddled his brain, and her soft laughter seemed to vibrate through him with the close proximity.

"Only the pretty ones," he teased. "Turns out I have quite the soft spot for spunky blondes."

He'd meant for it to come out as a joke, but the truth of it hit him like a full-grown ram. Grace must have sensed as much as she grew quiet once more. Eager to break the sudden unease, Micah cleared his throat and nodded his head toward the ewe.

"We'll need to move her so we can get the rest of the wool." Giving Grace some room, he continued to talk her through the next steps. "Now, grab the front legs, and once you have a secure grip, roll her over onto her back and rest her against the fronts of your legs."

Grace did as he said and let out another slight squeal as the sheep responded to her guidance.

"Good. Keep her laying on her sides with her shoulders resting on your foot and her head between your ankles to keep her calm and subdued. And if she puts up a fight, just squat down and sit on her head."

"Excuse me?" Grace jerked back, almost elbowing him in the face.

Micah chuckled. "Don't worry. You won't hurt her. If it makes you feel any better, the first time I did this, the sheep ended up wrestling *me* to the ground." He'd been red in the face for days and would have given up right then and there if it hadn't been for his dad's patient instructions. "God did this amazing thing with sheep where when you lay them on their backs, they immediately relax."

"Like a shark?" Her smile was infectious.

"Exactly."

Once she had the animal in position, Grace worked her way around the back hip, and the lamb's tail began to thump against the floor. "She actually seems to like it."

Micah brushed his hand over the buzzed wool and smiled down at Grace with pride. "It means she trusts you." Much like him. "That, and imagine having over seven pounds of hair removed at once."

"If it feels half as good as my regular cut and color, I don't blame her." Grace went back to shearing the last bit and sighed as she freed the remainder of the heavy fleece.

Stepping back, he released the sheep, and the animal bounded over to her other freshly shaved friends, tail wagging. They watched in silence for a moment as the gentle animals relaxed in the shade of the barn. Now freed of their heavy burdens, they seemed content to munch on the carpet of fresh hay.

Micah tried to see them through Grace's eyes—stubborn, easily-distracted animals with a penchant for eating brightly colored clothing. They were defenseless and had to be led to water, but they could also be kind, peaceful, innocent to a fault, and trusting beyond measure.

It always struck him just how similar people could be to sheep. How many times had he relied on God to lead him to water when all he wanted was to go his own way?

"Think I'm ready for the pros?" Grace teased. She smiled up at him, close enough that he could feel her breath on his shoulder. He didn't know who had stepped closer, but he could make out nearly every pale freckle across the bridge of her nose.

"Almost." He reached out to adjust his hat on her head. The wide brim engulfed her face in shadow, so he tilted it back slightly until he was looking down into her eyes. He swallowed. "Perfect."

Something flashed behind them, and Micah turned to see Callie in the doorway with her camera poised for another shot.

"What?" She had her free hand raised innocently in front of her. "Someone has to take pictures."

"Of this?" Grace asked, half laughing—the same kind of breathy laughter she used when she was embarrassed.

Micah wasn't too pleased with Callie's timing either, but he was filled with a sense of self-satisfaction knowing he'd stirred something in Grace the same way she did him.

Callie shrugged in a way that communicated *sorry-not-sorry*. "Who knows? Maybe someday I'll sell yarn. Then I'll be grateful to have some photos."

The two women stared at each other as if in a silent conversation before Grace cracked first. Once again, her laughter bubbled out into the cavernous barn, and soon, Micah joined in as well.

CHAPTER

Twenty-Three

GRACE CLOSED HER phone on the two new voicemails—one from Katrina and the other from her coworker, Betsy—and tossed it back onto her suitcase. She didn't need the reminder from her friend that she'd been gone almost three weeks. She knew Betsy meant well, and there was probably a warning in there about Katrina not being happy about the situation, but she'd as good as promised to see this through.

She knew she couldn't stay there forever, no matter the peaceful stirring in her soul that grew each day, but a few more couldn't hurt. Besides, Tony had yet to call back about her car, and she wasn't about to leave until she knew the ranch was safe and Callie's business was in good hands. Then there was Olive to think about.

And a handsome cowboy might have a thing or two to do with it as well.

"Are you sure this isn't too much?" Callie did a twirl in front of the hallway mirror, sending the floral pleated skirt swishing about her ankles. Grace had helped her with her hair, and the coppery curls now fell in waves around her shoulders.

"It's perfect. Caden won't know what hit him."

Callie's freckles stood out against the slight flush of pink. Grasping the material, she flicked the skirt a few more times and smiled. "It does feel nice to wear something other than overalls."

A shower and change of clothes had done wonders for them both, and despite Grace's tired muscles, her body hummed with a similar energy. After settling on the dark green dress dotted with golden mums, Callie had encouraged Grace to pick out one to borrow as well. The simple mint green skirt went beautifully with the blush tones of her sweater, and for once, she agreed with Callie's taste in clothes.

Downstairs, a buzzer sounded.

"That'll be the food. Would you mind looking for the rest of the lights while I check on it?" With a rustle of fabric, Callie turned from the mirror and flitted down the steps. After a few seconds, the buzzer stopped, and the sweet scent of roasted vegetables and balsamic vinegar wafted through the house.

Faint music floated up from the patio through the open second-story window. Any minute now, Micah and Caden would be there for their celebratory dinner. Which meant she had a few minutes to find the lanterns supposedly buried in the hall closet.

Rolling up the sleeves of her sweater, Grace opened the door and gaped at the mess inside. Wedged between the towels and linens were more empty jars, ribbons, and mismatched pots and pans than she could count. Bags of dried flowers lined the top shelf, the scents of lavender and rose spilling into the hallway while she held the door ajar.

"Are you sure those lanterns are up here?" she called downstairs. She bent down and picked up a handful of crumpled towels, pushing them to the side to create some space.

Footsteps echoed up the stairwell.

"Not that I'm questioning you, but it might take all night to find them." Grace pushed open the door to show Callie, but she froze when she saw Micah ascending the last step.

Freshly showered and dressed in a crisp white shirt and jeans, he looked the perfect gentleman. He'd even shaved. Grace hadn't noticed the dimples before now, not through that scruff of his she'd grown used to. Now when he smiled, those faint but oh-so-present creases framed his mouth in a way that made her wish for the hundredth time that Callie hadn't snuck up on them in the barn, camera poised and ready to capture whatever it was that had almost happened between them.

"I'm not sure about lanterns, but if you keep going, you might find Narnia in there." His deep voice soothed her runaway thoughts. Reaching to the floor, he picked up the first discarded towel and proceeded to fold it into a neat bundle. When he handed it to her, their fingers touched, sending shivers up Grace's arm.

Micah's attention shifted from the closet to her and lingered. "Is that a new dress?"

Grace hugged the soft knit against her body like a blanket and blushed. "Actually, I borrowed it from Callie."

"It suits you." His presence and appreciative gaze made her feel more feminine by the second. Even today in the barn, hay and wool clinging to her clothes and hair, his attention hadn't gone unnoticed.

"You clean up pretty nicely, yourself."

Those dimples reappeared. "Careful. All that sweet talk could give a guy the wrong idea."

As if she wasn't already there.

"Dinner's ready!" Callie called from the kitchen. There was the unmistakable sound of clattering dishes and silverware before a door opened somewhere downstairs.

"I guess we'll have to do without the lanterns, then." Grace took the folded towels and shoved them back into the only available space she could find in the closet. And when she turned around, Micah stood right beside her.

He stepped toward her and leaned in. Heart pounding, Grace stood there like a statue, afraid to move. His breath tickled the top of her head, and she closed her eyes. His sleeve brushed hers, filling her with warmth. But a second later, cool air rushed into the space between them.

"Is this what you were looking for?"

Grace snapped her eyes open.

In his hand, Micah held a small metal lantern. He placed it into her numb hands, and from beneath a mountain of yarn, lifted out another. The vanilla-scented candles inside brought her back to reality by the time he'd dug up a third.

"Once again, you saved the day." Grace wanted to pinch herself for having thought he might actually kiss her at the top of the stairs.

He shrugged a shoulder, making the lantern dance from the handle. "Habit, I guess."

Taking his cue, Grace followed him down the steps and onto the back patio where Callie and Caden were busy setting the table. String lights hung from the wooden crossbeams of the pergola, bathing the space in a warm glow as they bobbed in the breeze. With Callie's instructions, Grace and Micah arranged the lanterns around the wooden deck, lit the tea candles, and closed the glass panels on the small flames.

In a word, Grace could only describe the display as magical.

Once everything was ready, Caden popped open the bottle of rhubarb wine he and Micah had brought, and they all raised a toast to a successful day. As they clinked their glasses together, Micah and Grace exchanged a knowing smile.

They all moved to sit, and Caden rushed to pull out Callie's chair. She smiled up at him in response before he took the seat beside her.

"Micah, would you like to say grace?" Callie asked once they were all seated.

"Sure." He bowed his head, and Grace and the others joined in as he prayed a blessing over the meal. After the *amen*, the four of them dug into the feast before them.

A bowl of cereal would have tasted amazing after the day they'd had. Good thing Callie had been in charge of the cooking instead of Grace. The roasted chicken from the freezer and balsamic glazed vegetables were heavenly, and with homemade strawberry white chocolate ice cream for dessert, Grace wondered how she'd ever been content with takeout and freezer meals back home.

A few times during dinner, Grace caught Micah stealing glances at her from across the table. When their eyes met, he didn't look away, and his soft smile felt like a treasured secret.

When the last plate was cleared, Callie pushed away from her seat and stood. "Well, I guess the dishes won't wash themselves."

Grace was about to stand when Caden stood abruptly, his chair nearly toppling over behind him.

"I can help with that." Swooping in, he reached for the empty serving trays while Callie finished stacking the plates and silverware.

Grace stifled a giggle at the man's enthusiasm. "Looks like you found a keeper there, Callie."

A flush crept up the woman's neck. Peering over at Caden and his full arms, she smiled. "Hmm, I think you're right."

He sent her a conspicuous wink. "Whenever you need someone to wash dishes for you, you know where to find me."

With the plates in hand, the two of them disappeared into the kitchen, leaving Grace and Micah alone outside. The pair's laughter trickled through the open windows, loud in the otherwise quiet backyard.

Unsure what to do now, Grace turned toward Micah, who stood beside the trellis and the climbing honeysuckle. They both watched as a bee hovered above one of the delicate flowers for a moment before flying away toward the garden.

Micah tilted his head in the direction of the small bench nestled between the rose bushes and lavender. "Care to join me?"

Only a person with incredible self-control would have said no to his invitation.

The wooden bench creaked and groaned as she lowered onto the seat beside him. For what seemed like minutes, they sat in silence, watching through the semi-darkness as the bees flitted from flower to flower. They made a slow dance, floating between each bud, collecting nectar to take back to the hives before eventually making their way back home.

The longer they sat there, the more aware she became of Micah's nearness—every movement, every tap of his foot, the rise and fall of his chest. She wondered what it would feel like to run her fingers through the loose curls at the nape of his neck again, trace a fingertip over the scar and along his temple ...

You're leaving in a few days, Grace. What are you thinking?

She obviously *wasn't* thinking. That was the problem. Any other self-respecting associate would have gotten the contract signed and been gone before the bridge flooded. They most definitely wouldn't have stuck around to help out. Nor would they have fallen for a cowboy.

Micah shifted beside her, his voice catching as he started to speak. "That night you came over ... You were trying to chop wood and I ..."

"Kissed me?" Grace finished the sentence for him.

"Yeah," he said, sheepishly. "Sorry about that."

He seemed as flustered by it as she'd been at the time. An accident, a spur-of-the-moment event neither of them had seen coming. It had been such a surprise, but she couldn't help replaying that moment, wondering what it would be like to kiss him again. "Don't be."

He gave her a curious expression before growing serious again. "That night, you asked how I could accuse my dad of starting the fire."

Grace sobered at the quick change in topic. "I shouldn't have said that. You were right to be angry with me."

Micah silenced her with a hand on her shoulder. "No. You were right." The last ounce of fight seemed to drain from him with the admission. Grace could hear his breathing slow before he turned to face her again.

"I didn't make things easy for my parents when I was a kid. My brother Tye was the straight-A student, but all I wanted was to be on the ranch. My dad used to give me such a hard time about it. We'd get into these huge arguments, yelling matches, really. My mom said we argued because we were so alike, and I think that's what he was most afraid of—that I'd end up like him and never leave." His words trailed off until Grace thought he'd decided against sharing the rest of the story.

"I'm sure he was only looking out for you." Of course, she'd never met Micah's dad, but based on how his son turned out, he had to have done something right.

"Yeah, that's what everyone keeps trying to tell me." He gave a halfhearted nod and seemed to study the dirt at his feet. "What are your parents like? You probably have a much better relationship with them than I ever did with mine."

A part of her wanted to pull her knees to her chest, shrink within the large garden and disappear. But if Micah could lower his walls and share his past with her, so could she.

"I don't really remember much. They passed away when I was a kid."

He shifted beside her, but she didn't look up. "Grace, I'm so sorry. I had no idea."

Somehow, his apology didn't feel hollow. He understood her pain as much as she did his. Which is why she knew there was still more to his story left to be shared. "Thanks, I appreciate that. I've been on my own for a while now, but I would have given anything to have whatever extra time with them. Even if we did argue once in a while." She raised her face and searched for his in the darkness.

The hum of bees reverberated through the evening air as they sat side-by-side on the patio bench. Faint light spilled through the double glass doors from the kitchen, obscuring his features in long shadows. She might not be able to pick out the color of his eyes—which she knew to be rich and golden like polished leather—but the way his body seemed to relax beside hers told her everything she needed to know.

"The night of the fire, we'd gotten into it again. The funny thing is, I can't even remember what we were arguing about. I just remember storming out of the barn so angry at him. Next thing I knew, the hayloft was on fire." He paused and rubbed his palms over his jeans. "It wasn't Jack who drove him to smoke that night. It was me."

It all made sense. The outburst, his hatred toward Jack, why he worked so hard to preserve the ranch. All her life, she'd been trying to avoid her past while Micah had chosen to confront it day after day.

He shrugged. "After that, Mom sort of slipped into a depression, and I've been running the place ever since."

Grace reached out her hand and wove her fingers around his. A silent gesture that she hoped told him he wasn't alone. The slight squeeze of his hand told her he understood.

"At first, I didn't want to stay. I wanted to run away like Tye did as soon as he graduated high school and never look back. But someone needed to take care of this place and Mom. So, I took all my savings and applied for a loan. It got easier with time, running it all. But now, with the drought, the bank is calling in everyone's loans, whether we can afford them or not."

He'd poured his heart and soul into this earth. She could see it now. It was family pride, and more than a little guilt, that seemed to push him forward. He felt responsible for this place—and afraid to let others down.

He had dreams for the future—but was still trying to atone for the past.

"Micah, I ..." She didn't know what to say. Before, she'd thought she had all the facts, had blazed ahead, thinking she knew what it was he needed to hear. She could remind him that he didn't have to do it all on his own, that Caden and Callie were right there willing to help. That the people in this community cared for him as he did for them.

If only he'd let them in.

She knew how it felt to be left behind. To carry that heavy weight of responsibility to right some event in the past that could never be undone. Sometimes all it took was to let someone be heard and to know their scars didn't need to be covered.

"Thank you for telling me."

He remained silent for a moment and seemed to soak in her words before he spoke again. "Thank you, Grace. It is such a relief to talk with someone about this." He hiked an eyebrow and slid her a wary glance. "Sure you're not ready to run for the hills now?"

Grace felt something inside her relax. "If you didn't scare me off on the side of the highway, you won't now."

Micah chuckled. And oh, how it made her heart soar. "Was that before or after you attacked me with an umbrella?" His teasing lightened the moment.

"I didn't attack you." She gave him a playful shove that hardly made him budge.

"You did, and I had the bruise to prove it. Lucky for you, though, I have a tough head." His shoulder grazed hers, closing the distance between them.

Grace's breath hitched as every imagined thought of the past few weeks flashed through her mind. The what-ifs and possibilities drowned out the second-guessing as he shifted just enough to face her in the twilight.

Her fingers still laced through his, Micah tugged her a little closer and angled his head toward hers. When there was only a breath between them, he paused, a question hovering between them as if waiting for her to run or lean in.

And then he kissed her—softly—with a tenderness unlike before. Rough and calloused hands sifted through her hair, pulling her ever so close as he deepened the kiss. This wasn't a man who was fighting the world, he was searching for peace, and for reasons that maybe she would never understand, he'd found solace in her. Everything about him spoke of his regard for his family, the ranch, the community, and now her. In that moment, she found herself falling, and all she wanted was for this moment to never end.

She broke away first, but only enough to catch her breath with a deep lungful of cool air. "How's your head, now?" she asked sheepishly, her brain still trying to catch up to her emotions.

Micah's fingers trailed across her temple as he tucked a loose hair behind her ear. He smiled. "Never better."

With the way he was looking at her, Grace couldn't have cared less if she was supposed to go home in a few days. For the first time in her life, she knew where she was supposed to be.

She'd seen past Micah's defenses, and there was no going back.

CHAPTER

Twenty-Four

CADEN HAD NEVER felt so light as after he'd said goodnight to Callie on her front porch last night. Even now, as he raked fresh hay into the sheep's pens, he couldn't help but replay every moment they'd spent together the past few days.

"What's got you smiling?" Micah tossed a heap of alfalfa over the fence, a trail of dust hovering in the crisp morning air.

Caden propped himself against the pitchfork and watched his cousin take his time with the feed, the most relaxed he'd seen him in months. No doubt it was because of a certain blonde. "Probably the same thing as you."

Micah shot him a scowl, but they both knew he didn't mean it.

"Admit it. She's not the worst thing that could have happened to this place."

Micah's silent smile was enough of a response.

The sound of rustling hay and the bleating of nearby sheep filled the space while they worked. The sun warmed their backs as they moved down the fence toward the barn, working to separate the bales and distribute the hay around the temporary paddock. Hungry sheep trailed behind, snatching up the fibrous grain the moment it hit the ground.

"Still thinking about heading back to California?" Micah asked the question so casually that Caden almost missed it.

The contentment he'd felt moments before dissipated like the fine hay dust. "How'd you know? I haven't told anyone." Especially not Callie. Sure, he'd thought about it on more than one occasion, but the timing had never seemed right to leave.

Micah shrugged, never breaking his stride. "I've been wondering about it for some time. When you first came here, I figured it'd only be for a few months, but it's been over a year now. Not that I want you to leave," he added with a soft but matter-of-fact tone. "I wouldn't have gotten through the last few months without you. But I know you probably have plans that don't include baling hay and herding sheep for the rest of your life."

Everything Micah said was true. However, that insatiable need to keep moving didn't seem so urgent anymore. He'd only meant for this to be a stop-off in his search for the next adventure, not the destination. Of all the places he'd thought to settle down one day, the ranch had never even made the list.

He also hadn't counted on meeting Callie or finding such peace within these quiet mountains.

What if this *was* the plan?

Caden wrung his gloved hands around the wooden handle, still unsure about the future but no longer afraid. "I haven't thought it through, but if it's okay with you, I think I might like to stay."

Micah studied him for a second before he tossed another forkful of hay over the fence. "As long as you want to stay, I'm happy to have you."

And he knew Micah meant it.

They resumed their work in silence until they ran out of bales.

"Give me a hand with the rest of the wool?" Finished spreading the hay, Micah leaned his pitchfork against the nearby wall and took a step toward the barn. When Caden didn't follow, he turned and grinned. "Gotta earn your keep if you plan on sticking around."

Caden laughed—no, he flat out howled—at his cousin's joke and gladly followed.

Almost all the wool from the day before had been sorted into white plastic bags and lined into neat rows inside the barn. Only a few partially filled containers remained open in the middle of the enclosed space. Working together, they slid the nearly two-hundred-pound bags toward the others against the back wall.

Caden heard Olive's faint bleats through the gaps in the wood as he moved about.

"From what Callie says, it sounds like Grace is doing a fine job taking care of that one."

Micah nodded, another faint smile tugging at his mouth. "Another week or two, and she'll be ready to rejoin the rest of the flock."

Caden bent to retrieve a few tufts of wool that had escaped one of the open bags and tossed them back inside. He didn't want to bring up the fact that Grace would eventually have to go back home as well, leaving Micah and the lamb behind. Not that long-distance relationships couldn't work. He just didn't want to see his cousin get hurt. Not when he was in the best mood he'd been in for months.

"Do you think it'll be enough to save the ranch?" Caden nodded toward the wall of wool and the sheep on the other side. He'd done his own calculations earlier, glanced through the books when he knew Micah wasn't looking, and knew it would be close.

Micah must have been wondering the same thing and released a long breath. "God has gotten us this far. I'll trust Him to see us through."

Caden knew that was the right answer, but he still couldn't help but worry. In another week, they'd know for sure, but until then, he supposed Micah was right. All they could do was wait and pray.

Two-hundred ninety-nine, three hundred.

Good. The sheep set apart for the sale were all accounted for, and Micah had already seen to it that they had fresh water and food to last them through tomorrow. He'd stuck around long after he and Caden had finished distributing the hay—a few last-minute inspections before Frank's brother-in-law came the next morning.

Convinced everything was as it should be, he rounded the barn with Finn on his heels and stopped at the gate of the smaller pen. Olive slept soundly in the corner, still bundled in the little sweater Grace had knit for her. The stitches were crooked in places, but the simple gesture touched him more than he could express. In a few more days, she'd be back with the others, another sheep in the flock. But for now, her presence was a reminder. She was the one they'd almost lost.

And the one they'd found.

Micah cherished these quiet moments. There was nothing remarkably special about this lamb. No unique markings or lauded pedigree. She was just one lamb, but her unwavering trust made Micah feel as if he was doing something right.

Finn's ears twitched, and the dog took off around the barn.

A few seconds later, Micah lifted his head at the sound of an engine rumbling up the drive. His heart rate kicked up a notch as Grace's moonlit face from last night came to mind.

He'd teased Caden earlier about being love-struck when the truth was, so was he. It didn't matter that it made no sense. For once in his life, he didn't have a plan.

And that didn't scare him.

Leaving Olive to her rest, Micah pushed away from the gate and made his way toward the yard. Images of him sweeping Grace off her feet flooded his thoughts, and he smiled at the prospect of her in his arms again.

With a lightness in his steps, he picked up his pace. Once outside the barn's shadow, he had to shield his eyes with his hands from the blinding sunlight. Grace still had his hat from yesterday, and he could feel the refreshing gust of wind blow through his hair. Autumn was nearly here. In a few more weeks, all the trees would be a brilliant gold blanket stretching down the valley, and if all went according to plan, he'd still be here to enjoy it.

Finn's excited yips greeted Micah as he reached the yard, but it wasn't Grace who was petting the cattle dog.

Standing beside what looked to be a brand new Lexus was a woman far from home. The first thing he noticed besides her black pants and heavy makeup were her bright red heels. Bold, impractical, and dangerous.

"Can I help you?" Micah stopped a few yards away, his guard back in place.

"Hi, I'm Katrina." Stepping closer, she stuck out a manicured hand and greeted him with a firm handshake.

"Micah." He tipped his head in greeting, but until he knew why this woman was here, he'd keep his distance.

Her face lit with recognition, and what he could only describe as a calculating smile spread across her matching red lips. "Of course. The elusive rancher. I should have guessed."

The way she said *rancher* grated like road rash, but he reigned in his growing irritation.

"I'm sorry, but do I know you?"

She reached into her leather purse and extracted a sleek business card. "I'm from Prospect & Gould. I believe you've already met my associate, Miss Riley."

The modern typeface stared back at him, the truth in black and white. So, *this* was Grace's boss. But what was she doing all the way out here?

The woman closed her car door and took a few uninvited steps onto the property. The direction of the breeze shifted, and Micah got a lungful of her cloying perfume. "You know," she began, withdrawing a pair of oversized sunglasses from her bag, "you really should post a sign on the road to find this place. Luckily, I was able to ask a nice gentleman for directions about a mile back."

Micah frowned. The only property within a few miles of his was Callie's. However, he didn't have long to ponder over her words before they were interrupted.

A hummed melody floated on the breeze moments before Grace stepped out from behind the barn. She must have cut across the field from Callie's house because a few blades of prairie grass clung to her pants. Finn raced to greet her. A half-smile rested on her lips, and she raised a hand in greeting toward Micah but froze the moment she spotted Katrina.

"Grace! There you are," the woman said in her airy voice. Waving, she motioned for her to join them as her gaze dipped to

Grace's jeans and muddy boots. "Heavens, what are you wearing?"

At the woman's question, Grace's smile dimmed. Micah wanted to throttle this new stranger. She might look fancy in pressed trousers and a silky blouse, but if anyone looked out of place, it was her. Not Grace.

"Katrina, what are you doing here? Didn't you listen to my voicemails?" Grace's confused gaze shifted from Katrina to Micah.

"Just checking in. Someone had to after you'd nearly disappeared on us." The woman waved her off and made a show of studying the property.

Grace seemed to grow smaller beside her. Arms wrapped around her stomach, she looked the same as the day he'd confronted her in his kitchen. Like Finn, he stepped toward her, itching to comfort her distress.

Katrina's lips pulled into a slight frown as her gaze lingered on the barn and its faded paint. "Grace told me the place had seen better days in her report, and she wasn't kidding."

Micah told himself to brush off the remark. People had been saying things about his family and the ranch for years. This was no different.

"We're not interested in selling."

Her expression turned placating, each new mask more ingenuine than the last. "I can see why you might want to hold on to the place. All those memories, although the past has a way of haunting us if we let it. Isn't that right, Grace?"

Grace's face grew pink, and Micah clenched his mouth shut to keep from saying something he'd later regret. He refused to let his anger get the better of him. The quicker he could convince the woman to leave, the better for all of them.

"I'm sorry you drove all the way out here for nothing."

Katrina simpered, looking pleased with herself. "Oh, you misunderstand me, Mr. Prescott. We'll still honor our original price. After all, it's not the house we're after. A property of this size must extend well beyond the river. I've already spoken with one of your neighbors, a Mr. Flanagan, and he assures me the water rights are tied to the land."

So that was Jack's big plan—not a development but selling the valley's lifeblood to the highest bidder. Somehow, the truth didn't sit any easier with him, especially with the way Katrina was smiling at them.

Grace shifted beside him. She wasn't saying a word, and Micah couldn't blame her. Her boss seemed anything but friendly. Why she'd ever work for someone like that, he couldn't understand. But then again, they hadn't known each other for very long.

"Like I said, I'm not interested."

"Now, Micah. Can I call you Micah?" Katrina didn't wait for him to tell her no before continuing with her rehearsed speech. "My company is willing to pay handsomely for the place. More than enough to pay off your debts and start fresh."

He flinched. The only people he'd told about the loan were Caden, Callie, and now Grace. He trusted Callie and his cousin with his life, and Grace wouldn't have said anything, not after all they'd been through together.

Right?

He rested his hand on Grace's shoulder, hoping to calm the nervous energy he felt spilling from her small frame.

The woman's calculating gaze bounced between them, giving Micah the sense of a wolf zeroing in on its prey. Instead of dialing up her persuasion tactics, she surprised him and turned her attention to Grace.

"I'll be sure to tell the partners you were instrumental in trying to secure this deal. Whichever way this goes, the promotion is all but yours."

"Promotion?" Micah failed to restrain his shock.

Grace remained suspiciously quiet. He glanced down at her, and she seemed to be looking anywhere but at him. What exactly was happening?

Katrina's eyes rounded in surprise. "You didn't know?" She clicked her tongue like a mother hen. "Pity. I thought she'd have told you what with all the time you've been spending together. Anyway, I'm staying in town until tomorrow, in case you change your mind." She opened her car door and stepped inside, smiling. "Oh, and Grace, I look forward to seeing you in the office first thing Wednesday morning." She sent her a pointed look that seemed anything but friendly.

She disappeared in a cloud of dust, leaving Micah to pick up the pieces in her wake. Had he heard the woman correctly? Had Grace tricked him? And for a promotion, nonetheless.

"Tell me it's not true." He didn't want to believe a word of it, but what could Katrina possibly gain by lying? "Grace?"

At her down-turned expression, he knew he had his answer. Micah slid his hand from her shoulder and kneaded the back of his neck. "That's why you were asking about Jack the other day, wasn't it? To put a face to the name."

Her eyes rounded, and she shook her head. "No. I mean, yes, I thought the name sounded familiar. Someone else must have spoken with him about the deal before I joined, but it wasn't me. I must have read his name somewhere in the case file."

He couldn't believe he'd been so blind. *Of course* she'd known. She'd lied to him from the very beginning. Why was it so hard for him to accept the possibility that it had all been an act?

"And the rest? How did Katrina know about the loan?" It took an insurmountable effort to keep his tone as even as possible.

Grace's shoulders went rigid, and Finn nuzzled her leg with his nose to try to comfort her. "I don't know. Maybe she talked with someone in town or did her research before coming. The first day I was here, it was for work. How was I supposed to know how things would change between us once I'd gotten here?"

Micah couldn't believe this. After all this time, all these weeks of working side by side, she'd only been playing him. He'd been a fool to think Grace was on his side. "So, is that all this has been to you? Work?"

"Of course not. You know how I feel about you and this ranch." She reached out to touch him, but he stepped back.

For all he knew, it could have been part of the plan. Seduce the poor rancher into signing over his property. She and Katrina would have a good laugh and then move on.

The truth hit him in the chest like a full-grown ram until he could hardly breathe. "I barely know you, Grace. I thought I did, but we're nearly strangers."

He turned to leave and got as far as his parked truck when she called after him.

"You're so stubbornly attached to this land, it's clouding your judgment."

Swiveling on his heels, he retraced his steps until there was hardly a breath between them. "I'm stubborn?" he asked, struggling to keep a lid on the anger threatening to consume him. His temples pulsed, blood rushing in his ears.

"Yes." She stood to her full height, the top of her head barely reaching his chin.

Every harsh word and name he'd called himself over the years came flooding back all at once. Stubborn. Coward. Weak. Guilty. Nothing people said about him had been worse than what he'd already thought about himself, but Grace's betrayal stung the worst of all.

"Well, that may be, but at least I'm not afraid to fight for what I believe in." He watched her reaction, telling himself he didn't care when her eyes widened in shock before plowing ahead.

"I think you're perfectly content to waste time on other people's dreams rather than focus on your own. I think you're too afraid to step outside your comfort zone and take a chance, to really risk something for a change. Your shoes are rooted to the ground, Grace. And no matter how much you say you want to fly, you'll never do so much as walk if you don't pick up your feet and decide for yourself."

The moisture in her eyes was nearly his undoing.

Maybe he was like his dad after all. As much as he'd tried to keep his emotions in check these past fifteen years, all it had taken was one woman in a broken-down VW Bug to unravel his poorly woven safety net.

He didn't know which was worse: that Grace didn't agree with him or that she didn't defend herself.

His voice cracked as he laid bare his final question.

"What do you believe in, Grace? Because I don't even think you know."

CHAPTER

Twenty-Five

GRACE STORMED DOWN the driveway, ready to put as much distance between her and Micah as possible. She made a right at the corner and kept walking and didn't even stop to fish out the pebbles from her shoes.

After all this time, how could he accuse her of trying to sabotage him? Even from day one, she never would have stooped to such levels. That was Katrina's style, not hers.

A gust of wind tugged at her loose hair, tying it in knots at the nape of her neck. She fished around in her pockets for a hair tie but came up empty. Just as well. Her world was already falling apart. What were a few tangled ends in comparison?

She walked the two-mile stretch with nothing but her jumbled thoughts to keep her company.

Blisters bit at her heels by the time she reached the house. What she needed was a hot bath and some lavender-scented candles. And maybe some of Callie's healing ointment for her feet.

She paused at the top of the driveway, not ready to deal with Callie's questions, and forcefully drew in three calming breaths.

In and out. In and out...

Micah was right. She *was* afraid of taking risks. Callie was the brave one, going after her dreams without a second thought, and here she was, quite literally running away from the very things she'd grown to care about.

Namely, one specific person she'd come to care for.

Grace checked the mailbox before turning down the gravel drive and almost ran into the sedan parked at the entrance. Katrina.

Any hope vanished that her boss would head straight back to her hotel and leave her alone.

Grace looked up at the passing clouds and blew out a long breath. Could this day get any worse?

Inside, her stomach clenched the moment she heard Katrina's voice drift down the hall. An airy, high-pitched tone that reminded her of an adult trying to humor a child. Grace never knew if she was on the woman's good side or not, but after today's encounter, she was convinced it wasn't the former.

She took her time spreading the mail out on the dining table before dredging up the strength to face the woman a second time in less than an hour. Running a hand over her wrinkled shirt, she took a fortifying breath and stepped into the kitchen.

"Grace, there you are." Callie smiled as she reached for a plate from the cupboard. "Look who stopped by." True to form, she'd already made Katrina a cup of tea and, by the looks of it, was now trying to offer her one of the dandelion muffins.

While too polite to refuse, Katrina picked around the edges before turning to face Grace. "I figured you'd have to be staying somewhere near the ranch, and when I drove by here, I knew this had to be the place." She took a small sip of her tea and plastered on a smile. "I can see why you stayed away so long. It has such a lovely cottage feel."

Callie beamed at the woman's praise and passed her a jar of honey.

For the first time since meeting her, Grace wished Callie didn't always insist on seeing the best in people. Not everyone could be trusted, especially strangers.

Micah's harsh words came back to her. He'd trusted her, and despite her best intentions, she'd let him down. Maybe not directly, but she was the reason Katrina was here and sitting at the small table in Callie's kitchen.

Katrina stirred a spoonful of honey into her tea and took another small sip. Her face curved into the first genuine smile Grace had seen on her all day. "This is absolutely wonderful. Where do you buy your honey?"

Callie looked delighted. "Thanks, although it's the bees you should really be thanking. After all, they did the work."

Katrina's brow wrinkled in confusion, so Grace stepped in. "Callie has her own hives. It's really quite something. She's even starting her own business." If anything came from this visit, at least she could promote her friend's startup.

"Is that so?" Katrina's French-tipped fingernails clicked against the jar as she inspected the label. Her feigned interest shifted to approval. "I always admire a woman who's willing to take initiative. Good for you."

Callie fidgeted with the end of her braid as if unsure what to do with the praise, but after a few seconds, her face lit with an idea. "Grace, why don't you show your friend around the place? You could take her to the beehives and around the gardens."

"Me?" Grace shifted her wide eyes from Callie to Katrina and back. "I don't know. I'm sure she's tired after the long drive. And Callie, it's *your* house, after all. Not mine." Her stomach soured at the simple fact. Another reminder that she didn't truly belong here.

"Actually, that sounds like a wonderful idea. We can catch up while we walk." Katrina set down her cup and stood. "Where would you like to start, Grace?"

She'd been pinned into a corner and couldn't back out without offending someone. With no other option, Grace directed her boss toward the patio doors that lead out onto the herb garden. Callie gave her a thumbs up as the double doors closed behind them, leaving them alone to talk.

Against her better judgment, Grace showed her around the spacious backyard, pointing out the different flowers and medicinal plants that went into Callie's blends. Katrina listened without a word, her suspicious silence the only reply.

When they reached the edge of the garden, Grace stopped and looked back at the house to make sure Callie was out of earshot. She'd had enough of the veiled comments and politely worded barbs. She wanted answers. Now.

"How did you know about the loan, Katrina?" The question had been bugging her since her argument with Micah. It was enough that he thought she'd betrayed his trust. He might never listen to her, but she had to find a way to prove her innocence.

Katrina's face went slack with surprise before settling into a calculated grin. "Oh, that was pure coincidence, really." She waved her hand as if brushing off an invisible honeybee. "Like I said earlier, I talked with one of the other landowners. When I told him I was coming here next, he was all too happy to fill me in on a few details." Unconcerned, she reached for a nearby rose and closed her eyes as she took a deep breath.

Grace's body tensed despite the calming scents that encircled her. "I don't want the promotion, Katrina. Not like this."

Katrina let go of the flower, the pink and white petals swaying back into place. "Good. Because you're not getting it."

Grace froze, struggling to find the right words. "But back at the ranch you said—"

"I was trying to make a sale, Grace. Something you should have managed in the three weeks you've been up here."

Grace tried not to cringe at the harshness in Katrina's voice. For years, she'd learned to brush it off, but something in her refused to back down now. "You know I couldn't leave. Not with the bridge out."

Katrina raised a single eyebrow. "Seemed to be in perfect working order when I drove here."

Grace couldn't argue the facts, but that did little to alleviate the growing tightness at the back of her throat. "He'll never agree to it." At least she had that knowledge to ease her conscience.

Katrina seemed unconcerned by the threat and began to walk back toward the house. "Give it a few weeks, tops. Once he realizes this is too good a deal to pass up, he'll call."

"What makes you so sure?"

Her eyes got that dangerous look in them, like when she was closing in on a client, and Grace didn't like it one bit. "Every man has his price."

Once they were back inside, Callie invited Katrina to stay for lunch, but she declined the offer. "Lots of work to do and contracts to draft up," she'd said, pinning Grace with a look before saying her goodbyes.

Grace didn't breathe a sigh of relief until the sound of the engine faded into the distance.

"Did you have a nice time catching up?" Callie asked as she chopped vegetables for a salad.

Grace didn't want to worry her friend, so she pasted on a flat smile and stepped in to help. "It was fine. A little unexpected, but I suppose I have been gone for a while." She crumbled a square of feta over the leafy spinach and watched as it broke into a hundred pieces with such little effort. *Just like my life.*

"Must be nice to have someone who cares enough to check in on you like that." Callie's curls bounced as she whisked together the oil and vinegar. Once combined, she poured the dressing over the salad and dished out two platefuls. She handed one to Grace. "I'm sure people back home miss you. I know I would."

Callie's admission was like a comforting blanket on a cold day. But the reality was anything but. In truth, she had precious few friends. She knew for certain Katrina's visit wasn't out of concern but had more to do with the company's bottom line.

Callie was the one true friend she could count on—the closest thing to a sister she'd ever had.

Grace speared a forkful of lettuce but tasted nothing other than grass.

Her continued presence here would only bring more heartache. She knew that now. She'd already ruined things between her and Micah. She'd never forgive herself if she got in the way of Callie's happiness as well. After all, Caden was Micah's cousin. Sooner or later, he'd have to pick a side, and knowing Callie, she'd get caught in the middle.

Grace swallowed, her throat constricting around the lump of spinach as it went down.

Of all the days, why did Katrina have to come now? A few moments of happiness was all she wanted, but even that seemed too much to hope for.

Grace zipped her suitcase shut with a finality that made her heart ache.

What had she been thinking? With so much water under the bridge, how could she ever have hoped she and Micah might have a future together? So why did his rejection still sting so much? She'd wanted to tell Micah that none of Katrina's accusations were true, that she hadn't sold him out. But she knew he wouldn't listen.

She brushed her sleeve against her face and it came back wet.

No. It would be better for everyone if she left. It didn't matter that her car was still at Tony's. She'd call an Uber and pray it wouldn't cost half a month's salary to get her back home.

Home. She stilled at the thought. Where was that, exactly? Physically, it was her small studio apartment back in Denver, but her heart had never truly been there. She'd lost that sense of belonging the day her parents died, and she'd been searching for it ever since. For a blessed moment, she'd almost found it here, but she'd ruined that chance just like all the others.

Back in her slacks and ridiculous heels, Grace folded the clothes Callie had lent her and laid them on the bed. The letter sat on top, a far easier way to say goodbye than to face the tears.

A clean break. That's what they all needed.

Grace reached for the wooden knitting needles and ball of yarn left on the chair. The green wool had grown dingy with dirt, and the end was frayed from where Olive had chewed on it.

She managed a wobbly smile.

Before she left, she had one more item to take care of. As much as Micah must hate her right now, she couldn't leave without seeing their lamb one last time. She'd cut through the forest like before and be in and out before anyone knew she was there.

Then she'd be on her way.

Grace slipped through the garden and followed the trail by heart until she reached the edges of the meadow. It was getting late, and the sun had already begun to set behind the mountains. Like the first time, she paused, her brain telling her to keep going, but her feet refused to budge.

Maybe this was a bad idea. After all, Micah made it clear by the way he'd stormed off that he never wanted to see her again. But what bothered her the most, above all the distrust and hurt in his eyes, was his parting question.

What do you believe in, Grace?

He'd seen through her outer confidence to the scared girl within, stirring up all the old fears and questions she'd buried long ago.

For years, she'd been searching for something secure to hold onto—a *true north*, so to speak. But every time she felt she was getting closer, life dealt her another blow.

She slumped against a nearby tree and sank to the ground. Cool earth met her fingertips as she ran them through the dirt, stopping only when she reached the tree's roots. For decades, this tree had probably watched over the meadow, witnessing the changing seasons. Everything about it represented what Grace was not. Solid. Steady. Unmoving.

Trust in Me.

Like a whisper carried by the wind, the voice spoke straight to her heart. Closing her eyes, she listened as the leaves rustled above her—speaking in hushed tones—and waited to hear it once again.

Slowly, as if reluctant, a memory surfaced. Two smiling faces, her playing in the grass, a summer breeze that made the flowers dance in the garden. Nothing special, just an ordinary Saturday in the backyard. But the love in her parents' eyes made it the most important thing in the world.

Another gust blew through the branches, interrupting the scene. But that sense of belonging remained.

Her old life might be gone, but there was Someone else who'd always be with her.

Looking up again, Grace studied the tree more closely, noticing the intricate pattern of the bark. If God could make something so simple seem so beautiful, what might He do in her own life if she let Him? Maybe that meant she needed to trust Him enough to leave and start over. However much it might hurt, she could trust the unseen plan.

Something rustled in the tall grasses, and she looked away from the swaying branches. A flicker of movement caught her eye as a shadow disappeared behind a copse of trees in the middle of the field.

"Finn?" She listened for the dog's excited yip.

Nothing.

Grace pushed to her feet and stepped out into the last rays of sunshine. She paused on the edge of the meadow and listened. Only the wind seemed to stir the blades of grass. Despite wearing her sweater, a slight chill crept up her arms and down her spine.

Someone, or something, was watching her.

All reason told her to turn around and head back to Callie's, grab her bags, and get as far away from here as possible. But she couldn't. She needed to call Micah and warn him. It wasn't that long ago that Olive's mom had been attacked by the river, and apparently another rancher had lost a few head of cattle. What if whatever had attacked those animals was back? Or worse, if it wasn't alone?

Grace reached for her back pocket, only to realize she'd left her phone at the house. Just as well. No matter how well-intentioned her call might be, she was probably the last person he wanted to hear from right now. Especially if she was wrong.

She continued to watch, yet still, nothing moved.

Grace relaxed. The likelihood of whatever was out there having seen her by now was high, but so far, nothing had happened. Maybe she was overreacting. It could have easily been a bird or even a fox that had startled her.

Curiosity won out, and she put one foot in front of the other. She was careful not to stir the ground cover, so as not to scare off whatever animal was hiding. A woodsy scent tickled her nose as she drew closer, something musty and herbaceous that wafted on the feeble breeze.

The ground dipped toward a small spring, the bushy alders forming a screen around the protected alcove.

There couldn't have been a worse time for Grace to have changed back into her heels. Not wanting to risk a twisted ankle, she slipped each foot from the leather straps and left her shoes at the top of the rise.

The smell grew stronger, and she choked back a cough. Cigarette smoke tinged the air. Unless a fox had recently picked up the habit, someone was hiding in the trees less than ten feet in front of her. And knowing Micah's opinion on smoking, it wasn't him or Caden.

A voice inside her screamed to get out of there. Praying she hadn't been seen yet, she took a few cautious steps backward through the weeds. Something sharp stabbed the underside of her arch, and she yelped, breaking the silence.

A hooded figure raced from the thicket. "Hey!" she shouted, reaching out to stop whoever it was. But the person knocked her over in their rush to escape. Pulse racing, she pushed herself up from the ground as they sprinted toward the road.

She could have followed, but they were already too far away. Even if she tried, there'd be no way to catch up to the person in bare feet.

A trickle of something warm ran down her arm. The sleeve of her sweater was torn, and she lifted her arm to inspect the small gash from her fall. Drawing a tissue from her pocket, she applied some pressure until the bleeding stopped.

As she lowered the red-stained tissue, something small and white caught her attention. Unprepared for any more surprises, she paused before searching through the grass and lifting a smoldering cigarette from the brush. White, with blue wings printed across the top—the same kind Micah had found earlier by the fence line.

Grace's stomach dropped. Micah was right, someone had been sneaking around the place. But why?

Snapping her head up, she looked in the direction the man had come from, and her breath hitched.

Beyond the trees and across the field rose a few wisps of smoke.

CHAPTER

Twenty-Six

MICAH STOOD AT the fence to the upper pasture and surveyed what was soon to be his remaining flock. Freshly shorn, they appeared smaller, making them look all the more vulnerable.

He'd put Violet with the sheep set for tomorrow's sale while Fiona stood guard a few yards in the distance. So far, they'd yet to have any more suspicious incidents, but he wouldn't be able to relax until he knew they were in the clear with the bank.

He brushed a hand through his hair and sighed.

There were so many things he wished he could change. For starters, he'd take back every harsh word he'd said to Grace yesterday. Even if she had told Katrina about the loan, it was hardly a secret. And the promotion? He couldn't think of a person who was a harder worker or deserved it more.

He knew things could never be the same between them, not after the way he'd treated her, but he needed to try and set things right.

Fiona's chatter drew Micah's attention back to the field. Agitated, she paced toward the house, stopping at the fence. Ears up and forward, she scanned the fields like a sentinel. All of a sudden, the alpaca made a screeching sound that pierced the calm silence.

Micah's hands flew to his ears. "What on God's green earth?" He turned his back on the animal to drown out the high-pitched noise.

Even Finn went on high alert, the coarse hair along his spine having gone rigid.

The sound lasted for about five seconds before Micah could finally breathe another sigh of relief, but the tension in his chest remained.

Turning back, he followed the track of Fiona's gaze and froze.

Oh, no. His stomach dropped. What looked to be a gray cloud rose from the valley below, carrying with it the faintest scent of smoke.

Not again.

With Finn hot on his heels, he scrambled to the top of the hill and looked down in horror. Black smoke rose from the second-story hayloft, engulfing the barn in a cloud of charcoal mist. In an instant, he was eighteen again, watching everything go up in flames.

God, help us.

He raced down the hill as fast as his feet would carry him, all the while praying for a miracle.

A wave of heat hit him as he reached the open yard, the dry hay and wool already fueling the growing blaze. He couldn't stop to dwell on the fact that it was as good as lost already. If he didn't hurry, they could very well lose more than a stocked barn.

Caden and Callie were already running between the house and the barn with buckets of water in hand, the small amount of liquid doing little to fight the growing flames.

This was exactly how it had happened last time. Their families had set up a bucket brigade, but not before the fire spread to the rest of the valley. By then, families up and down the river were calling in for backup, and soon only Micah, his dad, and Callie's uncle remained. No one had expected the fire to reach the natural gas line, but when it had, the explosion was deafening.

Micah had survived with only a laceration to the head and a few cracked ribs, but the others weren't so lucky.

The next year, he'd expanded the hydroelectric system to replace the gas line all together.

He stopped Callie before she ran past with another empty bucket and pulled her a safe distance from the flames.

She struggled, but he held her firmly in place. "Micah, of all the stupid—"

"That's not going to work."

Caden raced up beside them. "What do you suggest we do, then?"

Micah looked from the barn to the road that went to the river. He wasn't exactly sure how far of a distance it was—one thousand feet. Maybe more. It would be a long shot, but it was the best option they had. "Find every hose you can. We can disconnect the generator and direct the water up straight from the river."

"Do you think we'll have enough for that?" Caden asked, voicing Micah's concerns.

"I don't know, but it's worth a try."

Nodding, Caden raced toward the river while Callie made for the storage shed, her flaming red hair trailing behind her.

While the other two were busy, Micah quickly ducked into the smoky interior to free the horses. Once he knew they were safe, he'd move onto the sheep pens at the rear of the barn.

Already, smoke had begun to fill the cavernous interior. Reaching Dune's stall first, Micah held his breath as he fumbled with the latch. After a few tries, he managed to unlock it as Dune bolted through the open door, nearly trampling Micah in his escape. Choking back the smoke, he moved to the next stall, where Roper stamped the earth with his front hooves.

"I'm working as fast as I can, boy." The latch clicked, and he swung open the door. He had to coax the large animal out, and once Roper was clear of the door, he took off at a sprint.

Micah raced after him through the doors, inhaling a lungful of fresh air the moment he was outside.

Finn barked at him as he emerged, the dog's excited yelps turning to a whine as Micah marched by. He was halfway to the pens when Grace stumbled into the yard. Hair a mess, and what looked to be a bloodstain on her sweater, she looked as if she'd fought off a coyote.

Panic clawed inside him. "Grace? Are you okay? What happened?"

From the way she was panting, she must have run there. And with bare feet, nonetheless. She bypassed the first question and went straight to the second. "I ran into someone fleeing your property. *And* I found this." She fished around in the pocket of her soiled pants and shoved the cigarette into his hands. "I saw the smoke and came as fast as I could." Bending over, she held her side and took a few steadying breaths.

He frowned at the familiar label. His hopes that it had been an accident evaporated, but right now, it didn't matter how the fire had started, only that they got it out in time.

"Are you sure you're okay?" He scanned the rest of her, noticing every stain, scrape, and tear of fabric from where she'd stumbled.

"I'm fine." She released her hand from her waist and stood as if to prove herself. "Really, I'm okay. What can I do to help?"

Something welled inside him. For a second, he forgot about the barn and the sheep until their loud bleats punctuated the air. Before he could respond, Grace took off for the pens, her mind as much on the animals as his had been moments earlier.

Despite her lead, he reached the gate first and flung it open.

"We're letting them run loose?" she asked as sheep flooded the yard and adjacent open field.

Micah watched as the sheep funneled through the open gate, taking the ranch's future with them. "We can round them up later, but for now, they need to get as far away from here as possible." As did the two of them, but he wouldn't leave until he could ensure that everyone was safe.

It took a while for the two of them to encourage the last of the sheep from their pens, by which time Caden and Callie had returned with every hose and scrap of tubing on the property. Callie had uncovered an old garden nozzle, which she affixed to the end, and soon, they had a thousand-foot-long fire hose trained on the barn.

The air grew thicker with smoke by the minute, and a layer of ash already dusted the ground.

Micah watched the final sheep race through the gate. His eyes were watering, and his throat burned, but at least they'd managed to free all the animals.

Grace was busy herding a few stragglers as far away from the barn as possible when her eyes went wide. Frantically, she scanned the yard until she pinned Micah with a pain-stricken expression. "Where's Olive? I don't see her."

Micah stopped what he was doing and looked around the yard. No sign of the green sweater. That's when he remembered the last pen on the other side of the barn. In their hurry, he'd forgotten all about it. "Grace, stay here. I'll go get her."

He hopped over the fence in one fluid motion and started to round the barn.

Just then, there was a loud explosion of shattering glass. Micah turned in time to see another window blow out of the barn. Angry tongues of fire spilled from the opening and up the sides, black trails following in their wake.

Micah couldn't look away as the fire consumed the old wooden barn. It was mesmerizing in a horrific sort of way, and he knew in that moment there would be no saving it.

He shielded his face as another window shattered, barely registering the shards of glass that bit into the backs of his arms. Something firm curled over his shoulder and yanked. He stumbled backward and fell right into Caden.

"It's not working. The fire's too out of control to put it out." Sweat trailed in rivulets down his cousin's ash-covered skin, revealing the red flush beneath. He heaved in one breath after another, and he looked ready to bolt like Dune had.

Micah had never seen his cousin so spooked. "It's only a barn," he tried reassuring him, but even he heard how insignificant those words sounded as the structure burned beside them. Everything he'd worked for was literally going up in smoke, and he didn't know if he had enough fight left in him to start over again.

The ringing in his ears finally subsided, and he turned around to take one last look. Charred debris littered the yard as the flames grew higher, engulfing the entire hayloft in a single terrifying blaze. Smoke poured out the open double doors, casting a shadow over the entire scene.

Callie was busy manning the hose, the single stream of water doing little to keep the fire at bay. But Grace was nowhere to be seen.

"Where's Grace?" he asked Caden. Last he'd seen her, she'd been asking about Olive, and then there'd been the explosion.

Micah's gut clenched.

Without thinking, he charged toward the inferno, Caden's raised voice fading behind him as he plunged into the fire in search of Grace.

The heat was unbearable. Grace could feel the sweat pouring down her face as she struggled to find her way through the smoke and debris. She could barely see anything through the glowing haze, but she knew she had to find Olive before it was too late.

"Come on, come on," she whispered, her heart racing with every step. Fallen timbers and smoke clouded her vision, and soon she was lost in a maze inside the barn.

Suddenly, she heard Micah through the thick smoke.

"Grace! Grace, where are you?" His voice was ragged and strained, but it gave her hope.

"I'm over here!" she yelled back, hoping he could hear her. Something like burning hair stung her nostrils, and she fought the urge to scream.

They called to each other through the chaos, their voices piercing the wall of fire until he emerged through the smoke. His arms wrapped around her in a tight embrace, and she nearly collapsed into him, dark streaks of soot marring his light blue shirt.

"We have to get out of here!" he yelled over the roaring flames.

There was a loud crack above them as a beam collapsed a few yards away, sending a shower of sparks in their direction.

Grace shook her head, the pressure pounding against her skull with every movement. "Not without Olive."

"There isn't time, Grace." His voice shook as the orange glow cast flickering shadows across his face. His hands dropped to her shoulders, refusing to let her go.

She fought every urge to cling to his solid strength in the middle of that burning building. But the longer she took, the greater the chance she'd never find the lamb.

"Please, Micah."

A coughing fit interrupted her argument, and she felt him scoop her into his arms. Her legs too weak to stand, she didn't protest as he lifted her from the ground and held her against his chest. Her vision grew blurry, and black spots threatened to snuff out the blazing inferno around them. She'd been in here for too long, her lungs starved of fresh air and polluted with smoke.

"Stay with me, Grace." Micah's plea echoed in her ears as another beam cracked in the rafters, causing another shower of embers to rain on top of them. Smoke and flames engulfed them like in a nightmare.

Her body jostled against his as he maneuvered them around fallen timbers back toward the barn's entrance.

Either an eternity or a minute later, he lowered her onto soft grass. The cold air was like a shock to the system, and shivers overtook her without Micah's warmth. She pried her eyes open, squinting against the grit caught in them as a flash of light blue disappeared within the barn's glow.

The fire's orange glow cast eerie shadows across the ground, engulfing the building in flames. She could hear Finn barking somewhere in the distance, only to be drowned out again by a loud hissing sound. She looked over to see Caden and Callie fighting the flames with a hose, but Micah was nowhere to be seen.

She tried to call after him, but another round of coughs overtook her. Throat burning, she dragged in another wheezy breath.

The inferno flamed to life, growing ever brighter as it consumed the barn. Grace watched in horror, and in an instant, she was taken back to that night—twin headlights heading straight for their car, the collision, waking up alone in the hospital.

The flames crackled, and the heat bore down on her in the open field.

The mental fog began to clear, bringing with it the sickening realization of where Micah was. Pushing up from the ground, she stumbled toward the smoldering building. Voices called out behind her, but she didn't stop. She couldn't lose another person she loved. Not again.

The bright flames against the inky sky made it difficult to see. A few yards from the entrance, Grace tripped over a piece of splintered wood and pitched forward, shards of glass biting into her hands and bare feet. There was a muffled cry; hers or someone else's, she wasn't sure. She blinked, trying to make sense of the dancing shadows before her. Sparks flew as the barn door gave way, and someone staggered out.

She hardly registered the stinging in her feet as she took a few steps forward, hope rising as the form began to take shape.

"Micah!"

He turned his head, and their eyes locked. He was covered in soot from head to toe, but he was alive. And he held something clutched to his chest.

A wave of relief flooded through her.

Micah rushed to her side, shielding the blackened lamb as he ran. His rough and blistered hand wrapped around hers, and he pulled her away from the barn as a final sickening crash echoed behind them.

CHAPTER

Twenty-Seven

FOR THE SECOND time in his life, Micah stared at the burnt shell of the barn—the same charred remains, the same stench of firewood and smoldering hay permeating the air. Even the brilliant sunrise beyond the smoky haze reminded him of last time.

By God's grace, they'd contained the fire to only the barn. And while it meant he'd have to rebuild it yet again, the rest of his world hadn't gone up in smoke along with it.

This time, he hadn't lost those closest to him.

To his surprise, Frank had shown up with nearly half the valley in tow. With everyone's help, they'd managed to put out the last of the fire, but not before the entire structure had been lost. Now, they were busy rounding up the sheep he and Grace had released last night. The old paddocks were a jumbled mess, but one of Frank's men had brought enough fencing wire to cordon off a section of the upper pasture as a temporary holding pen. Even Pauline had come, bringing enough coffee and food from the café to feed a small army.

Beside him, Caden lowered the phone and spoke. "That was Frank's brother-in-law. He's a couple of hours out and wants to know if we'll have the sheep ready by then. He heard about the fire."

Who hadn't? It seemed everyone was either already here or had called, asking how they could help. Micah couldn't believe the outpouring of support this community had shown in the past twelve hours. He didn't deserve it, but he appreciated it more than they'd ever know.

"Tell him we'll be ready when he gets here." Barely, but one look at the crowded makeshift pens told him they were nearly there.

Caden nodded and repeated the message into the phone.

While his cousin sorted out the details, Micah took a break from combing through the debris to watch the others work. He hadn't asked for their help, yet here they all were, rounding up sheep by whatever means necessary.

He smiled as the memory of Grace trying to shoo the creatures away from the gate came to mind. Caked in mud and dressed in those overalls, she'd been a sight to behold.

Micah squinted against the sun, hoping for another glimpse of that pink sweater.

"Looking for someone?" Caden had hung up and was watching Micah with a slightly amused expression.

"What? No."

His smile widened. "It's Grace, isn't it?"

Not that it was any of Caden's business. However, he had a way of inserting himself into the middle of everything.

"She's ... been a big help." It wasn't what he'd planned to say. Far from it. But what could he say? Everything was so complicated between the ranch, the fire, the loan, and his budding feelings for Grace. He sighed, knowing it was useless to lie to Caden. "She's leaving." That was the truth. It didn't matter how he felt. He had to accept the situation for what it was and be content with what he had.

Caden gave him a knowing smirk. "You love her, and you know it."

"Said the kettle to the pot."

His cousin gave him a friendly shove, chuckling beside him. "Fair enough." There was a moment of silence as they stood side by side, surveying the ranch. "So, what now?"

In the distance, the flock grazed peacefully in the fields. Despite being relocated, they seemed somehow unshaken by the events of last night. The sheep followed his and the other's instructions with blind trust, even though they had ample reason to question their security.

"The fire stole my last chance of proving to the bank that I'm not a risky investment. Not to mention the hay and wool that burned along with it. The sheep sale will cover a portion of the loan, but unless you've got another thirty thousand dollars lying around somewhere ..." Micah released a dry laugh, trying not to lose it with their neighbors present.

"So, that's it? We're just going to give up?"

Micah ran a hand through his hair, the grit from last night scraping against his fingernails. "I don't know." Oh, there were options, all right. But he cringed at what they might cost him.

Caden clapped a hand on Micah's back in a show of support. "Whatever happens, we'll figure it out together."

Micah returned the gesture, his chest expanding at his cousin's show of support. He knew Caden had been thinking about staying, but he hadn't let himself believe it until now.

Movement near the house caught his attention, and he saw Frank talking with Pauline. She turned in their direction, and the man made a beeline for Micah and Caden, the downward curve of his mouth putting Micah back on edge.

"Frank, what's up?"

A cloud of black dust settled at the man's feet as he pinned his gaze on them. "Either of you drive a brown-and-white Ford Bronco?"

They shook their heads in unison.

"That's what I thought. One of my men found it tucked behind some trees away from the road. Abandoned, from the looks of it." Face somber, Frank reached inside his jacket and handed Micah a small blue and white box. "This was in the grass, not too far from the vehicle. Last I knew, neither of you smoked."

Micah stared at the half-empty box of cigarettes, the memories of last night flooding back. He fished around in his pocket and withdrew the cigarette Grace had given him.

Flipping open the lid, he tipped the box over and slid the contents of it into his palm. It was a perfect match.

Another memory flashed before him. Fifteen years ago, his dad smoking behind the barn after another one of their fights. A truck pulling into the yard and a rough, familiar voice. He'd only caught a glimpse of the dingy Bronco driving off a half hour later and the pile of white cigarette butts left behind. In that entire time, his dad hadn't left the barn.

And a few minutes later, the hayloft had been in flames.

Frank's bushy eyebrows drew together as if drawing a similar conclusion, and he tipped his cowboy hat in thought. "Come to think of it, Jack used to drive a Bronco. Haven't seen it in years, but it had a similar look to it."

Micah looked at Caden, whose clenched jaw matched his. "Grace said she saw someone running from the ranch as the fire started. You think that could have been him?"

He scratched at his mustache and frowned. "Hard to tell. That man can be a right pain to work with sometimes, but I can't imagine how he'd be mixed up in something like this."

Neither could Micah, but he couldn't ignore the facts. Someone had been trespassing on the ranch for weeks. There was the cut fence line and the matching cigarette butts. He didn't know why, but it all fit. "Has anybody seen him?"

Frank stopped fidgeting with the brim of his hat and directed his steady gaze at the two of them. From the tensed wrinkles around his eyes, it wasn't good news. "I tried calling him while driving here, but he never answered."

Micah's pulse sped up. The headache that had been building since last night now pounded against his temples. "We need to find Jack." To set the story straight and prove them wrong or find the truth. Either way, Micah was left with no other option but to go searching for the man he'd spent half a lifetime avoiding. And this time, he'd settle things once and for all.

Micah nudged his heels against Roper's sides, scanning the fields for anything out of the ordinary. Caden rode beside him, reigning in Dune's nervous energy. The fire had spooked the horses, but they were their best shot at finding Jack across the few hundred acres of pasture and shrubs.

Frank and a few of his men had gone back for their own horses, leaving the two cousins to begin the search over an hour ago.

"I could eat an entire batch of Callie's dandelion muffins right about now." Caden held the reins with one hand and rubbed a circle across his flat stomach with the other.

Micah groaned. He didn't even want to think about food right now. Sleep-deprived and bleary-eyed, nothing sounded better than a warm shower and a pillow to crash his head on. Every inch of his body ached, and his lungs still burned from breathing in smoke fumes all night.

"You sure he's still out here?" Caden had been the first to start saddling up the horses the moment Frank organized the search party, but he had to be getting tired as well.

"His car is here, and he couldn't have gotten too far on foot." They'd already found his cigarette in the field—a veritable needle in a haystack. A man should be much easier to find. At least, that's what he'd thought. So far, they'd searched the field between his and Callie's place where Grace had first run into the man. Then they'd slowly made their way toward the river, but still no sign of him.

Micah was beginning to worry this had been a fool's errand. Maybe he should have stayed with the flock to make sure they were all right. Frank's brother-in-law would be arriving shortly and would expect him to be there.

Finn's black-and-white body darted between the trees ahead of them, ears alert to every sound along the river's reedy banks. A few times, he'd broken the silence with his loud barking, but each had been a false alarm.

Water splashed across the smooth river rocks, the constant chatter working to soothe his runaway thoughts. Another cool breeze rustled through the changing leaves, and he drank in a deep breath.

Finn's low growl snapped him back to attention. Pulling on the reins, Micah came to a stop and motioned for Caden to do the same. He'd lost sight of the dog, but another guttural sound drew his focus toward the northern bank of the river.

Micah dismounted. Watching the twigs and loose rocks at his feet, he took a few steps toward the sounds. Caden stopped a couple feet behind him and lowered himself from Dune in the same quiet manner.

Finn's growling stopped, and for a moment, Micah wondered if it hadn't been yet another squirrel or stay rabbit.

But then, something moved.

Finn lunged forward behind a giant boulder, releasing a series of barks, and a man dressed in jeans and a black hoodie came bolting from his hiding spot.

"Finn. Look back." Micah shouted the familiar command, and Finn raced toward the edge of the water.

The man ducked when he saw Micah and Caden, then swerved around them out of reach.

Micah let out a loud whistle, and Finn responded by moving in a counterclockwise circle, driving the man toward him and Caden. The dog nipped at the man's heels, herding him toward a cluster of dense oak brush.

Voices rose in the distance. The others must have heard the commotion, and after a few seconds, five men on horseback crested the hill, blocking the man's escape.

The man stuttered to a stop, head moving back and forth with jerky movements, searching for a way out.

Finn remained on point as the men drew in closer, closing the circle until there was no way he could slip out.

"That'll do, Finn."

As if a switch had flipped, the dog pivoted and raced back toward Micah, grinning with self-satisfaction.

"You okay, boys?" Frank spoke from atop his gray-and-white quarter horse. He made it clear by their very presence that he and his men were there to help, but this was Micah's to deal with as he saw fit.

Micah nodded his appreciation and approached the man from behind. He stopped a few feet away and waited for him to turn around and face him.

Slowly, two leathery hands reached up and pulled down the hood, and Jack Flanagan stared back at him.

The years had been harsher on him than he'd realized. The past faded as Micah looked into the man's wide eyes. Guilt was written all over his face, from the furtive glances around the circle to the pale color of his skin, and Micah knew they'd found their man.

All the arguments he'd rehearsed faded away, and the two of them stood there in silence. Every slowing heartbeat reverberated through Micah's body, a drummer's march drawing him toward the truth. But now that it was within reach, he couldn't convince his feet to move the final few steps. Heart racing, the events of last night and fifteen years ago blurred into one.

You were the one who drove your dad to smoke behind the barn that day. You were the reason he was flustered and careless enough to catch the hayloft on fire. You're the reason your dad and Callie's uncle aren't here anymore.

It was nearly too much to handle as his past fears collided with the present. He tried to shove them down like he always had, but they refused to be silenced any longer.

The lies he'd spent fifteen years telling himself flew at him from all angles and fell limp at his feet as he stood beside the rushing river. His entire life had been driven by those accusations: staying behind, taking over the ranch, living in isolation as he slowly worked to atone for his sins.

His sins. Or so he'd always thought. The past decade and a half he'd been trying to earn the town's, and ultimately God's, forgiveness. He'd never paused to think there might have been another way forward until now.

Jack shuffled his feet, the rustling of dry leaves catching Micah's attention again. All the fight seemed to drain out of the man, and after a few awkward moments, he finally spoke. "I can't lose it all. It's no excuse for the things I've done, but you have to understand, I was going to lose everything."

"What are you talking about?" Micah barked. At Jack's flinch, he clamped his mouth shut before he said anything else to make the man clam up.

After a few painfully silent moments, Jack muttered something under his breath that Micah didn't quite catch.

"Out with it, Jack," Frank spoke in a commanding voice. He and the other men had dismounted their horses and stood shoulder-to-shoulder, blocking any chance of an escape.

The old man seemed to sense as much and sighed, his shoulders slumping in defeat. He turned to face Micah and Caden, but his eyes remained focused on the trees behind them as he spoke. "Last year, I made the mistake of investing some of the town's funds in a new development. I invested myself and put my ranch up as collateral, thinking it was a safe bet, but then it fell apart. It wasn't like I could tell anyone, but it was only a matter of time before someone found out. Then a few months back, some company reached out to me. They said they were willing to buy my land, no questions asked. I thought this was my way out, to fix the situation before anyone else knew. But that all came crashing down the moment you turned down their offer."

Micah stared at him, more confused than ever.

Jack peered over at Frank, who was watching him like a hawk, and sighed. "It was an all-or-nothing deal. Get all the properties along the river to sign over their water rights, convince people it was in their best interests to sell."

Micah understood the unspoken admission, *by whatever means necessary.* "The hole in the fence and the generator. That was you?"

Jack nodded, his head dipping with the weight of his confession. "Not my finest moments. I figured you'd cut your losses and move on. I never thought it'd come to this..."

Micah's chest grew tight. He tried to shake it off, but the sensation grew until he could no longer fight it. He had the right to be angry with this man, to hold him accountable for all the pain he'd put him and everyone else through just like he'd blamed himself all these years. But no matter how much he wanted to judge him, see him brought to justice for his actions, he couldn't bring himself to do so. He'd spent too many years harboring unforgiveness and lingering bitterness toward others who had wronged him in his life. And maybe he wouldn't always be quick to forgive, but he could be slow to anger. Show mercy instead of wrath. And that could start now— when he had every right and reason to do the opposite.

As Micah studied the man's slumped shoulders and face twisted in grief, a sense of overwhelming calm washed over him.

"I forgive you." The words came easily, the last bit of his anger falling to the ground in surrender. He'd spent too long holding onto guilt and resentment. He didn't want to waste another day beneath that weight.

Jack stared back at him, his mouth going slack. "Why?" he croaked out, his voice cracking on the single word. Moisture clung to the corners of his eyes, and he dropped his gaze once more. "I don't deserve your forgiveness."

And that was it. It was as if God were speaking to Micah right there along the riverbank. Micah didn't deserve His forgiveness any more than Jack deserved his, but God, in His mercy, had already given it to him a long time ago. All this time, he'd been too blinded by his pride to see it until now.

"I forgive you, Jack." Micah spoke the words with more confidence this time. In a moment of clarity, he saw himself in the man—the bitterness, the fear, the willingness to do anything to protect what was his—and knew if he didn't make a change, he'd end up just like him.

Not anymore.

Neither Frank nor Caden questioned him as they led Jack away. It didn't matter if they understood. And maybe they never would. But for the first time in years, Micah felt as if he were finally free.

The man went willingly toward the horses, where they all saddled up to take him back to the house.

He didn't want to end up like Jack. And if that meant letting go of his sense of control and trusting God with the future, he would. It wasn't giving up but rather giving in to the embrace of the Good Shepherd. He didn't need to keep running anymore, because he'd already been found.

CHAPTER

Twenty-Eight

MICAH DOUBLE-CHECKED the latch of the livestock trailer, satisfied that the sheep were secure and had ample food and water for the trip to their new home. He hated to see any of them go but knew this was the right decision.

Frank's brother-in-law Davis came around the truck and joined him at the back. "Thanks for all the help."

Between the Levis, boots, and brand new Stetson, he could have posed for *Western Horseman*, or any other cowboy magazine for that matter. Newly retired, he'd told Micah how he'd decided to follow his dream and switch out engineering for ranching and had purchased a plot of land down by Montrose a few hours' drive west.

The man was friendly enough and, despite his lack of experience, seemed to have a good head on his shoulders. Micah immediately felt comfortable with his amiable smile and relaxed demeanor. "It's me who should be thanking you."

Micah no longer worried about the money. The fire had seen to that. There wasn't much more he could do to save the ranch, even with the sale, but that didn't matter. The support he'd received from friends and strangers in the past twelve hours filled his soul in a way he never would have expected.

"I know it came together fast, but I appreciate it all the same. I'm awfully sorry to hear about your barn, though. And to think it was deliberate." Davis closed his eyes and shook his head at the thought. His sincere gaze drifted over the blackened remains of the building and back to Micah. "Was anything else damaged in the fire? I hope no one was hurt."

Micah breathed in a lungful of air, the smell of smoke almost forgotten. "Luckily, the barn was all we lost."

Davis seemed relieved to hear it. After a few beats of silence, he bobbed his head as if sealing the matter. "Well, if you need anything, and I mean it, don't hesitate to ask. I may be retired, but I still know a few people who could help you rebuild." He extended a beefy hand, which Micah took.

As Micah stepped back, a thought suddenly came to him. "Actually, can you drop something off in town for me?"

The man shrugged. "Sure thing."

He left Davis by the truck and ducked into the house. He returned a minute later and handed over a crisp manila envelope.

"This it?" The man raised his eyebrows in question.

Micah nodded. God had given him this ranch to watch over years ago, and he'd been trying to hold on to it with clenched fists ever since. Like a man who buries his treasure in a field and leaves it—too afraid to use it lest it be stolen—he'd been blind to all the other blessings around him.

One couldn't accept a gift if their hands were already full. Nor could they give anything if they refused to let go.

Micah didn't want to continue living life that way. He was tired of holding back, of keeping those he loved at arm's length. No amount of land was more important than people. He could buy a new home with the money from the sale and have more than enough left over to ensure Callie and her business would be fine. He'd do anything for those he loved. And that included Grace.

Compared to running into a burning building, this was a simple decision.

With a final tip of his hat, Davis tucked the envelope beneath his arm and climbed into the truck.

The moment the trailer disappeared around the corner, Micah released a slow breath.

No going back now.

As Davis drove off with the signed contract, he braced himself for the wave of doubt to hit him, but he felt nothing but peace.

He was tired of clinging to the past. As much as he tried to force it, the future of the ranch was out of his hands. He could make all the right decisions, manage the finances, write out a business plan, and stick to it like glue. But at the end of the day, what was he really in control of? The rains came and went, the economy was an ever-changing animal, and every season brought its own unique surprises.

So, in answer to his own question—*nothing*. He could ensure the future of this place no more than he could convince the skies to rain. Only one person had that kind of power, and it definitely wasn't him.

The sooner he learned to live life with open hands, the better. Whatever God entrusted him with, he'd cherish with all his heart. And when the time came for something new, he'd be ready and willing to accept it.

Grace sat on the edge of the tub and winced as Callie dabbed the soaked cotton against a cut on her forehead. The amber liquid's sharp scent made her eyes sting, and she blinked back the moisture gathering along her lashes.

Now that she had a moment to relax, she felt every cut, scrape, and burn. Muscles she didn't even know about ached, and it was all she could do to keep her eyes open and not fall asleep where she sat.

Callie moved to the next cut, and Grace sucked in a quick breath.

"Sorry about that." Pulling away, she dropped the soiled rag into the trash can and ran a clean towel under the bathroom faucet.

With a sigh of relief, Grace took the soft, light blue towel and gently ran it over her face and neck. It came back a dark gray, the same color the water had turned when she'd finally washed her hands twenty minutes ago.

She massaged one of Callie's homemade creams over her freshly cleaned skin—a mixture of honey, lavender, and aloe vera—and immediately, the pain subsided. When she'd finished rubbing the salve over the tender flesh, she handed the jar back to Callie, who applied some to the red marks on her own hands and face. Dark circles framed her friend's usually bright eyes, and her coppery hair looked as dingy as a tarnished penny.

Grace feared she didn't look much better herself. Not that it mattered, though. Here, there was no pressure to put on a brave face or disguise the pain. She could be herself, scars and all.

Sagging against the wall behind her, she briefly closed her eyes and let her muscles relax.

She was exhausted. Without a fire to put out, or sheep to round up, it was all starting to catch up with her.

Uncovering the last of her freckles from beneath the soot, Callie tossed the dirty towel onto the growing pile in the tub and sat down beside Grace. She bumped her shoulder against hers and spoke with a sad smile. "So, are we going to talk about it, or are we just going to ignore the packed bags in your bedroom?"

While Grace had been expecting the question, she'd hoped she would have a few more hours of peace before having to face it. As far as she knew, Callie hadn't heard about her and Micah's argument the day before. But one look at her concerned expression said her friend understood more than she'd realized.

Grace sighed, looking up at the ceiling instead of Callie. "I made a mess of things, and I don't know how to fix them."

The ceramic tub squeaked as Callie turned to face her. "You know you can always talk to me, Grace. I might not have all the answers, but I can be a good listener. Sometimes, it's enough to share our burdens with a friend."

Grace could appreciate that. After all, she'd wanted the same for Micah.

Callie listened in silence while Grace poured out every detail of Katrina's surprise visit to the ranch, her argument with Micah, and Katrina's words to her in the garden, stopping at the part when she saw the smoke coming from the barn.

Hands in her lap, Callie remained unusually still until the story was over. Grace wasn't sure what was going through her head, but she had little time to worry before her friend's hand reached out to grasp hers. "I'm sure it was a difficult decision." Her face was soft and full of understanding.

Grace squeezed her hand before releasing it to fidget with the frayed end of her sweater. "I just don't know what to do anymore. I had a life before coming here. Friends, too. Or at least, I thought I did." Katrina wasn't really her friend. She'd already proved as much. "I just want to be able to fix everything."

"You've done so much already." Callie offered her a small smile and continued. "For starters, I wouldn't have been able to get my business up and running without your help."

Grace released a laugh, unwilling to accept the praise. "That was all you. All I did was put together a few spreadsheets."

Callie sent her a pointed look. "You did far more than that, and you know it. And as for Micah ... You gave him something to hope for. And that's no small thing."

There was a long stretch of silence as Grace absorbed her friend's encouraging words. "Do you think he'll make it?" she finally asked.

Shifting on the edge of the tub, Callie turned to face her. "Anything is possible, but I have a good feeling about this."

Grace stared at her. "How are you always so positive? Even after everything that's happened to you, you refuse to see all the bad in the world."

Callie was quiet for a moment, eyes studying the colorful bathroom rug at their feet before she finally spoke. "It's not that I don't notice it, Grace. There is a lot of pain and suffering in this world. I can either let it control me, or I can choose to focus on the good and trust that God has a plan. It might not be what I think is best—and oftentimes it's the complete opposite—but He is always in control."

"Even in this?" Grace asked, wanting to share in her friend's hope.

Callie smiled. "Even in this."

CHAPTER

Twenty-Nine

GRACE DRANK IN the morning sunshine as she sat on the edge of the patio, watching the lavender sway in the light breeze. The first sprigs had begun to turn brown, and soon, the entire garden would go to sleep for the coming winter.

She tugged the wool sweater tighter around her shoulders, the same blue and white one Callie had been working on for the past few weeks. "A gift for you," she'd said last night as they ate ice cream in the kitchen. After everything that happened, Grace shouldn't have been surprised by the woman's kindness, but her overwhelming generosity still brought tears to her eyes.

Blinking them back, Grace was about to head inside when a low rumbling caught her attention. It didn't sound like Micah's truck, and Callie was still inside working on her latest creation. Curious, Grace stood and went to investigate. Like the first day she'd arrived, she traversed the edges of the raised beds, avoiding the few patches of mud that dotted the garden, and swung open the gate.

There, sitting in the driveway, was none other than her VW bug. A little cleaner and more polished than before, but she'd recognize Cordelia's bright orange paint and dented fender anywhere.

A man climbed out of the driver's side. A few inches shorter than Micah, he wore Carhartts jeans and a T-shirt with the words *Los Piños Ranch* printed across the front in faded letters.

"You must be Grace," he said as he closed the door. "It's a pleasure to meet you." The man looked to be a couple years younger than Micah. His friendly smile put her at ease, and his faint Southern accent connected the dots.

"And you must be Tony. I've heard Micah mention you a few times." She'd seen him among the people who'd come to help with the fire and sheep but hadn't stopped at the time to talk.

"Don't believe a word he says." He winked. "I've got a few stories of my own from when we were kids that would make even his mother blush."

Grace chuckled, imagining a younger version of Micah running around the ranch and getting into trouble. She'd love to hear a few of those stories, if only to give her another reason to stay longer. "Your secret's safe with me."

He flashed her a grin as he stepped around to the front of the car. "Anyway, I brought your car back. Sorry it took so long."

"That's okay. I had enough here to keep me busy for a while." In all the excitement of the past few weeks and hours, she'd nearly forgotten about it. "How much do I owe you for all the work?"

He waved aside her question. "Don't worry about it. I owe Micah a few favors, so after this, we can call it even." Before Grace could protest, he unlatched the hood and propped it up, inviting her to inspect his work. "I did everything I could to get her up and running again—replaced a few hoses, rewired the electrical system, and put a temporary seal on the engine block. I'm not a licensed mechanic by any means, so I'd have it checked out at a garage before taking it on any major road trips. But it should get you where you need to go."

The sunlight reflected off the familiar, polished surface, but she didn't immediately reach for the keys. "I'm not sure I want to leave anymore." She hadn't meant to say it out loud, but Tony didn't seem to mind.

"Yeah, I know what you mean. I've got quite a few memories of this place. I sure will miss it." Crossing his arms, he leaned against the metal frame and peered around the yard and surrounding forest.

"Are you going somewhere?" Grace asked.

His back went rigid, as if he'd said too much. Standing, he pushed away from the car and popped the hood closed. "Forget I said anything."

Like that was possible.

Tony pulled a dirty rag from his back pocket and ran it over his hands. He seemed to study the greasy cloth before shoving it back into his pocket. "He told me not to tell anyone, but I guess you'll find out soon enough."

Grace didn't like the sound of that. "Tony, what's going on?"

His shoulders lifted and fell. "I don't know the details. Something about a contract and not having to worry about the bank's loan anymore. That's all he told me."

Grace's stomach sank. Micah wouldn't have sold the ranch after all he'd put into saving it. Would he? She didn't want to believe Katrina had gotten to him like that.

But one look at Tony's resigned expression confirmed it.

The front door opened, and Callie descended the front porch steps. She spotted the two of them and waved. "Tony, hey! What brings you here?" Her eyes moved to the orange VW Bug parked in her driveway and went wide.

Tony greeted her with an enthusiastic smile, the worry from moments ago gone. "I was just showing Grace how I'd fixed up her car. Took me a while, but now it's good as new." He set the keys on top of the car and paused, rethinking his answer. "Well, not quite brand new. But she runs, and that's the important thing."

He made no mention of the bombshell he'd dropped on Grace moments earlier. Not that she expected him to. But if he was hoping she'd forget it, he was very much mistaken.

"I heard you were the toast of the farmer's market the other day," Tony said, changing the subject. "My mom can't stop raving about the lotion she bought from you—said it's all but cured her eczema."

Callie beamed under the praise.

Grace smiled. At least she hadn't ruined things for everyone. She couldn't be happier about her friend's success, truly. But she wished she could somehow fix the rest of the mess she'd made.

"Say, do you think one of you could give me a ride to Micah's place?" Tony asked. He tucked his hands in his pockets and squinted against the bright sunlight. "Not that I don't mind walking, but I promised him I'd be back to help out some more with the cleanup. My folks and I have been over there most of the day, but I wanted to get this back to you in case you needed it." He nodded toward the car.

Callie looked from Grace to Tony and smiled. "Grace and I were about to head over ourselves. If you don't mind waiting a few minutes while I pack up some more supplies, you could ride over with us."

"Ready to go when you are."

Grace only half listened to their conversation, head still spinning around the news Tony had told her minutes ago. Callie turned for the porch steps and, in a split-second decision, Grace scooped her keys off the car's hood and yanked open her car door.

"Grace, where are you going?" Callie asked, spinning on the top step. "I thought we were taking the truck."

"I'm sorry, but I need to sort out a few things in town. I'll be back, though. I promise." With a slight twinge of guilt, Grace closed her car door before Callie could pelt her with another question and started the engine. The Volkswagen hummed to life, and she reversed it up the short drive toward the road.

Something inside the car rattled as she drove over the rutted road toward town. It didn't sound good, but she couldn't stop now.

She had to catch Katrina before she left. Maybe there was a way she could convince her boss to rework the contract. There had to be some middle ground where Micah could get help paying back the loan and still have a future on his family's land.

She had no idea what she was going to say, but she had the entire car ride to devise a plan.

Everything seemed quiet as Micah stood on the front porch of Callie's house. Sunlight poured through the stained-glass window embedded in the door, painting him in shards of color while he waited for someone to answer.

Silence.

He'd hoped to speak with Grace earlier when he saw Callie's truck at the ranch, but she hadn't been there. He would have asked Callie if she'd stuck around for more than a few minutes before driving off again. Something about it all didn't seem right, but not much of the last few days seemed to make much sense.

He lifted his hand to knock a second time when a faint humming drifted from out back.

Micah smiled. Grace. So this was where she'd been hiding out. He descended the steps two at a time until his feet were on solid ground and made his way through the small gate. The hinges screeched with the movement, and the humming stopped.

Frowning at the old hardware, Micah eased the gate closed in search of where he'd last heard the music coming from. Past the tomato vines and down a row of kale and assorted leafy greens, he sidestepped a large puddle before the path emptied out into the backyard.

Beside the lavender bushes was Callie, garden scissors in hand as she trimmed another handful of the purple flowers. Micah inspected the rest of the garden, but Grace was nowhere to be seen.

"Micah, what a nice surprise." She dusted her hands off on her overalls and met him with a smile.

In all the years he'd known Callie, she'd hardly changed. Same girl focused on saving the world one flower at a time. If he'd ever had a sister, he would have hoped she'd have been just like her.

Stripping off her gloves, she shoved them into a pocket as she watched him with a steady gaze. "How are you doing? Really?"

He knew better than to lie to her. She'd read between the lines, anyway. There were so many reasons why the past twenty-four hours hadn't been easy, but none of that compared to the peace he'd felt since confronting Jack by the river. "Honestly, I think I'm okay."

The worry lines between her eyebrows relaxed, and she seemed to breathe a sigh of relief. "I'm glad to hear it. And Caden? How is he?"

Micah smiled and nodded. "He's doing fine as well." He'd left him in charge of the ranch, confident he could trust him to manage the cleanup while he was out.

"Actually, I'm glad that you're here." Callie ducked inside for a moment and came out holding a small white envelope. "I was planning to drive back over later today to give this to you, but it looks like you've saved me another trip."

She handed it over, and he stared at the blank envelope in confusion. The seal broke under his fingertip, revealing a check with his name on it. His gaze caught on the large sum, and he snapped his attention back to Callie. "What's this?"

She casually rested a hand on her hip and smiled as if she hadn't just handed him a check for two-thousand dollars. "It's the first installment of what I owe you for the past three years. I've been saving up for a while, and with Saturday's sales, I can finally start paying you back."

While he appreciated the offer, there was no way he was taking Callie's money. His family was the one responsible for hers leaving in the first place. No way was he about to ask for her to give up anything else. It was one thing signing the paperwork when he'd been confident she'd be okay. "I can't accept this." He held out the check to her.

"You can. And you will." There was a note of stubbornness in her voice. She propped her other hand against her hip and took a step back, obviously trying to distance herself from the outstretched check in his grasp. "You've been kind enough to let me stay here rent-free all these years, but it's time I start making my own way. You don't have to carry the weight of an entire mountain on your own, you know."

Micah shook his head and extended the envelope out further. "No. You need this money for your business. You've earned it."

She shrugged. "So, I'll start next year. Besides, it might be a tad self-serving."

"And how's that?" He tilted his head, trying to decipher her cryptic logic.

She scooped up a twig of lavender, twirling it between her fingertips before sending him a funny look. "I could end up with a horrible new neighbor who doesn't appreciate my bees."

He couldn't help but chuckle. "You and your bees."

She shrugged and smiled. "They're like family. And family sticks together."

He knew she was talking more about him than her insect friends, and the knowledge warmed him. "You'll always be like family to me, Cal. But that doesn't mean I'm accepting this." He went to set the check on the table when she stopped him.

"You are one of the most stubborn men I know, Micah Prescott." Her lips pressed into a firm line before she continued. "Take the money or don't. But I won't let you throw away the best thing that's happened to this place in years."

He took a step back. "What are you talking about?"

Callie looked heavenward before blowing out a forceful breath. "You're willing to let Grace walk away thinking you still hate her when it's clear as day you have feelings for her."

He'd just signed over the ranch for her. Of course, Callie didn't know that, but the accusation stung, nonetheless. She was about to say something else when he opened his mouth to stop her.

"I don't hate her. I love her."

Callie went silent, as did Micah.

The moment he'd said it, the words settled in his soul like a whisper from God, filling up the empty spaces and breathing new life into his parched soul. He'd thought seeing her leave would be easier than losing the ranch. Instead, it felt like a part of him was missing whenever she wasn't there.

But that was crazy. He'd only known her a few weeks, and half of that time they'd been enemies. Everything he did was measured and controlled, prudent, and at times, shrewd. He couldn't see how any kind of a future between them could work—she lived in the city and worked for a big firm, and he had nothing left to offer other than some sheep.

"I already signed the paperwork." The riverside property, the ranch. All of it. The knowledge that Grace no longer had a reason to stay made his insides ache, but then again, neither did he since signing that contract. His future gaped before him, an empty field waiting to be planted.

Micah kneaded the back of his neck, unsure of where to go from there.

Callie startled him out of his thoughts with a hand on his forearm. She patted his sleeve and gave him a sad smile. "I wondered as much. But you don't need a piece of paper to keep her in your life. All you have to do is talk to her and be honest."

She turned toward the house, leaving the opened envelope exactly where Micah had set it. "And by the way, Grace left for town about an hour ago. Just in case you were wondering where to find her." With a smile, she scooped up the pile of flowers and carried them into the house.

Micah didn't need any further prompting.

He ate up the distance to the truck with long strides and climbed in. As long as Grace was here, he still had a chance to tell her how he felt. Maybe it was sudden and didn't make sense, but he wasn't going to let this opportunity slip through his hands.

In a cloud of dust, he revved up the hill and made a right toward town, praying he'd be able to catch her.

Fields and forests rushed past him, the first hints of fall painting his peripherals in oranges and gold as he drove down the length of the valley with the mountains watching in silent expectation. The newly restored bridge rattled beneath his tires. Once clear of the river, he directed the truck around the next curve and pumped his foot against the brakes.

There, on the side of the road, was a suspiciously familiar Volkswagen.

Micah couldn't contain his smile. For the second time in a month, he pulled up behind the ridiculously orange car.

And he prayed for just one more miracle.

CHAPTER

Thirty

GRACE TRIED THE ignition again but with no success—the thing gave one last pitiful hum before going completely silent.

So much for Tony's repairs.

"Come on, Cordelia. Don't do this to me again." She slumped against the seat, willing the car to come back to life before Katrina left town. A quick drive in and back was all she'd wanted, but based on her track record, she should have known that to be wishful thinking.

Now, for the second time in three weeks, she was stranded along the side of the road with nowhere to go.

"At least it's not raining." She wanted to cry—and if given the chance, she very well might have if she hadn't been interrupted by the sound of an approaching car. Turning, she looked at the curve of the road that disappeared behind the trees until a white truck emerged.

Out here in the middle of the mountains, it could have been any old white truck. But the skip in her chest told her otherwise.

Like a memory from a dream, the truck slowed and pulled to a stop on the side of the road behind her. Grace held her breath as the door opened and a pair of familiar cowboy boots belonging to an even more familiar man stepped out of the vehicle.

"Micah, what are you doing here?" she asked, stepping out of her car. She specifically hadn't told him where she was going, but from the look on his face, it was as if he'd expected to find her here all along.

He took one look at her car and the open door and frowned. "Car troubles?"

When Grace only nodded—still too surprised by his sudden arrival to formulate a response—he took a few steps forward. He looked as if he were about to pop open the hood when she stopped him with a hand to his elbow, finally finding her voice again. "It's fine. I'll just call Callie and ask her to have Tony come get it again."

The line between his eyebrows deepened. A shadow of dark stubble had grown in since the other day, softening his jawline in a not altogether unpleasant way. "I thought he'd fixed it."

"Yeah, well" —she shrugged— "maybe some things just can't be fixed." She wanted to believe otherwise, though. To hope that no matter how far gone someone might be, they were still worth saving.

That whatever the two of them had was worth saving.

Suddenly self-conscious under his serious gaze, Grace turned away from Micah and leaned against the hood. "I've been thinking..." She trailed off mid-sentence, wanting to lay everything bare but unsure how to begin.

"That sounds dangerous." His dimples appeared beneath the layer of scruff. Despite the shadows of exhaustion, he was smiling. At her.

It was enough to make her breath hitch as he closed the small distance between them. He reached out his arms to lean against the hood, trapping her between them.

"You're not making this easy on me," she said, suddenly breathless. "I've been rehearsing what I want to say to you the entire drive, and your presence is making it very difficult to think."

"Is that so?" His voice turned husky.

"So, I'm just going to say it before I forget completely." Which, based on his close proximity and his woodsy cologne muddling her brain, it was a very real possibility. "You're stubborn, work way too hard, and refuse to accept help from anyone. And you could really stand to own a pair of shoes other than cowboy boots."

"I thought you liked my cowboy boots." His mouth hiked up in the corner, and it took all Grace's willpower not to fixate on it.

"Tricking you into letting me stay was never the plan. You have to believe me when I say that. But now I can't imagine spending a single day away from this place, these people..." She looked down at her fingers, which wrung themselves into the fabric of her shirt. "You."

She barely got the last word out before he pulled her into a kiss that laid her fears to rest and let all her hopes and wishes for the future run wild. Rising onto her toes, she wrapped her arms around his neck and kissed him back—confident for the first time in her life that she was exactly where she was supposed to be.

Everything—all the heartache, the wandering, the searching—had been leading to this. All these years, she'd been too afraid to risk anything for fear of what she might lose when she should have been focusing on all the blessings she could gain.

And she wasn't afraid anymore.

She pulled back, not wanting to stop but trying to process the millions of questions and dreams ricocheting inside her when the first one popped out. "I have to go back home."

"You're not getting rid of me that easily."

"I have to figure things out with Katrina. I know you signed the contract, and before you say anything," she hurried to include before he could protest, "I fully intend to convince her of some changes. Because you see, I'll need a place to come back to once she fires me. And we've already decided you need more help if you keep insisting on running the ranch all by yourself."

"We?" he said, his mouth hiking up at one corner.

"Callie and I."

"I don't think Callie would object to you staying. She seems pretty taken with you."

"Only Callie?" she teased.

"I can think of someone else."

She laughed as he kissed her cheek. She couldn't believe how much she'd come to care for this man, who'd once seemed so distant and unapproachable. He'd softened and changed over the past few weeks, but then, so had she.

He leaned back and looked down at her, eyebrows pinched together as if unsure how to proceed. "I'm sorry for accusing you of telling Katrina about the loan. I should know by now that's not the kind of person you are."

That was the least of her concerns, but his words touched her all the same. "To be fair, I gave you plenty of reasons not to trust me when we first met."

"I wasn't much of a gentleman that day, either." Those dimples reappeared as he relaxed, putting her at ease.

My, how far they'd come in three weeks.

"What about Jack? Will you be pressing charges?"

Micah shook his head. "I'm sure Frank and the other ranchers will have their own opinions. After all, I wasn't the only one he'd been trying to convince to sell. But I'm done holding onto so much anger. It's time to move on and start thinking about the future."

The way he held her gaze when he spoke of the future made her heart soar. She swiped a piece of unruly hair from his forehead. "You're a wonderful man, Micah Prescott." For his generosity, his forgiveness, and for not giving up on her when any normal person would have.

His arms tightened around her. "If anyone deserves that praise, it's you. And I fully intend on convincing you of that as often as I can for the rest of my life."

If it weren't for the car supporting her, she might have melted right there.

He pulled her in once more, brushing another soft kiss against her lips. "But before I do that, I want to start by telling you that I love you. I don't care if the ranch's future is certain or not, but I *am* certain of this—of us."

"I love you, too." And to her surprise, she meant it. Every single word. Her fingers skimmed the side of his face, the remnants of soot still rough against her skin, and she paused at the old scar. It still amazed her how two people with such difficult pasts could find their way to each other. But God was in the business of miracles, and she'd never question the goodness of His plans ever again.

"You don't suppose I could offer you a lift back to the house?" he whispered against her lips. "As long as you promise to leave the umbrella in the car."

Smiling, Grace couldn't help but recall Callie's words about him riding in to rescue her on a white horse. She'd corrected her by saying it was only a white truck, but right now, the moment felt as enchanting as the stories her mom used to read to her at night.

"For old time's sake?"

He stepped closer and tipped his head once more. "How about we call it *to new beginnings*?"

She quite liked the sound of that. "To new beginnings."

EPILOGUE

FINAL ENTRY OF GRACE'S GRATITUDE JOURNAL, MARCH 20TH:

THINGS I'M GRATEFUL for, number one thousand ...

Do I have to pick just one? I feel I've been blessed in so many ways, and if these past few months have taught me anything, it's that we should cherish every gift, no matter how small it may seem. Who knows? It may turn out to be the beginning of something so much greater. I know a year ago I would have laughed at that line of thinking, but that was before I drove up a mountain valley and got stranded on the side of a deserted road.

Today is the first day of spring. Everything still feels quiet, as if slowly awakening from a deep, winter-long slumber, yet there are hints of new life everywhere. The bees have begun to venture out of their hives, much to Callie's delight, and we're right in the middle of lambing season.

Our first one arrived two weeks ago, all spindly legs and white wool. It was crazy and terrifying and miraculous all at the same time. Micah and I watched in silence as this little bundle of new life entered the world, and I couldn't help but think about how precious this life is and the people God's given us to share it with.

Since then, we've added twelve more lambs to the flock, with more on the way in the next few months. I still can't get over how cute they all are. So curious and innocent, they don't seem afraid of anything. Wherever the flock goes, they follow with excitement, even if it's only to rotate to a new pasture, because to them, it's a whole new adventure.

Had I known sheep could be so friendly, I wouldn't have run away from them my first week on the ranch. Okay, maybe I would have, but I can credit Olive with my drastic change of heart. Now, she is happily settled with the flock, although she gave us a few scares last fall. She's outgrown the sweater, no longer needing the extra layer of protection. But now I have a whole new set of lambs to knit my horrible sweaters for. Based on the scrap bin tucked in Callie's closet, it looks like this year's colors will be mustard yellow and magenta.

In my daily walk from Callie's house to the ranch, I'm reminded of how incredibly lucky I am to call this place home. Quitting my job was one of the best decisions I've ever made, followed by packing up my apartment and joining Callie as a partner in her growing business. She's already had four bulk requests from the shops in town who want to stock her teas and honey. We can hardly keep up with the demand, but with Caden stopping by most nights to help, I think we'll manage just fine.

I haven't said anything to her yet, seeing as it's not my secret to tell, but I believe I saw a jewelry catalog in his car when he drove me to town last week. I didn't pry, but anyone with eyes can see those two are perfect for one another.

And the ranch. How could I forget the very thing that brought me here in the first place?

Before leaving Prospect & Gould, I managed to convince Katrina of a few changes to the contract. I don't know what brought about her change of heart. Maybe it was the fear that Jack could implicate her and the company in his upcoming trial, but she was surprisingly more gracious than I'd expected, which made it all the easier to get them approved. Maybe it was Callie's honey that did the trick, but for whatever reason, she agreed to a reduced settlement for a fraction of the riverfront property. Between that money and the proceeds of the sheep sale last fall, it barely covered the bank's loan. And with less than a week to spare!

A few weeks later, Micah talked with Davis, Frank's brother-in-law, who offered to build them a new barn. Everyone else in the community pitched in for the supplies. At first, Micah refused their generosity, but they put up a good fight. That afternoon, Pauline pulled me aside and told me how this was their way of repaying him for all he'd done for them over the years without complaint.

I know exactly what she meant.

She also may have mentioned something about trying to convince him to run for the Planning Commission now that

Jack was gone, and while he didn't exactly say yes, I have a feeling he might reconsider.

Micah has been the greatest surprise of all. So maybe things got off to a rough start between us, but now I can't imagine any other life without him in it. He's taught me the value of perseverance, the joy of family, and most importantly, the peace of putting my trust in the greatest Shepherd of all.

I've found over a thousand things to be grateful for, and I'm convinced I'll find a thousand more.

I don't know what the future holds, and there are sure to be both struggles and joys, but I can't imagine a better person to experience it all with than Micah.

My very own cowboy.

DID YOU LIKE THIS BOOK?

BookBub has a New Release alert. Not only can you check out the latest deals, but you can also receive an email when I release my next book by following me here:

https://www.bookbub.com/authors/alyssa-schwarz

Check out my website:

https://www.authoralyssaschwarz.com/

Follow me on Instagram:

https://www.instagram.com/alyssaschwarzauthor/

Leave a Review on Goodreads:

https://www.goodreads.com/author/show/21846420.Alyssa_Schwarz

Other ways you can help support this indie author:

Request my other books at your local library

Host a book club (I'd love to join via Zoom)

Give a copy as a gift

And tell your friends and family

Tomato Flatbread Pizza

Tomayto, tomahto...
It's no secret Callie loves her garden, and especially her tomatoes.
From the sweet sugar bomb cherry tomatoes to heirlooms and
giant beefsteak, you can't go wrong with this simple yet
impressively satisfying dinner. Get creative, and let your
imagination run wild with the possibilities.

<u>Ingredients</u>
1 cup warm water
1 tsp active dry yeast
2 ½ cups flour
1 tsp honey
½ tsp salt
2 Tbsp olive oil
(2 Tbsp olive oil & 2 Tbst water - combined for later)
coarse sea salt
cherry tomatoes, halved
*optional toppings: sliced red onion, halved olives, sun dried
tomatoes, fresh basil, goat cheese...)

In a stand mixer, combine lukewarm water and yeast and let
stand a few minutes until yeast is completely dissolved. Next, add
in the flour, honey, salt, and olive oil and mix with the hook
attachment until fully incorporated. Increase speed to
medium-high, and mix for about 7-10 minutes until the dough

forms a ball around the hook and becomes elastic and smooth. Cover the bowl with a tea towel and let rise 1 ½ - 2 hours in a warm place until doubled in size.

Preheat the oven to 450 degrees Fahrenheit.

Liberally coat a 9x13in pan with olive oil and turn the dough onto it. Press the dough toward the edges, cover, and let rise again for another 30-60 minutes. Once doubled in size again, use your fingertips to press into the dough to form large dimples across the surface. Combine the extra 2 Tbsp olive oil and 2 Tbsp water and drizzle over the dough. Arrange your tomatoes and other optional toppings across the surface and sprinkle with coarse sea salt to finish.

Bake for 15 - 20 minutes until the crust becomes golden. Once removed, drizzle lightly with more olive oil and ENJOY!

ACKNOWLEDGEMENTS

This book wouldn't have been possible without the help of so many people, from the encouragement of friends and family to the critique partners and editors who helped me stay sane while writing this story.

To the critique groups through ACFW, I can't even begin to thank you all for your help, the weekly chapter exchanges, for answering my endless list of questions. I'd like to especially thank my amazing editor, Caitlin Miller. Thank you for all the time you spent pouring over these pages to make this story the best it could be. Your encouraging comments and emojis in the margins made the revision process such a joy, and I can't wait to work with you on the next book after this.

To the amazing authors who encouraged me on this journey including Susan May Warren, Tari Faris, Alicia Whittle, Jeanne Takenaka, and all the other members of the My Book Therapy and ACFW communities.

Readers, reviewers, endorsers, and other bookworm friends. Thank you for journeying with me through these stories and allowing me to share a bit of my heart with you all. And if you follow me on Instagram, thank you for putting up with a lot of videos of sheep. I promise, it was (mostly) for the sake of research. Plus, they're just so cute!

To my parents, who have always believed in and supported me. You have been my biggest cheerleaders, and I am so incredibly grateful. You've taught me to never give up on my dreams.

And to the Good Shepherd, who leads us up mountains and walks with us through the valleys. "I can do all this through him who gives me strength."

FALL IN LOVE WITH THE ENTIRE PRESCOTT FAMILY

The Prescott Cousins

Tye	Abigail	Tess	Caden	Micah
A veterinarian who just moved back to the same small town he ran away from ... and the girl he left behind.	Dependable and down-to-earth. She's an old soul finding new lives for the items in their great-aunt's antique shop.	Professional triathlete, and older sister to Caden. She may race for a living, but what is she really trying to outrun?	A bit of a nomad, and the baby of the family. He's worked every job you can think of, but he never thought he'd find a home working on the ranch.	Older brother to Tye and in charge of the family ranch. Loyal and hardworking, he will do anything to protect those he loves.

A PRESCOTT FAMILY
ROMANCE

LET'S CONNECT!

Instagram — @AlyssaSchwarzAuthor
Facebook — Alyssa Schwarz, Author
Pinterest — Alyssa Schwarz Author

Leave a review on Goodreads, BookBub, and Amazon

Subscribe to Alyssa's email newsletter at
www.authoralyssaschwarz.com

(or use the QR code below)

ABOUT THE AUTHOR

Alyssa is a Colorado native who attended the Colorado School of Mines, got her masters in Geological Engineering, and promptly became a watercolor artist and author (as one does). A member of ACFW and Novel Academy, she loves writing heartfelt romances with happy endings, a bit of mystery, faith, humor, and second chances. You can connect with her online at www.authoralyssaschwarz.com

www.ingramcontent.com/pod-product-compliance
Lightning Source LLC
Chambersburg PA
CBHW051318250626
47155CB00007B/2371